C000018828

In a Sorry State

James Joughin

Paperback ISBN – 978-0-9931035-0-6
ePub ISBN - 978-0-9931035-2-0
Mobi ISBN - 978-0-9931035-1-3

"My understanding had been for too many years intimate with severe thinkers, with logic and the great masters of knowledge, not to be aware of the utter feebleness of the main herd of modern economists. I saw that these were generally the very dregs and rinsings of the human intellect; and that any man of sound head and practised in wielding logic with a scholastic adroitness might take up the whole academy of modern economists and throttle them between heaven and earth with his finger and thumb, or bray their fungus heads to powder with a lady's fan."

- De Quincey, Confessions of an English Opium-Eater

"For Keynes the short run was much more significant than the long run – that long run in which, he used to say, 'we are all dead'"

- A.C. Pigou, Proceedings of the British Academy, v32, p13

"One writes a repellent book ... not to be repellent but to represent the repellent, to air the repellent, ... to reveal how it looks and what it is."

- Philip Roth, Guardian 07/11/14

Everything in this story is true. One or two names were changed to protect the guilty.

Part I

ONE

November 2011

"I know somewhat too much; and from this knowledge, once one has been infected, there seems to be no recovering. I ought never to have taken my lantern to see what was going on in the hut by the granary. On the other hand, there was no way, once I had picked up the lantern, for me to put it down again. The knot loops in upon itself; I cannot find the end."
- J.M. Coetzee, Waiting for the Barbarians

A grubby room off a dingy corridor. It's like a student's residence, cheap carpet, cheap curtains, a desk, a poster of Millais' The Blind Girl on the back wall. In a regulation issue soft chair, a man sits forward, anxious, picking at his cuffs. He is barefoot. He is in white pyjamas. The shirt is collarless and loose, the trousers are baggy.

Across from him, sits a woman on a stool, two files on her lap. She shuffles some notes. 'Memories,' she says, kindly and soft around the eyes. 'Good for us. In the round.'

The man rubs his face, a nervy, stuttering gesture. He uses the back of his right hand, rather than his fingers which are bandaged.

The woman is short and trim and wears an antique gold wedding band. A small microphone is visible, clipped to the lapel of her white coat. 'Perhaps,' she says, in a low voice, 'if we could go over it again, get the history straight.'

He shakes his head, seems bewildered, looks down.

'I know,' she looks at the notes, 'that we've been through this before but I'm still a bit confused.'

He says nothing.

'Perhaps you could start by telling me, in your own words of course, how it all began. Take your time.'

He stares at the floor then begins to sway slightly. Back and forth, back and forth. Like an animal in a cage.

'Or maybe you could tell me why you think you're here. What are your expectations? What do you think *we* can do?'

He frowns.

She looks at the notes again. 'Are you still having, er, panic attacks?'

He shakes his head and makes a noise, something like a whimper.

'You said you felt nauseous. What did you mean?'

She smiles encouragingly, waits for a moment and when nothing comes, scribbles something in the notes. 'OK, let's try a different angle. Let's try the Uganda stuff. Talk me through it. In your own words.'

Still he is unable to start.

'Tell me about Uganda. The country.'

'What about it?'

Three words, that's good. 'You know,' she pauses, 'as I was preparing for this session, I was reminded that my uncle was there, in the old days, before independence I suppose. He was a surgeon in the hospital. One of the great hospitals of East Africa, I always understood.'

'Mulago.'

'Yes.'

'That's where they took me.'

She waits for him to go on but he doesn't. 'And then? What happened?'

He laughs. Maybe it's more a giggle or a yelp of pain. At any rate, it is redolent of a man close to the wrong side of good reason. 'You like the Millais?' he asks, nodding towards the poster.

'Don't you?'

He shrugs. 'A bit sentimental for me.'

'You like more, what should I call it, reality?'

'I think it's important not to avoid it.'

The doctor smiles, patiently, waiting for him to continue.

'There was,' he says, in a tone that suggests he might be going to describe a dream he'd had, 'on my ward, a suspected Ebola case.' He rubs his face again, trying to get real purchase on his skin, which is raw and flaky, as if it hasn't seen daylight for some time. 'He was inside some kind of plastic tent. You know what Ebola is yeah?'

'The *public* ward, is that what you're saying? Didn't you have insurance?' she asks.

He takes a deep breath. 'Uganda is famously gifted by nature,' he intones, as if he is suddenly doing a voice-over for the Natural History Channel, 'but it is also host to most of the dangerous and epidemic diseases of the world. The Congo-Sudan-Uganda Albertine ecosystem, you know what that is?'

She nods unconvincingly.

'It's the world's largest reservoir of viruses. Not just Ebola but Marburg, Rift Valley fever, anthrax, dengue, HIV, chikungunya, Human Foamy Virus, imagine what that is, O'nyongnyong fever. And plenty of unknown viruses too. Seventy per cent of all human and animal pathogens are found there. It's the main incubator for all the *seriously* contagious stuff in the world.'

One minute he won't say a word, the next he won't shut up.

'We can talk about this if you want,' she says, 'but I think I have to ask whether this is pertinent? Or might you be meaning it as a metaphor for other anxieties?'

He fixes her with a weird and terrible stare. As she looks at him, he seemed, as she thought about it later, full of an infinite sadness, as if he had heard some awful news as yet unknown to anyone else.

'Perhaps,' she tries again, 'the metaphor idea might be a good entry point, a sensible avenue of enquiry? What other pressing anxieties do you have?'

'What *other* pressing anxieties do I have?' For a moment, he seems like a tyre that is about to burst, but the possibility that something, anything, might be sensible seems then to help and, taking a deep breath, he resumes the narrative.

'So, Ebola, you bleed prodigiously from every orifice, just think about that for a moment, you bleed from *every* orifice. Nine of them aren't there?'

She nods, as if that at least is true.

'Your body melts from the inside out. In a matter of hours, *hours*, you turn into a blob of brown slime and leak away on to the carpet. Nothing left of you but a greasy stain.'

She's worried she's lost control of where this is going.

'I asked the nurse if the guy in the tent was *infectious*, what the advice was, y'know? She spoke to the sister, who spoke to the ward manager, who got the official guidelines and read out to me that, and I quote, "Ebola sufferers should avoid sexual intercourse". And if they couldn't? I asked. Well, she said, if they really couldn't abstain, and that was the word she used, they should try to use a condom. Assuming they'd had the training that is. That seemed to be important.'

Silence for at least a minute and it sits heavily in the small room.

The man fidgets with his bandages.

'The problem with too much reality,' the doctor says, 'of perhaps insisting we should *confront* reality, is that we risk locating the problem in the wrong place. For most people, the greatest danger is not complacency.'

He scowls at her but she smiles and continues, 'In truth, it's not given to many of us to be able to forget the evils of existence. It could be that the real danger is falling into rage, depression and despair, losing hope in the human project.'

Rain is falling outside, darkness stepping in. The doctor's gaze follows some geese as they fly high above then scrutinises the cars parked under the window. A middle-aged man is easing himself from the torn seats of an old Escort van. Sunningdale Hospital, it says, red letters emblazoned on the side. The fellow is in overalls. He could be a driver or a clerk or the bloke who fastens the straps on the ECT machine. A red Mercedes convertible pulls up next to him. Two people climb out. The doctor watches as they walk purposefully towards the main entrance, a striking young black woman in an expensive suit, short hair, designer shoes, and an elderly man with the build of a midget wrestler. They are both carrying high-end leather briefcases and top-of-the-line smartphones.

When the doctor looks back, the patient is staring once more, bug-eyed, thyroidal.

'Internal and external stakeholders,' he says, almost shouting, 'critical path analysis, delivery mechanisms, enabling approaches, systemic change, sustainable transformations in the functioning of market systems, addressing attribution, rigorous causal chains from activities to outcomes, longitudinal impact, input additionality, counterfactual analysis based on a control group, I could go on. Do you know what any of that fucking *means*?'

'I suppose it depends on the context...'

'What context do you want? The four Buddhist paths, the Ten Commandments, the seven deadly sins?'

'How long were you there?' the doctor tries again. 'On the ward?'

No response. He could be sulking or he could be a prisoner of war, giving only name, rank and number.

'It must have been tough,' she says.

And with that he finally smiles, a demented, simian grin which, if she hadn't read the notes, with their copious and expansive reassurances as to his benign and fundamentally gentle nature, would have had her reaching for the panic button under the table.

And then the phone rings, a loud interruption that makes the doctor start.

'Yes?'

She listens to what the caller has to say.

'For him? Are you sure?'

She puts the receiver down and turns slowly to her patient. 'Apparently, you have visitors.'

TWO

April 1st 2011

Then take a picture of this. Six months earlier, a young woman dragging a heavy suitcase towards the check-in queue at Heathrow. She is in her late twenties, tall, elegant, but serious, even a little severe. She is wearing metal-rimmed glasses, her long chestnut hair piled high on her head. In cotton skirt and flat sandals, she could be a physics teacher or a social worker.

'Entebbe, madam?'

'Yes please.'

'How is it there?'

'Very nice, I'm sure.'

The check-in staff at business class are always solicitous. And so they should be. She'd paid three thousand quid for the ticket. Or somebody had.

Next, security, the patient shuffle forward, the removal of shoes, the moving belt, the pat-down. Was this the moment after which there was no going back? Or was it all in motion long before? Even now she could have walked away, decided it was not for her after all. People do. They ask to have their bags returned, cite panic attacks or the death of a loved one, suddenly remember they've missed an important anniversary.

She headed for the business lounge. A trainee no longer, she was with the big boys now, hired on her merits, given the just rewards. There would be no more helping with the photocopying and making the tea. She'd worked hard for this, studied in the evenings, done a stint as a volunteer at CARE, and eventually been employed there on a derisory wage. The company, her company, the revered HSC Ltd (once the more formal Hilleard, Semple and Crooks) might not be paying her much yet but she was making contacts, finding her feet. 'We'll smuggle you on to a few small jobs and once you've learned a bit of the lingo we'll sell you in your own right,' Hilleard, the MD, had promised. And he'd been as good as his word. She'd only been with the company two months and here she was, on her second mission, a real consultant, with a frequent flyer number and her own business card, embossed logo and all.

She'd been to Africa before, in her gap year travels, and loved it, totally, the heat, the dampness, the sensuality. Somehow people seemed to enjoy themselves better there. If they felt an itch, they scratched. That was something the English could never imagine, locked away in their little houses, making plans to see each other by telephone, diaries in hand, for weeks or months in the future. Sorry I can't make it at all in October and November's no good because Ma-ma's coming but I'm not sure when. It'll have to be after Christmas. What about the 21st of April?

The business lounge was empty but for a large group over by the window, all in matching green T-shirts and baseball caps. They were mostly overweight and looked American. Could *they* be going to Uganda? What for? Were they soldiers? Couldn't be. A couple of them didn't look more than teenagers.

She'd left home, the small nowheresville of Glenbrook, New Zealand, eight years before to follow a boyfriend round the world. They'd ended up in Oxford, hoping to make a home, but it hadn't worked out. One day, as she'd sat in a café alone, nursing a latte and musing on the boyfriend's long slide into the medieval arcana of Brasenose, she'd seen a leaflet with an emaciated black baby and its hollow-eyed mother, accusatory spectres from another planet. Why had she never thought of that before? She could help.

Getting started was easy enough. CARE took her on enthusiastically and she spent a month as a fundraiser, selling wicker and macramé hangings to tourists, before moving on to petition the IMF to cancel Third World debt. She raised 20,000 signatures in a month and achieved minor celebrity-hood on the corridor. They gave her a nickname, The Commandante, and a morning job on the Fairtrade coffee stall and, at a benefit for landmine victims, she got to shake the hand of Sting. Encouraged, she started a doctorate at Oxford Brookes University, "The role of the agricultural sector in poverty reduction – identifying/ developing sustainable diversification pathways for poverty reduction", something she felt her Kiwi background might be a help with, and, quickly, she was in demand. A UN committee in New York sent her five thousand dollars towards the PhD, a subscription to their glossy journal and a promise of work one day. She got a promotion, was sent on a couple of overseas tours: water for the poor in India, housing for the destitute in Peru. Then, one day, as if by providence, out of the blue, Godfrey Hilleard had called. The development world was desperate for women, he said, and his company HSC, one of the top consultancy outfits in the country, had regular work for her, *serious* work. 'Start immediately and we'll provide you with a mentor. Skip Bifferty, you know him? One of our top guns.'

She was nervous. She didn't want to meet her colleagues any sooner than necessary. 'The team are very distinguished,' Hilleard had said. 'Extremely eminent.' Mind you, this was what he said on the last trip when she had accompanied five soil scientists to a UN Climate Conference in Bangkok. These fellows, she had been assured, were 'at the very top of their game'. She had never been able to verify this as all five had disappeared for the duration of the conference, seemingly locked into 'consultations' day and night. She barely saw any of them until the flight back when all five, exhausted by their efforts, had slept the entire way home.

'Uganda will be great for you,' Hilleard had explained. 'It's one of the development success stories. Fantastic place, lovely people. You'll be starting at the top.' The team was to do a review, a progress report, for a large agricultural project, the National Agricultural Development Service project it was

17

called, or, to use its commonly cited acronym, NADS. This was great, just the sort of stuff she was studying for her PhD.

'It's a showpiece project,' said Hilleard. 'Famously well-designed. Everyone loves it, the government, MODE, the other donors, and they all want to keep it going.'

The Ministry of Overseas Development, known by its acronym, MODE, was the formal client, the office that would pay for the trip. 'It's a good one for us,' said Hilleard. 'Working with MODE is where we want to be. It's the pre-eminent agency these days, leading the world in best practice and innovatory thinking. The staff are frightfully sharp and they keep us on our toes. We want this work. Working for them looks splendid on the company profile.'

Further explanation made it clear that a new phase for the project was scheduled and, highly productive as it had been so far, the MODE lawyers still needed an objective review, for the files 'as it were', and they required an independent team to do the necessary legwork. And they had turned to HSC to put together just that team.

'Actually, it's slightly more complicated than that,' said Hilleard. 'These days everything is done through "framework" contracts.'

He must have seen Faith's puzzled expression. 'It's a mechanism to give everyone a degree of distance, safety if you like. MODE contracts to X, they subcontract to Y, who subcontracts to Z, in this case us, and we put together a team. It's good for everyone. We all get a cut of the cake. All except for the fellow who actually does the job, of course.' He laughed a little sheepishly. 'In this case, our good friend Dr Bent Baxter.'

Had Hilleard remembered she had already met Baxter? It was at one of the company's rare Monday morning meetings where he had deigned to actually come in, the exigencies of management being otherwise assumed to be beneath him. Had he forgotten that she knew about Baxter's problems on HSC's recent Kazakhstan mission?

'Dear old Bent,' said Hilleard dreamily, 'a legend in the profession. He'll be Team Leader.' As Hilleard described him, Baxter, a MODE departmental head in the old days of long, long ago, was decent and friendly, and had a brain so big it was said to have pushed out much of his hair. Lord Pareto's planned contribution to the team, on the other hand, had a more thorny genesis.

'*Lord* Pareto, did you say?' said Faith, taken off guard.

'Yes,' said Hilleard, his voice dropping to a whisper, 'and, *entre nous*, it *is* a bit of a strange one.'

A crackle from the loudspeaker. The flight would be boarding in twenty minutes. Faith started to arrange what she would need on the aeroplane: some reading on Uganda, her special socks, her iPod.

Lord Pareto, Hilleard explained, had once been a mandarin at the Foreign Office, done a long tour in North Korea, everyone grateful for his efforts and fortitude. On retirement he had been co-opted on to the Board of COMPASSION. 'You know them, Faith? It's a campaigning NGO. As you know, the charities love an aristocrat on the payroll, it does wonders at the fundraising parties. Just as important, Pareto's wife's related to the Minister and he probably likes to get a bit of sun after a long European winter. It's all a bit messy but the point is, for us, having a scion of one of England's great and ancient families on the team is bound to open doors and, even though the old boy is getting on a bit now, he assured me he's still right at the cutting edge of theory and best practice.'

So, not for this mission dozy old colonials like the famous five soil scientists, shabby beardies in faded corduroy. No, Baxter and Pareto were to be the epitome of the modern consultant, super-aggressive storm trooper types with customised spreadsheets and PowerPoints for every eventuality, five thousand dollar suits and mobile, wireless super-fast Internet connections, all with GPS, just in case they got lost.

'We showed MODE your CV,' Hilleard had told her, beaming, 'and they jumped at it. They want *young* people these days. They want enthusiasm. The High Commissioner in Kampala fancies himself as a bit of do-gooder. Wants to raise his profile on the Geldof Scale, if you know what I mean, and he needs young people and young women especially, if you follow me. Quite right too. Truth is, in this game, experience is vastly overrated.'

The lounge door opened and an elderly man bustled in, pulling an attaché case on a trolley. Wearing a green safari suit and a Panama hat, he looked like a vicar on holiday. Fully the sociologist, Faith watched him warily, logging his details, noting the flash card hanging from a string around his neck. Could this be Pareto?

'But don't be fooled, Faith. MODE is a very demanding client. Brightest and best of the sons of the morning, dawn on our darkness, and lend us thine aid. And all that.'

She reached in her bag for her reading.

'And on that note,' Hilleard had added. 'Be wary of other consultancy reports. Pasted together by people who can't write for people who don't read. Stick with the old stuff and the people who know. Things don't change much. Bend in the River, that's a good one.'

And that was enough briefing. With still barely an acknowledgement from Bifferty, she was signing the disclaimer forms and climbing into the cab for the airport, clutching, despite Hilleard's warning, the latest volume on Uganda from the World Bank. 'Uganda is blessed,' she read on the first page, 'with a rich diversity of natural habitats, species and genetic resources in its forests. It is one of the most diverse countries in Africa, with 11% and 7% of the world's bird and mammal species respectively . The surface of the country is 241,548 km squared, of which about 35% is classified as farmland, 20% as forest, 29% as bush, grassland and swamps (including a tiny 0.2% designated as built-up areas), and 15% as open water. Average annual rainfall is above 600 mm in most of the country and above 1,000 mm for about half of it…'

She could hardly wait. On the Bangkok trip, her colleagues had been a disappointment but she realised it would be different this time. The soil scientists had *appeared* keen but none of them had written a word and Faith had been drafted in to compile the proceedings for the entire conference. Having not understood the discussions or having taken many notes, she had had to invent most of the findings, but nobody checked and she was pleased to be given a pat on the back by Hilleard. Later, while briefing the bureaucrats at the UN Climate Office in Geneva, she had seen the only written material the beardies had submitted, a shoebox full of expense claims with receipts from taxi companies, dry cleaning firms, pharmacies, shoeshine girls and that wonderful catch-all for the forgetful and innumerate, 'contingencies'.

'*Last call for BA063. Business class passengers please board from the front of the aircraft.*'

She followed the group of green-shirted Americans as they waddled out into the corridor and turned towards the gate. She could hear the vicar behind her, the clip of his brogues echoing along the linoleum. Still no sign of Baxter or Pareto. In the boarding tunnel queue, the green shirts ahead of her were huddled together, yakking loudly in a barely decipherable hillbilly discourse, and she was pushed up against a man she guessed must be the group leader, a genial bozo with his hat on backwards. As they all shuffled forward, she found herself, without exactly meaning to, drawn into conversation with the man about what his group was going to do in Uganda.

'Doin' the work of the good Lord, ma'am.'

She was thrown. Perhaps she had misheard. 'You're missionaries?'

'You bet.' He had a kindly smile but, still, mission work hadn't come into her development training.

'What will you all do?'

'We're working with the lost children of Uganda. If we can multiply ourselves in these young people, then we can reach multitudes. We can reach nations.'

She wasn't sure what to say. 'Are the children lost?'

'You bet, yes ma'am. But Africa is the fire pot of spiritual renewal and they can be found again.'

His name was Bill and he started to tell her how, ten years before, God had impressed on his heart the GRACE Project.

Another acronym, this *was* the development world.

'God Rescuing African Children from Evil, ma'am. We've been tasked with supporting Christian schools and street children ministries, trying to make an impact spiritually. Our goal is to glorify God by helping people come to know Him. We do this through the regular teaching and preaching of scripture and by functioning together as a community of believers.'

This was all a bit sudden but hadn't CARE once put it something like that, something about treasuring the vibrant spirit of service and love? Even Hilleard had talked about savouring the experience for self-evaluation and growth.

As the missionaries trundled forward, turning right into economy, she turned left and took her designated seat in the rear of the front cabin. Seat? A huge recliner with a TV screen and enough room to stretch out completely. Still pondering how much she had come to know God herself, she unloaded her necessities into the pocket of the chair in front, helped herself to the champagne the charming stewardess was proffering and settled into her reading: "Uganda enjoyed a period of sustained economic growth of about seven percent annually between 1990 and 2006, made possible by a stable ruling coalition, macro-economic stability, low inflation and relative peace. Poverty declined from 56 percent in 1991 to 25 percent in 2010…"

The vicar was making his way up the opposite aisle, struggling with a heavy bag. He smiled at her and walked on. Not Pareto then. The crew was doing a last-minute inspection. Stewardesses were moving among the cabin checking seat belts. Where were Pareto and Baxter? Had they missed the flight?

Then, just as a steward was adjusting the controls on the fuselage door, trying to swing it shut, there was shouting from outside the aircraft, urgent noises, arguing, and as everyone turned to look, an old duffer in a cricket blazer bursting through and into the cabin. He had a camera bag over his shoulder and was dragging a large case and several plastic carrier bags of duty-free goods, one of which dropped to the floor, the contents spilling across the carpet. 'Fuck!' he muttered, out of breath, as if he had been running.

A stewardess approached. 'I hope you've not been drinking,' she said, carefully stepping around the debris of miniature whisky bottles and cigarette cartons. She was a large, forbidding matron in a dark blue uniform and the man retreated a step.

He was gasping for air, so much so it seemed he might be fighting back asthma or a heart attack. 'I nodded off,' he stammered, 'I'm sorry, I…' He gawped around the cabin as if seeking a witness to come forward on his behalf. But the passengers had no wish to be involved. Most of those Faith could see were making careful and intense studies of their respective safety leaflets.

'Wait here,' said the stewardess and marched away.

Another, younger, woman approached, put a friendly hand on the man's shoulder, tried to steer him away from the main entrance.

'Get back,' he shouted, stumbling against the lavatory door, suddenly angry, suddenly red-faced. 'Don't touch me. Get *off*!'

'I'm sorry sir,' said the young woman, 'but it's forbidden for intoxicated persons to board the flight. If you're drunk, I'm afraid we will have to ask you to leave the aircraft.'

'Leave the aircraft?' he barked in the kind of chalk-on-blackboard voice only heard these days at Henley. 'Drunk? Leave the aircraft? I've just run half a mile to get here.' Then he was reaching for something inside his jacket, scrabbling at the pocket, and there followed that endless frozen moment, the one all air travellers fear. Eyes wide, Faith, and all around her, watched the hand plunge into the pocket, observed the contortions on the face, waited for the weapon to emerge, every movement stopped, every passenger, all the crew paralysed. So this was how it would be. Why had they gone along with the farce of being polite? Why had they not just jumped the ridiculous man then and there, battered him to the ground with their support cushions?

'You can't speak to *me* like that.' His arm jerked free, something in his hand, not a gun or even a knife but a wallet, battered and torn. He was brandishing it in the air now like a crazed cop in a cheap buddy movie. 'I'm with the United Nations. I've got full VIP accreditation. Look, I've got the *laissez-passer* right here.' There was an electric silence. The bodyguards had failed to shoot. Where were they, the trained marksmen, the hotshot marshals who would blast away before the fanatic could reach his weapon?

The man thrust his ID right into the stewardess' face as if it *were* a gun. He was so convincing he must have rehearsed it. 'Is that a way to treat a loyal customer? Is that a way to behave? I've got five million air miles and what do I get for them? I've never seen such rudeness, such appalling service. I'm here as a servant of the Crown and you treat me like some common oik.'

The stewardess flinched. 'I do beg your pardon sir,' she grovelled. 'My apologies. This is a terrible misunderstanding.

UN? I'm sorry we didn't know earlier. We might have...' She was stalling, trying to think. 'Perhaps we could have upgraded you but... unfortunately... first class is now completely full.'

'Never mind that,' the man snapped. He seemed to have regained a little control. 'There are other priorities now.'

Faith looked up for a moment, careful not to attract attention. She may have been inexperienced but she knew the first principle of long-distance air travel: celebrities and lunatics are to be avoided at all costs.

Presently the matron returned, accompanied by a burly policeman with a machine gun on his shoulder. He seemed pensive, perhaps sifting the evidence in his mind. 'Now then,' he said to the old man, 'have we all calmed down? Everything all right, sir? What do you say we get this show on the road?'

The man looked from the policeman to the older stewardess and back again then waved his arms as if directing the plane in some esoteric manner known only to himself. The other passengers seemed to be holding their collective breath even as the tension had relaxed a little. The man did his best to smile. He shrugged. 'Oh well, OK, where's my seat then?'

'Up there, on the right, sir,' said the stewardess, pointing up the aisle and quietly taking possession of his bags.

As he approached, Faith risked a quick, sideways glance. The fellow was in his mid-fifties maybe but his ruddy complexion and thin patchy hair had made him seem older. He stopped beside her as if to take another breath before trudging on, another step on some interminable journey. Then, before she could reflect and without even a warning, he was pushing his way over her, launching himself at the seat by the window, jerking and shoving against her legs, his shoulder bag swinging in her face.

'Just a minute,' said Faith, unable to hide her irritation. 'Excuse me! Is this your seat?' This was silly. There were empty seats all over the cabin and he wanted to sit next to her.

'Of course it is. Otherwise I wouldn't be trying to sit in it.'

She rose to let him past and within moments he had settled, lowered the backrest and completely crashed out, indifferent to the trouble he had caused. There were no signs of their departure although by now the flight was over an hour late. She tried to read some more but was fidgety and tense.

'This airline really is a disgrace,' slurred the man suddenly, from his near horizontal position. 'They simply don't care, can't even be bothered to be polite. One *has* to be firm with them.'

Faith frowned.

'Lord Pareto of Pangbourne, by the way. I suppose you're the trainee.' He stuck out a hand, soft and clammy as it slid through her fingers.

It was obvious of course. Their seats would have been booked together. But then what had happened to Baxter?

'What's that?'

'Dr Hilleard told me we were *all* booked on this flight,' said Faith.

Pareto scowled. 'I'm lost. Sorry. Baxter? Who's he?'

'Our team leader.'

'Is he the consultant?'

'We're *both* consultants, him and me, we're both with HSC. And I am *not* a trainee.'

'You're both with HSC?'

'Yes.'

'Shouldn't *you* know where he is then? How the hell would I know?'

Faith tried to remember what Pareto was supposed to do on the team but all the background Hilleard had rattled out had drained from her mind and the young stewardess was now leaning across her seat. 'Everything OK, sir?' she was asking. 'We have a take-off spot in fifteen minutes and we need to get going.'

Pareto pulled a face. He seemed to be considering whether to give permission for departure. 'What did I say?' he grunted. 'Rude and unhelpful. Let's hope their flying skills are better than their manners.'

The stewardess smiled graciously and walked back to her radio. A dull thud announced the closure of the aircraft door and BA's theme music began to ooze in from speakers in the fuselage, like sludge from a broken drain.

And that was it. There was no going back. She was locked in now. Oh wondrous world!

THREE

April 5th 2011

"The moment that the topic of the pre-European African past is raised, many individuals are concerned for various reasons to know about the existence of African "civilizations". Mainly, this stems from a desire to make comparisons with European "civilizations". This is not the context in which to evaluate the so-called civilizations of Europe. It is enough to note the behaviour of European capitalists from the epoch of slavery through colonialism, fascism, and genocidal wars in Asia and Africa. Such barbarism causes suspicion to attach to the use of the word "civilization" to describe Western Europe and North America."
- Walter Rodney, How Europe Underdeveloped Africa.

Four days later and Faith, once again in cotton skirt and flat sandals, no make-up, is perched on the edge of a fake leather chair in a recess just off the fake marble lobby of the Hotel Imperial, Kampala. She has managed to set up a meeting and she is watching her man, her appointee, approach.

The Hotel Imperial was not what Faith expected. Then again, what *does* one expect in Africa for three hundred dollars a night? On her Bangkok trip, half that money had bought luxury beyond anything she had ever experienced but this, as Hilleard had repeatedly warned her, was not Bangkok. Her first view of the Hotel Imperial was from the outskirts of town and she thought the huge, squat, windowless building on the skyline might have been a derelict grain silo or maybe the town jail or perchance a missile launch pad.

'Welcome,' said a grinning loon, sunk deep inside an oversize purple, green and gold doorman's uniform. He checked the glove compartment of the vehicle. 'Have you got a gun, madame?' he asked. Eventually he opened the barrier to the underground car park then clicked his heels and saluted twice.

'Who the fuck was that?' grunted Pareto, waking up in the back. 'For a moment I thought I was back in Pyongyang.'

Disgorged into total darkness, deep in the innards of the building, they were led by a man with a torch through what appeared to be air-conditioning tunnels, up a concrete staircase of which every step seemed a different size. At what Faith took to be the ground floor, they picked their way through the kitchen of a Chinese restaurant and around the back of a gaggle of stalls selling African masks. Faith was tired and when she saw the reception desk far off in the distance, she remembered her need of a bath and pushed on ahead, leaving Pareto confused and breathless, struggling with his luggage.

A large crowd was milling round the lobby and she had to shout over the din. 'Bookings for two? Dr Cullimore.'

The clerk checked the screen. And checked again. And again. 'Madame, I'm afraid...'

She knew what was coming.

'You see, madame, we have a conference....'

'Oh please, you must have *one* room. Please, we made bookings.' She gave him her slinkiest smile and thrust out her chest.

The clerk bit his lip, looked blank.

She scanned the lobby and the heaving throng. Who were all these people? She didn't really have to ask. She knew it was an NGO thing. So many beards. So many women in saris and young men in Palestinian scarves. So many furrowed brows.

'Just *one* room? Please...'

'Well, perhaps we may have *one*. There could have been a cancellation.'

She signed the form before he could change his mind, grabbed a porter and pushed her way towards the lifts. The place was absolutely *chocka*. Even as she waited for the lift, buses were pulling up outside, disgorging more delegates, more development workers, more consultants.

The porter bumped his trolley along the corridor and into her room, casually tossing her laptop on to the bed.

'Oi, be careful!' A touch of The Commandante but it was a brand new MacBook, property of HSC, and she didn't want it damaged.

'Sorry, madame,' grovelled the young lad, in a convincing display of servility, all the while pulling back the curtains, dusting the dormer, fiddling with the phone. She smiled graciously. He couldn't be expected to know what was in the little black bag and what would he think if he did? This tiny box of circuitry was worth half his life's income.

She walked to the window and slid it open. A spectacular view over the city and far in the distance, the sparkle of what could only be Lake Victoria. Immediately below a huge, circular swimming pool, a marquee, conference delegates doing their lengths, waiters in white suits, a band on the podium, the tinkle of glasses and, even at this distance, the sweet smell of barbecued pig.

And here was her appointee, sliding towards her through the throng of bean feasters and work-shoppers. He was moving among his people, seemed almost to be floating. It was a performance, reaching out to shake the many proffered hands like a great campaigner on the stump. It was as if he knew everyone in the place. Or they knew him.

She had been watching the crowd for some time and was already classifying the people by one or other distinguishing feature: with tie or without, western shirt or African, attaché case or rucksack. This was a socks and sandals scene without a doubt, charity people, do-gooders, a missionary or two, maybe even some of her old CARE colleagues. There was a guy with a CONCERN T-shirt. The opposition. Whatever the conference was about though, this was the cheap seats, three hundred bucks a night or not.

'Name's Tripp,' said the man. 'The Bank.' There is only one 'Bank' in the developing world and it doesn't operate ATM machines or let you cash cheques. Tripp was the World Bank number two in Kampala, your genuine big cheese. With his coy little boy smile and his perfect teeth, the man was clearly American. Maybe it was also the pale linen catalogue jacket and the matching candy stripe catalogue shirt. Young, barely older than her, with freckles and a healthy tan, he had the deepest of deep blue eyes and a grin to kill for, kind and serious and deeply sincere. 'You OK?'

She nodded. 'Seems I was lucky to get a room.'

'You bet, we got the World Poverty Conference next week, you heard? It's a big one, takes days just to get all the delegates settled in. The main event is at the Serena but they're holding the NGO forum here. The discount wing.'

'The activists?'

'I guess. These people,' he gestured with his hand, 'are the scout parties, the Sherpas.'

The Serena Hotel, on the other hand, down the road a bit, was an altogether more swankerous establishment where the marble and the leather were genuine, the only place in town for the great and the good and those with corporate Amex cards. And even that wasn't good enough for the various heads of state. They and their flunkies would be accommodated at the exclusive Munyonyo Resort, a purpose-built VIP gaff down by the lake, silky-thighed waitresses flown in from Thailand and men with bazookas on the gate. The Pope was expected to show at some stage but the chalet they were going to put him in was still a state secret.

'I was thinking...' Tripp started to say but, at that moment, a deafening burst of noise shook the entire lobby, seeming to shake the hotel to its very foundations.

'Renovations!' he shouted over the din. 'Well kind of. They haven't finished the place yet and are still building night and day.'

It was true. Since her arrival, there had been almost continuous drilling somewhere in the building. Sleep was impossible much before midnight.

'They've thrown it up in three months which is insufficient time for the concrete in a fourteen-floor building to harden. It should be one month per floor, you know what I'm saying?'

She wasn't sure she did.

'It means they need to do a lot of running repairs. It also means you don't want to be in here during an earthquake.'

Faith looked at the ceiling. None of the tiles were flush or even square to the wall. Above the main door a large crack snaked its way to the window.

'The question you have to ask yourself,' Tripp continued, 'is whether that noise is really the hammer drilling they claim it is or whether it is the sound of concrete failing and, if the place did collapse, would there be a warning? A few minutes perhaps, with the cement cracking and falling? Or would it all come down like a pack of cards, no chance at all?'

She looked again at the ceiling. How would one know?

'Now,' Tripp rattled on. 'My problem is that I need to get to Nairobi for a Bank briefing tomorrow and, with all this unrest, I need to leave plenty of time to get to the airport.'

She hadn't heard about any unrest.

'Thousands of arriving delegates is bad enough but the opposition are using the conference as cover, making a nuisance of themselves, trying to embarrass the government. There was trouble in the Katwe settlement last night and the police have been in there cracking heads. But I was thinking that you could come with me, in the car. How about it? It'll give us some quality time together.'

She must have looked surprised.

'Don't worry, the guys say the road is clear now.'

'The guys?'

'Security guys. At the Bank. They say the streets are quiet.' He spoke in a muted whisper as if he was talking to a friend or a partner in crime. 'You've had a security brief, yeah?'

She hadn't.

'Well, there *is* a bit of unease out there but it's not an issue. It's not like Jo'burg. You're not likely to be shot at or have your head sawn off by a meth'd up lunatic with a penknife.'

He had a car outside, a black Mercedes long wheelbase four-wheel drive with tinted windows and CD plates. It was sleek and shiny with room enough inside for him to spread out all his papers and still set up a pool table. They sat in the second row and Tripp told the driver to get going.

'Tripp! Is that your first name or your second?'

'Some people say Dr Tripp but Tripp'll do. But how's it going? How's the work? I heard you'd been in the field already.'

He was right, she *had* been in the field, wherever that exactly was, and she was still struggling with all she had seen, still trying to make sense of it. The flight from London had arrived just as the sun was coming up and no sooner had she stepped out of baggage reclaim into the warm African morning than a little Ugandan in spectacles and waterproof hat had launched himself out of the crowd, his handwritten welcome sign held up like a white flag. She couldn't remember whether he had offered a name but he did say he was a senior officer with the Ministry of Agriculture's National Agricultural Development Service, otherwise known as NADS. He was polite and friendly and he was insistent that the team should come with him, 'to see some farmers.'

She hesitated. Who *exactly* was this guy? Was he on their team, their *side*, or someone else's side? Was that the right way to look at it? Was he authorised to set up their programme? What had he to do with their brief? But she was exhausted after the long flight and Pareto was still inside the terminal somewhere, gathering up his gear.

'We'll visit some project sites, talk to some farmers,' said the man, in a voice somewhere between a mumble and a mutter. Two lackeys were already manhandling her luggage on to a trolley, hauling it towards a white Land Cruiser which was idling just the other side of the fence.

'Wait, wait, just a minute. What about Dr Baxter? Shouldn't we wait till he arrives? Maybe we need to check in with the authorities first?'

The man looked confused.

'Our team leader is not with us.' Was she being over formal? 'I'm concerned we don't jump the gun without him.'

'The Minister? You know him, yes?'

'No.'

'I think for him the team would like a what? A visit. That is what he seems to see.'

It had been a challenging few hours. On the plane she had wrestled to reconcile the behaviour of Lord Pareto with what she knew of COMPASSION and its commitment to 'social justice and human rights for all in the developing world'. Now she was faced with another kind of test. 'It's just a question of protocol,' she said, as convincingly as she could. 'I mean, won't the ministry expect a call from us before we start? Even as a courtesy?'

'That,' smiled the man, 'has been captured by what I said,' and, smiling reassuringly, he took her by the arm and began to steer her towards the car.

Just then, Pareto, photographer's bag strapped across his shoulder, stumbled out of the terminal. 'Care-*ful*!' he shouted at a porter who was pushing his trolley. Shouldn't they wait for Baxter, she tried to ask him. But Pareto, gaunt and worn out, probably hung-over from eight hours of drinking on the flight, was more concerned with his camera stuff. 'Don't drop it,' he snapped as their new friend helped ease the bag off his shoulder.

She let herself be shepherded into the Land Cruiser and strapped in. For a few minutes, Pareto was engaged in securing his gear but, eventually, he eased his considerable girth into the seat next to hers. 'Who is this guy,' he whispered, 'and where the fuck are we going?'

Finally they were out of the airport and racing along some kind of main road. 'Sit back,' said the man. 'It's an enjoyable drive.'

It was dual carriageway for a few miles and they sped along easily enough, weaving among the traffic, overtaking on the outside, scooting by on the inside, the driver winding his window down to shout cheerful abuse at anyone in earshot. Then they were on to a single lane road which in places had been cut from the hillside, great escarpments of mud hanging above them and dribbling away below. From what Faith could see, most of the vehicles were unfit for the road while, judging from their performance, three quarters of the drivers appeared to be drunk. Presumably few of them would have licences or insurance. She was glad their driver seemed to be taking care.

After an hour there was a sign for Kampala and then they slowed and came to a halt. There were cows on the road, the driver said, or was it a broken-down truck? They waited in a long tailback for forty-five minutes and then edged on to another stretch of dual carriageway with glimpses to the right of high-rise buildings, even skyscrapers. The modern city.

Then another hour easing through tin shacks, lean-tos, wooden houses, corrugated iron and everywhere mud and more mud. Faith was beginning to feel queasy. There was a faint smell of diesel. Was it coming from the car or was it just background clag? 'How much further is it?'

'Not far,' said the man from the ministry, somewhat gleefully.

'But we've already done two hours.'

'That is very true.'

'We've done two hours already...'

'Yes.'

Then, a worse smell, a miasmic stench. It was sweet and sour and gagging, like burning hair or rotting flesh and it seemed to thicken the very air they were breathing.

'What's that smell?'

'I'm not hearing you.'

'That stink. What is it?'

'Meat factory,' said the man proudly and he pointed to a walled compound. 'They are burning the horns. See the birds? They come to pick. Those big ones are marabou storks.'

Eventually, the carriageway opened out a little and the traffic began to speed up again. They were going north now, said the man. 'This is the road.'

As well as the constant stream of cars, there were also buses, big and small, lorries, single and double trailer, container trucks. There were bicycles and motorbikes, bullocks, sheep and chickens, market vendors lugging goods, often on their heads, uniformed children walking to school. Somehow Faith had imagined rural areas with farms and colourful farmers hoeing maize but this urban sprawl seemed to be all there was, not much to see but shanty towns, ragged people, scabby dogs.

On and on, more slums, more people, more cars. Weary as she was the buzz of the engine was boring into her head like a wasp in a bottle. At one moment, she felt as if she had been drugged and it was as if the car was hardly moving. The next they were going fast again, weaving and dodging, half of the vehicles going suicidally quick, the other half suicidally slow. But she was too tired to resist. Dead animals in the road: dogs, cats, monkeys. They passed some banana gardens and a settlement where a scattering of naked children danced and yelled by the side of the road. At another place, they crossed a bridge and

Faith saw several men, naked, getting ready to swim, their eyes a startling white against their black skins.

'My friend?' said Pareto, at one point, trying to get the attention of their minder. 'Am I right in thinking you have Pygmies here?'

'No need to worry, sir, Pygmies all gone.'

Faith was asleep when the vehicle crossed the Nile bridge at Karuma and she was still sleeping when they pulled into the district headquarters in Gulu at around one o'clock. 'This is the what? The guest house,' said the man from the ministry, as they pulled up next to what looked like a concrete pillbox. 'Welcome to what? To Northern Uganda. If this was a country, it would be the poorest in the world. You will stay in the guest house tonight. Have a short rest. Let me pick you later.'

The place was not inviting. The lobby stank like a common bordello – an ammoniac blend of cheap scent, rancid coconut oil and copious semen. And checking in was a trial. Under a huge picture of the President, a handsome man with a genuine smile, the manageress, a large woman in a voluminous black turban, tried to take their details. She spoke little English and Pareto, growing more exasperated by the minute, seemed to feel he had to spell out that he needed a smoking room, with a shower not a bath, a wake-up call with tea and mangoes at six (so he could catch the World Service news on his satellite radio) and no, repeat no, neighbours on either side. The whole process took nearly an hour.

By the time she got to her room, a hot, windowless cell with a small bed and one chair, Faith was shattered. She had just enough time to set the alarm before crashing into deep sleep.

And she was little better come the afternoon. She was still trying to wake up when a crowd of ululating women arrived along with an army of men in dark suits, all of them smiling, crowding around, offering hands. The district had laid on another vehicle, they said, just for the day. Another vehicle? Well, a fleet of vehicles. Three more Land Cruisers, two Pajero four-wheel drives, an old Land Rover and a couple of motorbikes.

Faith was unnerved. Was this the intimate meeting with the stakeholders specified in their brief?

'People have been drummed,' said their friend from the ministry, and Faith made a mental note to find out his name.

If the people had been drummed, it had certainly encouraged a good turnout. One by one the crowd introduced themselves. First, there was the political apparatus, that is the mayor, the LC5 Chairman, the District Security Officer and his entourage of uniformed security personnel, all with rifles and sunglasses, the Municipal Secretary, the LC3, the Provincial Commissioner, the LC1 vice-chairperson, the District NADS Co-ordinator, the Sub-county NADS Co-ordinator, the Parish Chief and the Sub-location Sub-chief. They all shook hands and said how pleased they were. Then followed the various district departmental heads, a bewildering array of Directors, Assistant Directors, Acting Directors, Deputy Directors, Commissioners, Department Heads and Subject-matter Specialists and, of the latter, there seemed to be a full complement for each department. That meant Agriculture, Forestry, Water, Veterinary, Natural Resources, Land Adjudication, Provincial Affairs, District Affairs, Regional Development, Environment, Planning, Roads, Works, Energy, Health, Gender, Trade and Commerce, Micro-Finance, and Education. Then, lurking at the back, almost hiding in the wings, were a handful of non-technical people whose stammered introductions Faith could barely hear but might as well have been the Supreme Custodian of the President's District-based Speed-dating Pool. Looking round Faith counted forty-three people in all.

'I thought it was just an informal thing,' she protested. 'All I want is to ask a few questions.'

Everyone smiled. One or two clapped.

Pareto leaned forward to whisper in her ear. 'I thought he said the Pygmies had gone.'

Eventually, the two of them were bundled into the fanciest of the three new Land Cruisers, Faith in the front with the driver, Pareto and the man from the ministry in the middle with the District NADS Co-ordinator and a few more in the side seats at the back, six vehicles in all, the motorcycles with a passenger apiece.

'Where are we going?' asked Faith.

'To find a farmer,' said the District NADS Co-ordinator who seemed to have assumed control.

Once out of town, the rough tarmac gave way first to a moonscape of potholes then to brown murram which, as the convoy raced along, sprayed out behind them in a giant cloud of fine orange dust. At one point, they entered a stretch of forest. It was dense and dark and the great trees, most of them swathed in creepers, pressed against the side of the road, almost as if ready to reach out and swallow them up. As they turned a bend on the side of a hill, Faith got a view back the way they had come and glimpsed a stretch of water reaching to the horizon: the Nile, mythic, legendary river, sought by Europeans for two thousand years and, here she was, riding along its flank in an air-conditioned Japanese 4x4.

On a bridge by a stream, an old woman was sitting on a log, her body wrapped in a swathe of white cloth, her face a matt black.

'Looks like a witch,' laughed the man from the ministry.

The woman didn't wave and for a curious fleeting moment, Faith felt as if she had seen a ghost or a presentiment of something from the future.

In the vehicle, the man from the ministry and the District NADS Co-ordinator took turns to try to explain what the project was about. NADS was a major initiative, the District NADS Co-ordinator said, to try to improve farmers' knowledge and to raise agricultural yields. It was based on helping groups of farmers to work together and on encouraging them to seek out services that small businesses, input dealers, grain traders and so on, would be able to provide.

'People here spent twenty years in camps,' said the man from the ministry. 'They lost everything and the fighting was terrible. All sorts of what? Atrocities.'

All sorts of projects were being implemented to help the villagers get back on their feet. NADS had been started as pilots in a small number of districts and its success had been such that the donors were falling over themselves to provide funds to expand it. MODE had been a leading light in the process. After six years, said the District NADS Co-ordinator, the project was famous. It was a model for other countries. Visitors came from far away, from China and Japan.

Faith was impressed. She had prepared a few questions but somehow she couldn't find a suitable pause in which to ask them. Like asking the man from the ministry's name, it seemed very easy to miss the moment. After an hour racing and bumping around what seemed like the murram road to nowhere, she was quite bewildered as to direction and time, all the while the man from the ministry was talking and talking and *talking*. 'The President has decreed prosperity. Prosperity for what? For all. Everyone will be prosperous. Every farmer will have an income of ten thousand dollars a year. The wounds of the war will be what? Healed.'

Faith was struggling to keep her eyes open and Pareto, sprawled listlessly across the back seat, had succumbed to the pleasures of total blackout. They passed a large machinery yard where a dozen or so sparkling new tractors were parked. 'Assembled in Uganda,' said the District NADS Co-ordinator proudly. 'We need tractors here, for modern agriculture.'

Struggle as she might, Faith just couldn't stay awake. It was so *hot*. And still they were driving, twenty miles, thirty, the forty-three dignitaries, the six vehicles, still in line, in formation, the road worse and worse. Occasionally they stopped and walked around for a minute or two, all forty-three people trying to locate the elusive farmer, determined to submit him or her to rigorous questioning, but on the one occasion they managed to trap one, an elderly lady in rags who spoke no English, the hubbub was too intense for Faith to get in a word. She was glad to return to the vehicle where the air con hummed and she could sink back into the soft seats. She was thankful to be in the front where no one could see her eyelids drooping.

'That one,' said the District NADS Co-ordinator, at one point, gesturing towards a red tractor by the side of the road, its exhaust belching black diesel smoke, 'is for ploughing.' In the driver's seat, bare-chested, his well-toned workman's muscles gleaming with sweat, a young man in a builder's helmet watched them as they passed. He looked Faith straight in the eye but he didn't smile.

FOUR

April 5th 2011

Q. How does the white man hide something from an African?
A. He writes it in a consultancy report.
- Ugandan joke

'The NADS project's been a huge success, Faith. All credit to MODE of course. Their input has been invaluable.' Tripp had explained they would try to beat the rush hour, always at its worst in the evening, by taking a shortcut through the Industrial Area, past the US Embassy, over the hill to Makinde from where they could drop down to the airport road. 'It's a bit of a rat run, but usually it's the better route.'

They'd made good time so far but were now at near standstill behind a green minibus, the driver of which was in some kind of shouting match with a group of motorbike drivers. With bars across the windows, Faith wondered what kind of vehicle it was especially when she realised there seemed only to be women inside, young girls. The one by the window had her face painted in bright colours, blue, red and yellow.

'NADS is our showpiece,' Tripp went on. 'Probably the best project in the Bank's entire agriculture portfolio. We've had two evaluations both of which have given it the highest marks. The farmers are benefiting in large numbers, with lots of positive spillovers. The rate of return on the loan is over two hundred per cent. It's hugely exciting.' Tripp was still unaware of the girls in the van, so deep was he in contemplation of the project's achievements. 'Green-lighting its expansion is a no-brainer.'

Faith was watching the girls. They had seen the two *muzungus* in the vehicle behind and were pointing and signalling in their direction.

'Uganda huh?' said Tripp when he finally realised he was being waved at. 'Not exactly the end of the world but you can certainly see it from here.' He liked his own jokes that was clear. 'Have you met the Minister yet, the Honourable?'

Unfortunately no, she had not. She'd called the Ministry of Agriculture on her first day back from the Gulu trip and tried to set up an appointment but the person she had spoken with had said the Minister was 'on safari'. She had visions of a man in tourist khaki, peering out from the top of a Land Rover, binoculars and a thousand dollar camera round his neck.

'You need to see him. I'll fix it. He's one of ours, top guy, very simpatico, right on message, you know what I'm saying?'

'Totally'.

'Another thing,' Tripp again, 'we've seen your terms of reference and we like the cross spectrum of analysts HSC has put together. We think your approach is sound, given the time available, although I expect MODE will be pushing you for more quantitative rigour.'

She waited.

'They like their quantitative rigour.'

She nodded. Do they? OK.

'By the way, is Dr Baxter here yet?'

She was relieved to be able to report that he was arriving tomorrow. 'You know him?'

'He did a paper on the Foster-Greer-Thorbecke weighted poverty gap index a few years back. Well, a note, or was it a memo? I forget.'

'And?' She was losing the thread a little now.

'I felt the dummy variables were a problem.' Tripp seemed to take this as a personal affront. 'There was an issue with heteroscedasticity.'

This guy certainly had the jargon. Like the missionaries of old, who had to learn Latin and Greek before being set loose on the natives, the development elite had to take an apprenticeship in Third World, a hybrid of acronyms and economic gobbledegook designed to deter all but the most persistent. While Faith was well on with the beginner's course she could see Tripp was far ahead of her. He had honed the basic demotic into a style of discourse so painful and confusing, it took on a perverse eloquence all its own.

'Some people were worried,' he was saying, 'y'all might get diverted by the static incidentals but I told them I'd appraise you as to NADS' dynamic possibilities.'

Faith was only half listening. The girls in front were leaping up and down now, banging on the van window, making strange, disturbing faces. Tripp turned and caught sight of them, pausing finally to watch for a moment.

'It's an ambulance,' he said, 'from the mental hospital in Butabika. You see them driving around occasionally. Probably when they need to hose down the cells.'

The van signalled to turn left and as it did, the girl with the painted face opened her shirt and, taking her large breasts in both hands, rubbed her nipples up against the glass.

'For the next phase of NADS,' said Tripp, not even pausing for breath, 'we must be sure all the modalities are fully leveraged. We must pursue sustainability, add value and elaborate mutually satisfactory goals.'

On her first morning at the Gulu guest house, the staff brought hot tea and ginger biscuits. Faith was sitting on the veranda watching the sun ease its way over distant trees only to have her reverie interrupted by Pareto, stumbling out of his room, bleary-eyed and grumpy, morning fag in hand. 'I told her,' he snapped, 'biscuits are no good to me, I must have mangoes. I need fibre. I mean, what's the problem?'

'Maybe they have bananas?' said Faith, trying to be helpful.

'One more night and that's it. I didn't come all this way to sleep in a fucking shed.'

The forty-three stooges had been dismissed the night before, all but the District NADS Co-ordinator, and the visitors had been told to prepare for a ride in a helicopter. 'A service for guests,' said their friend from the ministry. 'The Minister has ordered.'

'The Minister has a helicopter?' said Faith.

'Of course. He is a what? A general.'

'He prefers not to travel on the roads,' added the District NADS Co-ordinator. 'They are not for generals.'

It was the sheer volume of noise that struck her most, the metal clatter of the rotors echoing up the valley, the roar of the engines. Then the thing itself, the movie-familiar black insect, erupting sideways over the ridge, banking left, then right, swooping down on to the little concrete landing pad by the guest house, the pilot, a white man in helmet and headphones, Faith's holdall blown across the strip, hurtling away amid a miniature sandstorm.

'C'mon then, chop-chop,' said Pareto as he set off towards the helicopter, leaving Faith to follow behind. They ducked under the rotors, Pareto diving for the seat next to the pilot. Faith clambered into the back and the District NADS Co-ordinator handed her a helmet. A great vibration and she felt the machine lift, slowly at first and then, with a rush, up and rising, skating over the encampment below. The villagers who had gathered to see the commotion waved as the pilot pointed the nose out into the forest then, with the flick of a switch, they were away, moving east, towards the sun.

In a helicopter it is noisy and impossible to communicate without shouting and, after a few minutes, Faith was happy to retreat into her own world. She had come all this way to do something, to support this project, to help the people here. But already she was confused. What was this project trying to do? Was it going to help the poor? Who were the poor anyway? She wasn't even sure what questions to ask. What could she know that the people here didn't?

After half an hour and just as the unremitting roar was becoming truly oppressive, they turned north and made for a small village high on a ridge. There was some cloud on the hill and the pilot edged carefully around it, passing over the escarpment. Faith could see a piece of open ground and she felt the helicopter slide, crablike, towards it. Down they dropped and suddenly they were on the flat amidst a whirl of dust even thicker than that on take-off.

The pilot removed his helmet. 'They call this "the place of skulls",' he said, jumping out and running round to open the passenger door. 'I don't know why.' He was wearing shorts, tailored and tight, highlighting his thighs. An old colonial herself, she knew this was the dress of the white man outdoors, the uniform that distinguishes the honest bloke from the city slicker, the man of the soil from the joker in the business suit.

They walked, the man from the ministry first, then the District NADS Co-ordinator, then Pareto, who proceeded in a jerky, erratic manner, his head bent at an angle, as if he was searching for something in the long grass. Faith took up the rear. The path wound through a maize field and emerged in a clearing where an old woman was standing alone, holding a stick in the air. As they approached, Faith could see there was a snake speared on the end of the stick. It was wriggling, still alive.

'Boomslang,' said the man from the ministry, showing off his knowledge. 'Keep on the what? The track.'

'Of course,' Tripp was on autopilot by this time, 'the stakeholders have their differences but you'd expect that in any process, especially one as vibrant as this.' The car had travelled another four kilometres but had again been held up behind some sort of altercation. The driver edged his way past some small buses parked half in the road, angry crowds milling around. This was the same airport road she had travelled when they first arrived but, now, in the dark she could see nothing, and had no idea where they were, only the occasional flickering glow from a paraffin lamp lighting up a stall by the roadside.

From out of the shadows, some kids came running, sprinting along with the vehicle, banging on the window, shouting, jumping, checking over their shoulders, chased or being chased she couldn't tell. A truck edged past them, going the other way. In the blaze of its headlights, Faith saw Tripp in profile. His hair was exquisite. Luxuriant, thick, golden brown, and beautifully cut. His eyes were too small though and that little bit too ready to slide away.

Stopping and starting, they managed another kilometre before an even larger crowd forced the driver to a complete halt. As they waited, Faith saw a young boy, maybe twelve years old, falling to his knees. Sticks and stones were flying through the air as older youths leant over the boy, prodding him with what looked like fence posts. Even in the fading light, she could see the boy was bleeding badly, from his mouth and from his nose, and she could see too that he was crying, his eyes streaming. No one seemed to want to help him. Indeed people were pushing forward to get at him, kicking and flailing at him as he tried to escape.

'Shouldn't we *do* something?' she asked.

'Best not to get involved,' said Tripp, as the car began to move once more.

'What will they do to him?'

He looked away. There was nothing to say.

About a mile from the helicopter, they came to a little hamlet where some villagers were sitting under a tree. They were all women, Faith noticed, except for one very old man, bent over and grey.

'This is one of my NADS groups,' said the District NADS Co-ordinator. 'They all came from the camps.' He then began a long introduction, some of it in the local language, bits of it in English, and Faith was able to follow, more or less. The District NADS Co-ordinator said there were two people from 'Yookay' who had come to look at the project and they wanted to talk to farmers about their plans. He said he had been a NADS supervisor in this area for four years and he knew the people were keen for the project to expand so they would become prosperous and he hoped they would help the visitors. He explained that Madame Faith, as he now began calling her, wanted especially to talk to the ladies and that he would translate. This was the work Faith liked, talking to people, hearing their stories, understanding their lives. There were techniques for this of course, methodologies they were called in the textbooks, and she had learned them in her PhD fieldwork, practised there her interrogatory patter, the checklist in her head. She had the questions off by heart now, the nonintrusive ones to start, about income and working hours and time spent collecting water, innocent sounding chit-chat about gender roles and numbers of children and whether it was difficult to get medicine and how far away the fuel wood was and what crops the people grew. Then there was the little wealth-ranking exercise for when things were going really well, when she would try to chivvy people into arranging and classifying symbols drawn on the ground, when she could show her picture book with its quiz about local illnesses and disease and get people to identify who were the rich in the village and who were the poor.

Translation was sometimes a problem but she'd learned while doing her PhD that she had a real talent for intuiting what was going on underneath. The usual pattern was that the translator, in this case the District NADS Co-ordinator, would repeat her questions, sometimes in sentences so short she was surprised they imparted any meaning, other times in long embroidered stories or parables. There would then be a long pause and the women would confer among themselves, sometimes at length, eventually volunteering an answer. Sometimes this would occasion great mirth in one or other group, or it might provoke shouting and protests. At any rate, after some time, the translator would set to work providing an answer to the original question. If this answer made any sense, Faith would write it down in her notebook. This was the information she would later use to write her report. If, as seemed might be the case here, she could not understand the reply, she might try again, phrase the question differently. Sometimes she would use her discretion and pass on to a different topic.

After fifteen minutes of formal group talk between the District NADS Co-ordinator and a dozen or so women, Faith was able to gather a smaller group and sit alone with them on the ground.

'What do they think of the NADS project?' she asked.

There was a murmur which she took to be a positive response.

'Has NADS helped them? Was life better than it was in the camps?'

'Oh yes, missus,' they chorused.

'What benefits have they got?'

Government officers had 'sensitised' them, it seemed, and they'd been 'facilitated' and provided with 'resources'. Even some 'capacity-building' had been arranged. There would soon be prosperity for all. Gender was very good, thank you.

'Have they got money from the NADS work?'

They were quite sure they had.

'How would they spend it?'

They weren't sure. Maybe they would build a new meeting house in the village and get a DVD player. One woman said yes, and the men will buy beer and gamble on cards and dominoes and jigjig with other men's wives. Howls of glee all round.

'Maybe you would like to talk to this one special lady,' said the man from the ministry, coming over to interrupt. 'She is a model farmer.'

'OK. Great, yes,' said Faith, happy to oblige.

They proceeded through some trees to a large cement house with a small brick shed off to the side, a Friesian cow tethered to a post in the yard. The woman was waiting in the entrance. 'Good morning,' she said, in well enunciated English.

'Good morning,' said Faith and shook her hand.

The woman had recently retired from local government and NADS had given her the Friesian cow as well as a poultry "package" with three hundred layer hens and some complementary feed and medicines to get the enterprise going. Unfortunately, she had little experience of poultry farming and most of the birds had died.

'That's a pity,' said Faith, unclear what else to say. 'That barn is very impressive though.'

'Yes,' beamed the woman.

'Were you in a refugee camp?'

No, she was lucky, she said, she had friends in Kampala who looked out for her.

'Are you in a group?'

It seemed she had only joined a group since she'd got the birds. Perhaps that had been her problem. When the birds started dying she had no one to turn to.

'But you said she was a model farmer,' said Faith to the man from the ministry.

'Of course,' he said.

'But she seems quite well off.'

'Yes, the project has helped her.'

'Do others come to learn from her?'

'Three,' said the woman. The problem was that she was frequently out on other business so if people called she was often not there to receive them.

'Y'know,' said Faith, to no one in particular, as they walked back, 'everyone we met was a woman.'

'Of course,' said the man from the ministry, beaming. 'We are very gender positive on this project. Didn't you hear? They said gender was good.'

'Where are the men anyway?' asked Faith, looking round.

'In fact,' said the District NADS Co-ordinator, 'most of them are dead.'

She must have looked surprised.

'This is a place for that disease that goes around. The graves are over there under the trees.'

As they waited for the pilot to prepare the chopper for take-off, to go through his checklist, Faith sat on the grass, reflecting and writing in her notebook. Dispassionate observers might have speculated as to the quality of her information. They might have suggested that her questions revealed more about her than the answers did about the women of the village. But she was happy and her notebook was full.

'You like this place?' asked the man from the ministry.

'I love these *people*, their attitude, their approach to life.'

'Really?' said the man from the ministry. 'What do you mean?'

What *did* she mean? She knew this was a minefield. 'I dunno, easy-going?'

'You won't get development with easy-going,' grunted Pareto, coming up behind her.

She said nothing.

'But you sociologists are against development anyway, I suppose? Liberal capitalism and its inherently exploitative nature. And all that.'

She stayed silent. Was that a question or a statement?

'You see,' said the man from the ministry, taking on a pensive tone, 'these people are what? Pe-ezants.' He pronounced it to rhyme with green peas. 'Here the President's policy is to get them to where they *need* things. He wants them to get used to paying for school fees and health care and transportation. Then, when they need money to pay for these things, they will work and then they will look after their maize or their coffee or whatever they have. That's how you get what? Prosperity. *Development*.'

She was surprised. 'Is that the NADS line?'

'NADS,' said the District NADS Co-ordinator, 'doesn't have a line. NADS is flexible, bottom-up, demand-driven, farmer-led. '

Was that the line? 'But why can't we leave the people where they are?' asked Faith, suddenly wistful. 'They were quite happy before, with their bananas and their hunting.'

'Christ,' grunted Pareto, almost animated. 'Look over there. On the horizon.'

She turned to look and the two men laughed.

'The twenty-first century,' said Pareto. 'Population growth. It's on the way. Haven't you read the background papers, doctor?' He was quite the philosopher now. 'Our friend here is right. If this place is to have a hope, these people are going to have to buck up smartish. People must learn to buy and sell. They must learn to put values on things. Otherwise they're fucked.'

They'd barely managed fifty yards and still the noisy crowd and the boy, stumbling, tripping, falling, rising, falling again, someone clipping his ear with a stick. Then, at last, the car surged ahead and she lost sight of him.

As they reached the lakeshore, Faith could see a line of fires stretched out like beacons across waste ground to the right. A large crowd was silhouetted against the flames, some people carrying banners, one or two with old rifles. On the pavement, children were burning tyres, others beating oil drums in rhythm. Some of the drums had been filled with stones and were being rolled along the road, making an eerie thunderous rumble. The guys may have said the city was calm but had they been out here? The mood seemed ugly.

And then the car pulled up at the barrier for the airport compound, the driver fumbling to open the glove compartment for the security guards to check.

'See that old plane over there?' said Tripp, pointing to a rusted hulk not a stone's throw from the road. 'That's the one the Israelis stormed in 1976. The raid on Entebbe, you heard about that? They freed the hostages.'

Faith had seen the movie. 'And it's been there ever since?'
'Yup.'

'One thing,' said Faith, as they pulled away from the barrier. 'It was difficult to understand what was going on down there. Is NADS really helping the poor?'

Tripp appeared surprised by the question. 'Of course, I told you, it's one of our best projects. Washington loves it. *Everyone* loves it.'

She heard a pop-pop-pop, off in the distance. Fireworks? Or something else? Two soldiers sitting by the kerb, AK-47s cradled in their laps, rose to their feet and loped back along the road, fluent and graceful, cats on the prowl.

By the third day, the man from the ministry seemed mostly concerned with getting rid of them. 'But let us see one last group. You need to have a what? A representative sample.'

Back in the helicopter, they were soon roaring over the forest again, heading west. Faith was used to the rotor noise by now but still she couldn't hear a thing anyone said. So when, after a few minutes, the pilot shouted something to Pareto, his mouth almost in his ear, she took no notice. The man from the ministry was looking at a map and, like the other two, occasionally peering down, searching the ground below. The helicopter began a turn and they locked on to a small stream and followed it off to the left. After a minute, they swung around and made a pass back the way they had come. What were they trying to do? What were they hoping to see?

The pilot flicked a switch. 'There,' she heard him shout, but the rest was drowned in the fearsome clatter. He was pointing now to a small clearing on the edge of the forest, a tiny patch of brown by a sea of green.

They swooped over a village and Faith could see women running. They circled again, looking down on some huts and a huddle of people close by. They descended and she saw that the clearing was on a ridge, like a knife-edge, and that they were going to land in the centre of the precariously perched group of huts. Dust began to rise, almost engulfing them, and suddenly, just as they touched down, two of the huts started to lift off the ground. It was as if they were stretching at their bonds with the earth and then, as if ripped out, they abruptly flew backwards and away, down the side of the hill.

The engine was switched off and the roar began to subside. The rotors ground to a slow drone, then a purr and then silence, only the echo off the hillside now and the dust beginning to settle. The villagers, again almost entirely women, were standing in a huddle watching the place where the huts had been: a gap in the row now, as if a celestial dentist had pulled a festering tooth out by the roots.

The pilot removed his helmet and opened the door. A small ragged group, some in shoes, others not, shuffled cautiously to within twenty yards, apprehensive, scared even.

The pilot stood up and yelled. 'Where is the NADS office?'

Excited murmuring. The women wide-eyed, confused, several standing with their mouths open, in astonishment or even shock. Maybe they'd never seen a helicopter before, certainly not close up.

'NADS office?' the pilot tried again, impatient. 'D'you know where it is?'

Faith understood he was asking directions but were they really lost?

'NADS?'

The group conferred again and then, in an abrupt jerking action, one woman's arm shot out as if she was pointing. And she was pointing east, back the way they had come.

The pilot wasn't convinced. 'What's the name of this place?'

The woman looked anxious and pointed again, this time in the opposite direction.

The pilot shrugged, 'OK, thank you.' He had a chocolate bar on the dashboard and he tossed it to the woman who fumbled it awkwardly then dropped it through her fingers.

The pilot flicked some switches. 'It's got to be *that* way,' he said, as if talking to the machine, and, with a roar, the engine jumped into life once more.

The helicopter lifted off and, as it did, another house crashed into the valley. Amidst the swirling debris Faith could see women running, children screaming, a dog hiding its head in a bush.

'Quite extraordinary,' shouted Pareto gleefully, 'These people. They don't even know where they fucking are!'

At last they reached the terminal, uniformed porters running, one of them diving forward to open the door.

'Uganda, huh?' said Tripp. 'The sort of place people put up mirrors to make it look bigger.'

This time she laughed too.

'But, look, Faith, it's great. You're underway, you're moving. But keep it going, no let up, you know what I'm saying? Keep up the good work.'

And suddenly another limo, this time a monster stretch, cream with gilded paintwork, part showbiz, part Mafia: fat Elvis meets Dick Cheney. The man who climbed out was young. He wore a linen suit and a collarless shirt, aid industry chic. He had a laptop bag strung across his shoulder, not much thicker than a credit card. 'Tripp! Wha' happen', bro?' He raised his hand for a high five.

But Tripp knew his manners, was polite, motioned for the man to wait. He was a professional. He stayed with the matter in hand, didn't let himself get diverted. He put his hand on Faith's arm, firm and strong and purposeful. He looked her in the eye. 'Sorry I've got to leave just as you're starting. But it's only a couple of days, a conference. Did I say that already?'

'So many conferences…'

'Yeah, but this is a good one. Post Conflict Scenarios, it's the next big thing, the new paradigm.'

She smiled and waited.

'But as for NADS, remember the big picture. I'm sure you don't need me to tell you and MODE will repeat it ad nauseam. Keep the strategic context in sight at all times.'

'Yes, but...'

'The strategic context yeah?' He flicked away a lock of his gorgeous hair and, taking his colleague by the arm, ambled over to the first class check-in desk.

FIVE

April 8th 2011

"Western liberal capitalism, in its contradictory development and despite its inherently exploitative nature, ... is still capable of throwing up occasional relatively unselfish intellectuals and professionals, as it has done in Africa; people who ... from a kind of enlightened self-interest are motivated to throw in their lot with the oppressed peoples and classes and find genuine satisfaction and fulfilment in participation without dominance. They can help to work out solutions together with Africans in complementary equality, contributing their theory to be confronted and transformed by their companion's praxis until the theory of one becomes praxis and the praxis of the other becomes theory, in a progressive, mutual confrontation with the hard realities of our catastrophic age."
- Aidan Southall, 'The Recent Political Economy of Uganda' in Hansen and Twaddle (ed.), Uganda Now, 1988.

But what did 'good work' mean? Faith wasn't sure. Dr Julian Carruthers, the MODE Private Sector Adviser, as he was called, their ostensible contact in the system, had gone to Cape Town on a wine-tasting trip, or so his PA, Henrietta McNaughton-Balls, told her on the phone. 'Had to use up his travel allowance,' she explained. 'Before it expired.'

So she did some more phoning then spent a couple of days running around town, visiting NGOs, trying to catch donor reps, putting her face into the occasional desultory workshop, to not much avail. She tried to organise a participatory group feedback session with NADS staff and hoped Pareto would help.

'Participatory what?' he shouted, over a bad mobile phone line. 'No, no, not my style at all.'

She filled the empty moments with reading. You could never know too much about a place, she assumed. And so, on the morning of her sixth day, still no sign of Baxter, she was out on the tiny balcony of her ninth-floor hotel room with a pot of local coffee, the Lonely Planet Guide to Uganda and a pile of consultancy reports, the early morning sounds and smells of Kampala drifting in on the warm breeze from the lake. Above her, the ever-present, ugly-brute marabou storks circled on the thermals while, below, their young shuffled from foot to foot in colossal matted nests, each one woven into the tree canopy and substantial enough, it seemed, that, if the hotel was to collapse at that moment, she might be able to leap on to them like some kind of life raft.

She flicked through a pile of documents sent over by Tripp's office: a bibliography running to over a thousand reports, and those only from the last five years, some twenty of which Tripp had judged to be the *key* documents on NADS, stuff that she needed to have absorbed 'by yesterday'. Most of the reports seemed to rehash the ones that had gone before but Faith persevered doggedly nonetheless. "Uganda is blessed," she read, from a report near the top of the pile, "with a rich diversity of natural habitats, species and genetic resources in its forests. It is one of the most diverse countries in Africa, with for example 11% and 7% of the world's bird and mammal species respectively, in only 0.02% of the land area." Hadn't she read that before? Didn't it sound familiar?

"Sometimes known as the Pearl of Africa, the scenery is different, the vegetation is different, the climate is different, and, most of all, the people are different from anything elsewhere in the whole range of Africa."

She needed a drink. The minibar was full of delights but she restricted herself to white wine.

"All large mammal species suffered massive population declines in the years up to the early 1990s... This was a result of massive poaching during the terrible years of political instability..."

A brisk knock at the door.

'Just a minute.'

Another knock, rat-a-tat, louder this time, abrupt, invasive even.

'Hang on, *hang on.*'

She closed the file and climbed off the bed just as the door flew open with a violence that startled her, revealing, on the threshold, a curious figure. In his left hand, an old bush hat and, nestling by his feet, a sizeable tin case, so battered and torn it might once have been borne by porters on some great journey into the interior: on its side, stencilled boldly in white paint, big enough for all to see, the words Bent Beresford Quartermaine Baxter.

Taken off guard, Faith could do nothing but stare, the thump of the door still echoing in her ears. Baxter, in his turn, stood immobile for a moment, his eyes taking in the scene. He furrowed his brow and peered purposefully about, from the bed to the window, from the wall-mounted trouser press to the stack of reports on the floor. It was as if, puzzled as he obviously was, he hoped Faith might explain the reason for her presence, even as if he might be about to demand an answer to some metaphysical problem that was pressing desperately upon him.

There was silence for what seemed an age. Neither of them seemed to know what to say. 'Dr Baxter,' she managed eventually, as if suddenly remembering a long forgotten cue. 'Thank goodness you're here.'

Baxter responded with a smile all his own, moderately agreeable, moderately obliging, and ambled into the room, his shoulders rolling curiously as he walked, his manner suggesting an odd mixture of awkwardness and assurance. But he didn't speak and a further difficult silence ensued.

'Mmmm,' he finally managed, venturing to the window, picking his way across the room like one of the marabou storks she'd been watching, lifting his feet as if he might be tip-toeing across a swamp. He was a good-looking man, tall, willowy, a weary smile licking at the corners of his eyes. He had a thick, droopy moustache and pepper-and-salt hair, thinning and worn a little too long for a man of his age, giving him the look of an ageing Wyatt Earp.

Against the window, the light was behind him and for a curious moment, it seemed to Faith to cast him in an almost mythic aspect. Dr Bent Baxter, HSC's number one rural development *fundi*, celebrated (at least he *had* been until this unfortunate business in Kazakhstan) traveller and seasoned operative (one hundred countries under his belt, all the English-speaking African countries and lots of the non-English speaking ones too, years out in 'the bush' and 'the field', and it had to have been a grander version of the field than the one she had been to). At any rate, he was a maverick, a totally colourful guy, and 'a real friend in trouble', or so Hilleard had told her. Certainly his walk had about it something of an agricultural aspect.

His outfit was unorthodox for this business: white jeans (too tight and somewhat grubby), embroidered khaki shirt (also too tight, nasty epaulettes), snakeskin cowboy boots.

'My luggage was mislaid,' said Baxter. 'They gave me the pick of Lost Property.'

Faith was relieved. She'd been worried it might be an indication of some aspiration towards the role of white hunter. You never knew these days, dress etiquette was everywhere in flux, Denys Finch Hatton by Vivienne Westwood.

'How is it then?' he barked. 'Have you sorted it all out? I expect you've written the report already?' He was suddenly all business-like and formal.

'I *have* been to one of the project areas,' said Faith, 'but there wasn't an *awful* lot of time.'

He made a pensive face. 'And Lord Pareto? I asked for his room downstairs but they had no record of him even checking in.'

She wasn't sure what to say. 'I haven't seen him since we got here. He seems to have gone, eh, off-piste. Totally.'

Baxter shrugged and started on a long foray as to where he'd been and why it had taken him so long to get here. He'd been held up in London, he said, trying to track down all the sources they'd given him at the MODE briefing. 'They're so demanding these days. On the one hand they want you to follow every possible lead, Brits who've worked in Uganda, top academics, oil people, investors, opposition politicians, analysts likely to know the true score. On the other they just want you to approve the project.' Anyway he hadn't had much joy, he said. He'd met an anthropologist in Camberwell who had spent his life studying magic and loss in the swamps around Lake Albert and an elderly woman from Farnham who had once taught classical piano to the children of the Kabaka.

Looking back, she realised she should have seen he looked a little apprehensive, daunted perhaps. Was that it exactly? It seemed he was somehow undefined. Had he always been like that she wondered or was it something that had come over him, or was coming over him now? Certainly he was more indeterminate, she felt, than someone of his experience had a right to be.

'I suppose the fundamental point,' he said, 'is that MODE wants us to understand that NADS is doing very well thank you. Essentially they want us, if at all possible, to give the project, and all their friends here, top marks for effort.'

OK, he was taking control. He did know what he was doing and she was relieved. On her own, she'd been out of her depth. 'I did try to set up some meetings but there is a huge Poverty Conference coming up and the whole town is overrun with visiting experts. We don't seem to be very high on the pecking order.'

As Faith had discovered, the presence of development experts was not always the net addition to the common good that the textbooks predict. The professors might bring clear thinking to the pressing problems of the day but they also brought (what they themselves would have called) externalities. Never mind queues to see the minister, food prices had skyrocketed. The newspaper was reporting red snapper at twenty dollars a pound and you couldn't get tiger prawns at all. There were shortages of high-end French wine, this latter outage being so serious, the paper also said, that some government ministers had protested, one even writing in to say he was tempted to join the slum dwellers in their regular Friday food riots. And the sex industry had apparently gone haywire. While once you'd had to make firm appointments with the few local transsexuals, it seemed Kampala had now become so overrun with scantily clad six-foot beauties, that, to protect public morality, the authorities had proposed detaining them all for the duration of the conference. That exemplary upholder of standards in high places, the Mufti, had even suggested executing all 'the homos' or at least marooning them on an island in Lake Victoria. Such ideas were not popular with the development elite. After all, it was the very reason many of the silk suits were so keen to come in the first place.

'I'm sorry if I haven't got very far,' said Faith. 'But I'm only here to help.'

'Don't worry, love, you're doing fine, it'll be a doddle.' His face was kindly and reassuringly protective.

And with Baxter on the case things did start to speed up. Even as he checked into the hotel, he'd called the High Commission, always the first 'port of call' in MODE matters and secured a meeting with Dr Carruthers, finally back from his wine-tasting break in Cape Town.

Carruthers said he'd arrange a car from 'the pool' and, next morning, good as his word, the car was idling in the hotel atrium, ready and waiting, right on the dot of eight. Car? Actually it was a monster SUV with 'roo bars' and triple locks and the number plate stencilled on the roof in giant letters in case helicopters needed to track it down after a carjacking. The diplomatic plates were a gas, Faith had to admit as, at every junction, the police saluted, clicked their heels and waved their batons, all in a desperate effort to assist the visitors through the near gridlocked traffic. The windows were darkened and the air conditioning was cold. There was a magazine rack between the seats in front and a screen on the back of each headrest showing the latest movies. The driver wore a purple Ruritanian uniform and Faith felt like a rock star. The streets of the city edged past outside. People gawped but they couldn't see in. She was invisible.

'It's not like the old days,' sighed Baxter, lolling beside her in the back seats. The vehicle had paused at the Jinja Road crossing where a lorry was jack-knifed across the junction. Half a dozen policemen were trying to help, blowing whistles, yelling, running, signalling them forward. Some motorists had been forced on to the verge to let their vehicle through and Faith saw a number of them shouting with rage, waving their fists, one even spitting with despair.

'When I started in this racket,' Baxter went on, 'I was a MODE trainee. My first post was in Dar es Salaam. I used to walk to work in shorts and a T-shirt. Sometimes I'd run along the beach, in bare feet. And I didn't get there till after ten. I used to stop off sometimes to cut coconuts, maybe have a swim. Outside the town, you could drive for a day and never see a car. It was idyllic. That was the whole point of working in the tropics.'

At the junction of Kira Road, they waited another ten minutes while the driver eased on to the roundabout. 'It was simple then. Now look at it.' Baxter pointed to a man in a gas mask trying vainly to cross the road. 'It's like something out of Bosch. Wall to wall shanty towns, from Jo'burg to Cairo, sick people, skinny people, wasted people. Three million of 'em in this town, eighty per cent of them without lavatories.'

They drew up in front of an imposing metal gate set into a white stuccoed wall, fifteen-feet tall and topped with razor wire. In a tiny hut behind bulletproof glass, three men in green uniforms sat by a turnstile. One rose to sign them in while another frisked them, took their keys and their phones and their wallets and their ID, spun on his heel, saluted, spun again, and then ushered them through the metal detector machine and into the cavernous building beyond. The British High Commission in Kampala is spanking new, a gleaming white palace, a monument to the significant development effort underway. All the latest diplomatic requirements are in place: in the lobby, a life-size picture of the Duke of Kent giving prizes at Wimbledon and, at the back, a nine-hole pitch and putt with a machine gun nest behind the first tee.

Up the vast central staircase, along a mile of red carpet, left into reception, and there, behind another glass screen, a pneumatic blonde playing a computer game. Her plastic name tag proclaimed her to be Mrs H. McNaughton-Balls. Faith had to do a double take. What was the woman thinking? In an almost skin-tight leopard-skin T-shirt, her huge breasts were thrust forward like the torpedoes of a gunboat mounted for a punitive expedition.

'We've come to see Dr Carruthers,' said Baxter, trying not to look.

'Designation? ID?'

'He *is* expecting us,' said Faith, in her best Commandante mode. 'We spoke, you remember?' It hadn't been easy. She had been put on hold for ten full minutes, plugged straight into the muzak, Scott Joplin playing the theme tune to The Sting.

They sat with the magazines, under the same portrait of the President she'd seen at the Gulu guest house, Faith browsing through Helping the Hungry, the MODE house rag, a tabloid intended for the interested public. The first article was a piece about a dam in Pakistan. It was all set to transform the lives of a group of poor cotton-farming peasants on whose behalf MODE had marshalled its unparalleled resources and skills. The article was accompanied by several colour photographs of MODE experts at work: engineers, hydrologists, statisticians, plant pathologists, boll weevil specialists, bearded white men in long socks delivering earnest exegeses to puzzled natives in embroidered pyjamas. In one photograph, a Dr Peter J Piper, described in the caption as an econometrician, was strolling thoughtfully in a cotton field, some kind of tablet in his hands, apparently formulating non-linear functions.

'Yah?' A tall, languid man in a white shirt, sharking in from a door in the wings.

'We're from London,' said Baxter, fully the team leader now. 'We're here to see Julian Carruthers.'

'At your service,' said the man, doing his best to avoid looking either of them in the eye. 'I'm the Senior Economist here.'

They all shook hands. His hair was bushy with a reddish tint like rust, darker stains above the ears. Faith was transfixed. It was a wig, an elaborate construction to be sure but one which nevertheless failed to fit quite flush. He led them up a long corridor and into a small room at the back of the building. Other than a few chairs, the room was empty. It could have been an interrogation chamber.

'We were told you would help us,' said Baxter, pushing two HSC business cards across the table.

'We were told you were advising the government,' added Faith, not wanting to be left out.

Carruthers scowled and turned in her direction, again declining to meet her eye.

'They said you would help us set up meetings.'

Carruthers read her business card again and then risked a glance at her breasts. 'Dr Cullimore eh? Or can I call you Faith?'

She smiled uneasily.

'Well, Faith, the main point you have to understand,' continued Carruthers, going straight into his best dean of faculty mode, 'is that this is the best agriculture project in Uganda, in

Africa, maybe even in the whole developing world. Take it from me, it is a model of best practice and everyone loves it. It has been pored over by academics of every persuasion, visited by the bas bleu of every continent and it has passed every test there is. With flying colours.'

'What sort of tests?' said Baxter.

'NADS was conceived as a 25-year programme and it's some six years into the schedule now. There's no need for you to reinvent any wheels. Results on the ground have been excellent.'

'What sort of results?' said Baxter.

'The NADS staff,' said Carruthers stiffly, 'were hand-picked from across the entire ministry and are absolutely the best people available. They work hard, let me tell you. Excellent chaps.'

'But what exactly are the results?' asked Baxter again. 'Can we see…?'

'Look, I told you, it's a 25-year project. We wouldn't expect there to be massive changes yet.'

'The results though…'

At that moment Carruthers' mobile rang and he grabbed the handset, checked the screen, and scuttled out of the room.

'I should have warned you,' whispered Baxter, as they waited. 'MODE staff… people think they're all arrogant shits but actually they can't help it. They're all a bit aspergery. That's how you get the job.'

Faith laughed. 'I *had* wondered.' She knew that a post like this could be the next step up for her. 'How *do* you get a job here?'

'It's not hard. They tell you the hundred funniest jokes in the world and if you don't laugh once you're in.'

Carruthers reappeared. 'I will say one thing,' he smiled, his lips pale and thin as the paperknife in his hand, 'it's nice to see London sending out youngsters once again. We need people who've still got some passion, people open to new ideas. Some of the old hands,' he added, not looking at Baxter, 'get a little, eh, *tired*.' He sat down and, with his hands behind his head, pushed himself back in his chair. This must have increased the pressure on the back of his scalp because, at that moment, his wig began to stretch and then, to Faith's astonishment, to lift at the hairline.

'There's a number of areas,' Carruthers boomed out, 'we must insist that you cover while you're here. The team is generously resourced and we will expect state-of-play reports on,' he looked down at a notepad on the desk in front of him, "NADS' impact on climate change, gender for growth, corporate social responsibility, green growth and socially responsible investment, youth issues, energy consequences, the UN Principles on Human Rights, the "Protect, Respect and Remedy" framework, I believe they call it. And, what else? Oh yes, female genital mutilation, that's the new one coming in from London.'

'Is it a problem in the extension service?' said Baxter.

'That's for you to find out, squire. And, I'm sure I needn't tell you, but we will be looking for maximum rigour and exceptional quantitative robustness.'

Baxter nodded but said nothing.

'One thing though,' Carruthers again. 'You need to see the Minister. That will help you with the bigger picture.'

'The Minister? Will he know the details at project level?'

'Of course. This Minister is one of the best. And his support will be invaluable. It will ease your way through everything.' Carruthers' accent was that strange Etonian baritone long associated with halfwits and those brought up to run the Empire but, in these straitened times, now re-established as the key identifying feature of the natural governing class. 'And, I'll tell you what, Dr Baxter, you need to see some Ugandans, don't think you can get away with only meeting consultants and donor staff. There is *some* life outside this place you know.'

Faith was still staring into the dark fissure at the front of Carruthers' head, mesmerised by what was almost a cavern. She tried to concentrate, tried to draw her eyes away but instead found herself straining to see what was in there.

'And,' Carruthers added, as if thinking out loud, as if scanning the interactive address book in his head, '…what about Tripp? He talks the talk. He can give you the details you need.'

There followed a few moments of silence while Baxter, unaware that Tripp was virtually the only relevant person Faith had seen, scribbled down the name.

'I read,' said Baxter dreamily, as if it had just occurred to him, 'that some of the NADS budget might be being steered towards handouts to the party faithful, patronage to the President's family, that kind of thing.'

'Tittle-tattle, Dr Baxter. Don't believe everything you read in the papers. Take it from me, this is a good project. A lot of good people have put a lot of good time and money into it. We are quite confident. Anyway, your brief is to show that the project is technically consistent. Concentrate on that. We need to badger the other donors, get all our partners singing from the same hymn sheet...'

'Technically consistent,' said Baxter rolling the phrase around his mouth as if it was a suspect wine. 'What does that mean exactly?'

'You're the expert, Baxter.' Carruthers was clearly irritated now. 'And there is no need to get arsey. What we need, what we're paying you for, and the sooner you grasp this the better quite frankly, are a few insights into the internal mechanics of the project. Give us, and our partners, some easy-to-understand indication of how well the project has performed against its design frame. It's quite simple isn't it? We don't want all your usual bollocks about impact or outcomes or due diligence or value for money or any of that stuff. That is a different game of soldiers all together and we'll take care of that ourselves, when the time is right.' He looked at his watch. 'Oh dear, is that the time already? Your schedule is frightfully inopportune I'm afraid. We've got this big Poverty Conference on? Have you heard? Lots of bigwigs coming in, heads of state and all that.'

'*Important* people,' said Baxter.

'Indeed.'

'London needs our report in two weeks,' said Faith.

'Two weeks!' said Carruthers. 'Oodles of time then. They've been extraordinarily generous I must say.' He let this tail away before suddenly jumping to his feet. 'Look, leave it all with me. Where can I find you? Faith?'

'The Imperial.'

'The Imperial! Good God! Is that wise? Are you sure the place is safe? I've heard the City Engineer absolutely refuses to even enter the building.'

'There's no space at the Serena. It's full of all your important people.'

Carruthers allowed himself another long, studied stare at Faith's breasts. For a moment she thought he might be preparing a lewd proposal. 'By the way you've heard about the new security protocol I suppose. Did Mrs Mac give you the leaflet?'

'Leaflet?' said Baxter.

'There's a raised level of alert.'

'Alert?'

'Haven't you heard? Good God, man, where have you been? Of course it's just the usual troublemakers, but it's certainly been timed to cause maximum disruption to our conference.'

Baxter began to gather his papers. He seemed to be hardly listening and Carruthers was doing nothing to hide his annoyance. 'All expats have been warned to be careful,' he said. 'It's your responsibility to take care.'

'The rebels can be pretty horrid,' conceded Faith. 'I've read all about them. When I was in Gulu they told me how the rebels had abducted hundreds of schoolgirls and cut their arms off.'

'Bad business,' agreed Carruthers.

Baxter shrugged, which was a mistake. Beginner that she was, even Faith knew that, no matter how silly the story or how great the provocation, it's never wise to doubt an officer of Her Majesty's Government. Security anxiety is the medium of exchange for expatriates and if you want to be someone's friend, you have to humour their stories, indulge them a little. With an audience of credulous innocents to sit in attendance, the seasoned expatriate will quickly spin into an inexhaustible fund of dark tales: witchcraft and millenarian cults, child sacrifice, armed policemen running amok, gang rape, cannibals they have known. Once they're warmed up, you can jump in with the hard questions, that's OK, but with Carruthers just getting going, a display of impatience was no way to respond. His stories were for Faith anyway, not for leathered old wrinklies like Baxter.

'You've seen it all I suppose, Dr Baxter, yah? The world holds nothing that will surprise you?' Carruthers's eyes narrowed and his face began to redden.

Baxter said nothing, seemed as if he was entirely elsewhere.

'All those assignments for the United Nations, Dr Baxter. What a lot of experience! What a knowledgeable chap you must be!'

Baxter was on his feet, laughing, making it all much worse.

Faith looked at her shoes. She would have allowed Carruthers five minutes on civil unrest, narcotics abuse, weird diseases, mutilation, whatever. Just to get him on side. But then again, and remembering some of Hilleard's dreadful stories, she was glad not to have to listen to another exposition on the various uses for barbed wire and screwdrivers and the multiplicity of female orifices into which ingenious natives have squeezed boiling coals.

'Look,' Carruthers was suddenly angry, face almost as red as his wig. 'I've been here a full year. I know Uganda. I know the rest of Africa too.' He was shouting, quite carried away. 'I've worked for the IMF. I've consulted for the World Bank. I've done economic modelling in Tanzania. I did my PhD in Cote D'Ivoire. I've also been in Iraq, I may add, under heavy fire and bombardment. I've seen the world, Baxter, and I know people like you. I know your game.'

But Baxter didn't care. Still chuckling, he was turning on his heels, leaving the room. In a moment he was yards down the corridor.

Carruthers wasn't done though. Almost molten now, he scuttled after Baxter, in furious pursuit. 'Now you've finished fucking up Kazakhstan,' he shouted, loud enough for all the corridor to hear, 'you've come to fuck up Uganda. Is that it, Dr Baxter? Is *that* it?'

SIX

April 11th 2011

"The vanished terms: state, politics, power, classes, class struggle, social change, alternatives and revolutions, ideologies. Their insipid replacements: governance, communities, social partners, poverty, consensus."
- *Samir Amin, Beyond US Hegemony, 2006*

Fucking up Kazakhstan! What a cheek! This from the people who had carpet-bombed Baghdad and were now the army of occupation in Afghanistan. He'd been in Iraq had he? The man was plainly a missionary or a fanatic. Did he do the waterboarding himself or did he pay some other jobsworth to do it for him? Baxter may have looked calm but he wasn't. 'Your brief is only to show that the project is technically consistent!' What a fucking cheek.

But there was no point in getting upset. None at all. Faith may have been under the impression he was an expert, his passport even said as much, but, as he had learned at the Kazakh debriefing, no one else was likely to be under that illusion for a while. The Kazakh experience had shredded his nerves more or less completely and his major challenge now was just to get through the next few weeks. To do that, he had to find some composure, develop at least the *appearance* of calm, immerse himself in the job, most of all act like a professional. This meant concentrating on the task at hand. This meant settling in and settling *down*. One day at a time, Sweet Jesus, one day at time.

Mission protocol: he'd learned this, over the years, slowly but surely, how to pace yourself, how to develop routine. First, he had to get comfortable in the hotel. This might not be easy; the monstrous dump they'd booked him in had needed a day just to learn the way around. From the lobby, he had explored the place, looking for fire exits, the first thing he always did. With all the power cuts in Kampala, he knew it was unwise to take the lift, you'd be stuck in there for hours, even days, before the repairman came and levered you out. Much safer to walk the stairs, dark, dank and slippery as they were.

He'd reconnoitred the so-called mezzanine, essentially an aircraft hangar, empty but for one tatty sofa and a forlorn exhibition of the usual faded Africa photographs: tattooed tribal beauties with braided hair and impossible teenage tits and ancient spirit men with wise and wizened faces, each picture presumably selected by the management just in case guests should have any doubt they were actually *in* Africa.

On the next floor, there was something like a lounge, with a few plastic chairs and a coffee table. It seemed there to be forever teatime, a small group of elderly gentlefolk hammering out rinky-dink drum beats on what looked like an old tree trunk. From there he had taken a turn around the gym with its broken bikes and malfunctioning running machines and its swimming pool and two floors of conference rooms (dark, musty and packed with locals undergoing, according to the sign, an Empowerment Training Workshop).

Baxter's room was on the eighth floor. It was a generic international hotel apartment with the usual all-polysomething fitments, paper flowers and plastic fruit. A cheap plasma screen was sunk into the wall, the wiring awry and shoved down the back of the huge oblong bed that seemed to promise more than just sleep. From his tiny window he could see across to the roof garden with its casino and revolving restaurant (Please Abstain from Sticking Your Head Out the Window, it helpfully advised in the room folder).

He had insisted on an apartment in order to establish a working office and he'd already started assembling what he needed: first off, the reports of the consultants who'd been here before him. He needed to get going on the obligatory Inception Report. That meant nothing much more than rehashing the Terms of Reference but that's the nature of consulting. He wasn't there to write Hamlet.

Putting something on paper was always a good idea at this stage in the mission although it wasn't something every team managed to do. The point is that even in the worst situation, the client can be mollified by a report, an exposition with arguments for and against, options as to one course of uncertain action or another, SWOT analyses, logical frameworks, GANTT charts, flow diagrams etc. And if the whole mission was to fall apart in tears and recrimination (as missions sometimes did), he was a professional. If he had some evidence to support his side of the story, some analysis, however spurious, he would be able to spin his way out of it.

Making a report was easy enough for Baxter. Tedious yes, but straightforward. After a lifetime of consultancy, he had at least fifty project review documents on his laptop, many of them very similar to the one he had to do now. Judicious rejigging and regurgitating would get him seventy per cent of the way. Use the 'Find and Replace' key, find Kazakhstan and substitute with Uganda. Well, maybe Kazakhstan wasn't the best example. The office was out for blood on that one. But it wasn't fair. They should have been chasing Macpherson, he was the driver on that awful night.

He liked to start the day with a walk, not as far as the street which, like every other road in Africa these days, was clogged to bursting with lead-spewing traffic, but maybe around the hotel grounds. At the Imperial, this had meant befriending the vicious guard dogs deployed to deter intruders to the building site they called a garden and exchanging a nod or two with their minders, large men in sunglasses and ill-fitting suits, automatic rifles and cans of mace.

If he had meetings he would arrange them in the morning. Otherwise, it was reading in the afternoon, sauna and massage at four, followed by a swim. At night, he would take a stool by the bar, indulge a few thoughts, make a few plans for the morrow. Sure, the airline had lost his clothes. That had been a nuisance and he wouldn't look his best, attired day after day in charity shop donations, ill-fitting tat collected by old ladies in every small town around the western world, jet-planed 10,000 miles, hauled off the baggage carousel and held at the damp and mouldy Entebbe Lost Property Office for just this sort of occasion: wrathful tourists reduced to tears by the non-arrival of their spanking new Burberry suitcases.

But more important, lost luggage meant lost meds and that *was* a problem.

The pharmacy in the hotel was run by a Chinese lady who, when he entered her shop, had come scuttling out from behind the counter like a hyperactive squirrel, all big eyes and smiles. She was no longer in the morning of her years but she had a beguiling aroma of musky chestnut and her white coat was alluringly stained. Her enormous leathery hands seemed to hold hidden secrets from the east.

'I need some Remeron,' said Baxter.

The lady furrowed her brow.

'I've lost my luggage. My scripts were in .... my....' He let the sentence tail away.

'You like mass-a? Vay goo.'

Buying medication in these circumstances is sometimes difficult. He tried talking louder. 'I've lost my meds. I need some Remeron. Quite urgently.'

Still she seemed not to understand. 'I ting you like *mass-a*. Massa vay goo.' She leant closer, as if to get a better look at him, squinting, inspecting, poking.

'Remeron? Just a few, to get me through the next couple of weeks.'

She retreated to the back, rummaging in a cupboard, the sound of drawers being pulled open and shut. As he waited, he began what he hoped looked like an idle flick through a pile of brochures promoting what seemed to be cough syrup. When the pharmacist reappeared, grinning like a veritable Madame Mao, she was holding up a small blue bottle. 'Chinee medicine, vay ni.'

Baxter looked at the label. Huang Qin Gao, it said.

'Now mass-a?'

He took a step back. 'No, no...'

'Don like? How bow ginkgo leaf?'

'No, no, Remeron. Rem-ER-on. I'm sure the ginkgo leaf is good but...' He produced a wad of dollars to make his point but still she was unmoved.

'Look, I'm with the World Bank and… perhaps I should have said… I *am* a doctor.' He was on safe ground here as all white men in the developing world are with the World Bank, one way or another. And doctorates are, of course, an impenetrable minefield to all but a tiny few. Baxter's was from that great centre of medical learning the University of Edinburgh, albeit in marketing studies, a mere detail in the story.

'I was talking to the manager,' he tried, leafing once more through the money and, adopting a friendly, confidential tone, one eye on the door. 'He said that, as a long-term guest, my wish was his command.'

'I see, I see,' Madame Mao beamed again, pleased to be on good terms with friends of the management. 'No plobrem.'

'He told me you were fully qualified to handle my, shall we say, *account* yourself.'

'Cun? You li' cun?' She fluttered her eyelashes. 'My cun vay joozy.' And in a flash she was round the counter, homing in on him, those great hands reaching for his belt.

'No, no! I need Remeron. It's a brown pill.'

She stopped and frowned, looked as if someone had suggested something improper.

Baxter put some notes on the counter and eased another wad from his pocket. 'Remeron, yeah? How much is it? You must have some. Please. Twenty dollars? Fifty?'

Madame Mao narrowed her eyes. She was getting the idea at last.

'I don't need much. Say a bottle of twenty?'

She hesitated.

'Sometimes the pills are white. The box is blue. A hundred dollars, would that cover it?'

'Have Librium.'

'Librium?' He took a step back. 'Oh, dear… well… if…' But then, in that moment of pause, before she could move, Baxter somehow regrouped and nipped round the counter to scour the assorted bottles of potions and pills. There were drawers and open shelves, jars and vials and boxes, rows of packets, sachets of many colours. The first bottles he saw contained yellow tablets then there were some red capsules then some big black things that looked like lozenges.

'Oh, you've got Nardil, "a non-selective and irreversible monoamine oxidase inhibitor",' he read off the bottle. 'A bit fierce,' he said, 'but we're getting warmer I suppose. Oh you've got *these!*' he pulled a small white bottle from the shelf. 'These *are* interesting. Halcion? Banned in my country, you know, and well past their sell-by date. But still… Could be useful…'

Madame Mao was meanwhile unlocking a small drawer by the telephone. 'We have only capsules in the Librium,' she said, pulling out a little tray with an assortment of bottles. 'But we have these too. Perhaps you... eh...'

Baxter bent forward to read the label. 'Ketamine? Good grief! Why didn't you say so before?'

The pharmacist smiled nervously.

'How have you got this? This is for knocking out horses. Are you running a veterinary clinic too?'

She laughed nervously. Maybe she didn't understand. Finally she said 'It's very popular with expatriates.'

'Really? Gosh! Well, I suppose it does liven things up a bit. Brightens their pointless existences and all that.'

She smiled. 'Opposite. Calms them down. Sedative effect.'

'Well, it's a theory, but I tell you, madame, these are *very* special. Guangzhou Zuchang Chemicals. Best Quality,' he read from the label. '98.7% pure. This is the dog's bollocks and when you've this sort of stuff, my dear, you shouldn't be hoarding it. There are still a few old soldiers out there who *appreciate* this kind of gear. The manager was right! You certainly know your business.'

She beamed from ear to ear, happy now, allowing Baxter time to scour a few more shelves. Quickly though, the old watchfulness returned.

'Are you anx-ass bout any-ting?'

'Are your kidding me?' snapped Baxter. 'Do I look anxious?'

She came closer and seemed to peer into his face, as if looking for something behind his eyes.

'Look, I'm fine thank you, but I will take the Nardil and thirty of the kit kats. And I might as well take the Librium and the Halcion too.'

She started to put the bottles into a bag.

'But I also need Atorvastatin, Bisoprolol and Warfarin. A month's worth. Can you manage all that?'

She shrugged and went again to the rear of the shop. After a minute or two she re-emerged with a brown paper bag, folded neatly at the top.

'Gimme some Temazepam too,' Baxter grunted, picking up another small bottle. 'They do take the edge off things don't they? And maybe a few bennies, you never know when you might need them.'

'You sure you OK? Feel OK?'

'Absolutely.'

Madame Mao smiled graciously, hesitated, checked there was no one watching, and slowly palmed the money into a drawer under the desk.

'Now for mass-a?'

'If you insist,' he sighed. 'But let's make it quick.'

'When you leady,' she said, briskly pulling on her rubber gloves, 'do it here,' and she gestured to the lap of her grubby white coat.

Afterwards, as he lay immobile, virtually comatose, worn out by her punishing and taxing method, he watched with one eye while she opened a musty old ledger and, laying out some carbon paper, began what seemed a virtual essay, impressive Chinese characters dragged out over two pages. Baxter was pleased to note her attention to detail. You couldn't be too careful these days. He'd had experience of the MODE claims department before and knew that, if you wanted the taxpayer to pay for your stash, you needed receipts and all the proper documentation.

As it turned out, the pool at the Imperial was closed. It was leaking apparently; 'into the rooms below' according to the cheerful attendant. So, to get a swim, he had to make his way to the Serena, the only other pool around.

The Serena is a different kind of gaff to the Imperial. As he walked up the long bougainvillea-lined drive, Baxter's first sight of the place put him in mind of a Columbian drug boss's retirement villa, something out of Sam Peckinpah. He expected to see hirsute men in sombreros and dark-eyed senoritas with castanets but the lobby was instead heaving, like everywhere else in the town it seemed, with workshoppers and consultants. The only contrast, and it wasn't much, came from the occasional tour group, mostly overweight persons with mullet haircuts and a dress code leaning towards standard battle dress: khaki hats, knee-high boots and binoculars, as if they were hoping to find wildlife in the hotel grounds or as if they anticipated an attack by a local insurgent group, maybe the notorious Lord's Resistance Army with its infamous traditions, explicated at length the day before by Faith, of cutting up girl children and making magic charms from their genitals. As in Kenyan game parks, Thai hill lodges and Spanish beach resorts, your tourist tends to move en masse, minimising the danger of unplanned encounters with the indigenes. He or she venture out of the grounds only to queue for the tribal dancers or perhaps to photograph the marabou storks as they squat in the trees along Speke Avenue shitting on the fancy four-wheel drives parked nose to tail below.

The Serena pool was round the back of the main building. It was large, bright blue, tree-lined and inviting and Baxter was soon spread out on a sun lounger, idly browsing an academic paper on the macroeconomic underpinnings of public investment, showing off his charity shop micro trunks to the many air stewardesses and tennis club ladies stretched out around him. As he began to drift into sleep, the sweet waters of Lethe lapping at his toes, he became aware of a commotion at the entrance to the pool, just where a flight of stairs came in from a small hallway. He rolled over to get a better look, careful not to get suncream on the file.

A man was arguing with the attendant. He was wearing a charcoal grey suit with a leather pork-pie hat balanced jauntily atop a great mane of yellow hair. It was an unusual outfit 'poolside'. With him, on a lead, was a large Alsatian and it seemed the staff were trying to restrain the beast, clearly agitated as it was, trying to stop it coming into the pool area. There was another man there too, in the shadows, a short, squat figure in a yellow baseball cap, black shell suit zipped tight to the chin. This second man was standing back, avoiding the argument, more interested, it seemed, in the near-naked stewardesses and their flagrant displays.

Both men had the same wrap-around sunglasses and for a moment they made Baxter think of cartoon London gangsters, heavies from Eltham or Bow or some such outpost but he knew they were no cartoon. He had read somewhere about a phobia whose chief characteristic is recognising people from one's past in the faces of persons quite unconnected. These men were familiar but not because of any phobia.

They pushed past the attendant, the dog bounding ahead, barking at a group of children and knocking over cold drinks. Baxter rearranged his papers, made sure the file was conspicuously open.

They chose the long route, circumscribing an erratic arc through the basking ladies. The first man looked straight ahead, led, it seemed, by the dog, a white stick in his left hand, while the other, the track suit, patrolled the deckchairs, probing each of the bathers in turn, his robotic stare sweeping over and along the line, inexorably fastening on the women with the skimpiest costumes and the biggest breasts.

'Well, well, well, look who's 'ere?' grunted the long-haired man as he pulled up to Baxter's lounger. 'Dr Bent, development consultant. Hard at work are we?'

Bent was not a good name in this business but what could he do? It came from his father, a Danish sailor.

Meanwhile the ladies had woken up. Those on their stomachs, reached around behind themselves, stretching to fasten their bikini straps, alert to possible danger or distraction. It must be a movement unique to modern times and it was undertaken by a dozen women simultaneously.

Before Baxter could say much, the second man had barged in on them. He had a large, swollen head and was so small he verged on the stunted. He was clearly tense, edgy, on the move, like a boxer warming up. 'Bent!' he shouted. 'We heard ye might be here. I can see why!' The Glasgow accent was as brutal as ever and a couple of the ladies recoiled visibly.

'Jesus, Pugh, look at the jockeys on her. She's certainly excited aboot *something*.'

The long-haired man groaned. It was involuntary but unmistakable, a whimper of arousal, a moan of suppression, the sound of a man wrestling with years of what the economists call 'deferred gratification'.

'You know ma assistant, Bent? Dr Pugh?'

Know Dr Pugh? How could he not? Everyone knew Pugh. And even if you didn't, his reputation preceded him.

'He's just back from another tour in Afghanistan,' said the wee man, with a chuckle. 'Bringing development to the mullahs. He got a medal for it.'

With his splendid head of yellow hair Pugh could have been a venerable junkie jazz musician or the lost twin of General Custer. As he watched him, though, Baxter could see that, for all he might have wanted to look icy cool, the blind factotum was unsettled. He was sweating badly. Was it the heat or the proximity of the near-naked stewardesses he couldn't see, or was it something else? His skin was a deathly white and across it flitted the dark shadows of old acne scars. He was like a gecko in sunlight.

The midget was Zoo Adderbury, Permanent Secretary at MODE, the top man. Baxter had known him for years, at least since Adderbury had been a mere head of section and he had been a 'dogsbody', as Adderbury himself had once put it.

'And yer here on the NADS review? Is tha' wha' Ah hear, Bent?' Adderbury had always known everything going on in the office, who had borrowed what paper clip from who five years before. His attention to detail was legendary. 'It'll be straightforward Ah suppose. Is that why yer doon at the pool awready? NADS is one o' oor best programmes, you have taken *that* in Ah hope?'

He *had* it heard it somewhere. He tried a reassuring laugh but it came out like a strangled cough.

'And you've my old pal Pareto, the Duke of Pangbourne, with you I hear. How's he shaping up?'

'Well, actually, I haven't met him yet.'

'Oh aye?'

'He's out doing fieldwork.'

Adderbury smiled. 'I can see him now. Interviewing stakeholders, promoting empowerment, engendering the dialogue. Don't forget we need some real numbers, Bent, proper economics.'

Baxter nodded. 'But what brings you here, Zoo?' he asked, trying to change the subject.

But Adderbury wasn't finished. 'NADS is one o' oor rare successes, Bent. We need to big it up, pick the low hanging fruits, you know wha'hm saying? Ye sure you've got that?'

He was. Sure. Definitely.

'As for uz, it's the Poverty Conference. It's the curse o' senior management, Bent. I have to attend all these international shindigs. It's a diabolical imposition but somebody has to do it.'

'Took us three hours from the airport,' grunted Pugh, white stick in hand, dog lead tight around his wrist, eyes hidden behind his blacker than black sunglasses. 'Police and troops all over the place, armoured vehicles, sirens. Worse than fucking Helmand. Zoo thought there must've been a coup.'

Adderbury ignored him. 'It's a huge boost for Uganda,' he went on. 'They've had to build five new hotels just to fit aw'body in. The big cheeses are aw coming. World Bank, UN, IMF. The big man there, Dominique Straus Khan. Maybe even the Pope. Development is right up the agenda noo. We're gonnae end world poverty by 2020. Ah tell ye, Bent, yer lucky to have got rooms.'

'We didn't. We couldn't. Pareto is in an apartment block out in the suburbs and I'm at the Imperial.'

'Oh!' said Adderbury, surprised. 'Well at least you're cost saving. Good on ye!' Adderbury had always fancied himself as a funny man, but, with his hair grey now and razor cut, he had more the look of a comic-strip American general, a Patton or a miniature Schwarzkopf. This was strangely appropriate as, while in the very early Blair days, MODE had been a home for development *thinkers*, a place where intellectuals argued and fought over practice and theory, now, with Afghanistan and Iraq and Somalia and Libya and Yemen, and the need to take a more, how did they put it, *muscular* approach, the place needed a top man more comfortable with the complex, perhaps darker, requirements of the Foreign Office, someone more familiar with the delicate exigencies of the latest phase of the never-ending imperial adventure.

In Baxter's youth, the driver of development, as these things were called, was thought to be big engineering projects: high dams and motorways, honest bricks and mortar. These were an easy way of spending the aid budget: you could get shot of the money fast, most of it could be steered towards British contractors who would design and build the dam or whatever (and then get out before there was any trouble), and there was always something there at the end, something for the minister of the day to stick a blue plaque on. Adderbury had made his name hustling and plotting in that world but then the wheel of development fashion had turned, to *privilege*, as they described it then, gender empowerment and human rights, concepts whose operationalization required, at the minimum, an army of smooth-talkers able to bamboozle the host government into taking a barrel of snake oil and calling it development aid. And then the wheel had turned again, so much in fact that Baxter had to almost gasp in admiration at how Adderbury could survive, even prevail. Perhaps it was just that the new thinking had quickly sped its way past the soft notions of social capital and well-being and democracy only to find itself led inexorably on to liberal intervention and shock and awe. Before anyone had realised, General Adderbury was comfortably perched atop a new pile, a new milieu. As Baxter watched, he seemed almost to be able to read in Adderbury's dark moon face, now beaming up from behind impenetrable shades, a genuine accommodation with this opaque new world, a further iteration of the single-mindedness and determination for which he was so celebrated.

'Anyway, come and check us oot, Bent. We've got a whole MODE team in the Serena, aw the top floor, aw the guys and gals. We're doing a big presentation on the last day. You'll love it. It's cutting edge stuff. Best practice. Actually, good practice is, I think, what we modestly call it now. Anyway I'll get ye a pass. I'll leave it at reception. There'll be lots o' networking, barrels o' bevy, NGO totty, know what Ah'm saying?'

Part II

SEVEN

April 12th 2011

"The white man is very clever. He came quietly and peaceably with his religion. We were amused at his foolishness and allowed him to stay. Now he has won our brothers, and our clan can no longer act like one. He has put a knife on the things that held us together and we have fallen apart."
- Chinua Achebe, Things Fall Apart

He had the intense and startling features of the picture book Karamojong warrior, hair short above the forehead then heaped in a bun at the back, a heavy earring which had stretched his earlobe, beauty marks cut into his face and eyes so bright they might have been on fire, but when he strode into the lobby of the Hotel Imperial that same afternoon, wearing nothing much more than a red blanket and sandals cut from a car tyre, Faith found herself wondering if he was really the right man for the job.

'Know good gofer,' Tripp had texted her. 'Knows NADS story, got strat vis n fistful refs.'

Well, he *looked* totally great and she could see from the way a group of missionaries scuttled for cover in reception that he would be a good man to have on your side in a quarrel. She introduced herself and he scowled. He seemed like a prisoner waiting for the sentence to be read.

'They told me your name was Lodi.'

'My names are Alphonse Remi Amase Nakut.'

'Not Lodi Charles?'

'Come again?'

'Are you Lodi Charles?'

'Yes.'

Long pause.

She sneaked a glance at his scars. She had read they were to glorify the life of the warrior, or maybe a penitence for killing an enemy.

'Have you got more than one name?'

'I'm not getting you.'

She was flustered but he seemed keen to help so she told him what she knew. Although one of the team seemed to be rather 'doing his own thing', the team leader had got a grip and had a handle on the task ahead. The main problem was that, with the Poverty Conference taking everybody's time and energy, they had hardly managed to make any connections. No one seemed to want to talk to them and they were still awaiting a formal briefing.

'They have not quite got back to you?'

'Exactly.'

Dr Carruthers, she said, had assured them that everything at NADS was going just great and that the government supported a new phase of the project but the team was supposed to check this. And, as far as she was concerned, their deadline was hurtling towards them like one of those overloaded container trucks she'd seen careering along the Gulu road.

'Maybe I could fix some meetings for you?'

'Could you? Well, yeah, great.' She *had* tried, she said again, but either the secretaries wouldn't take her calls or they wanted to see authorisation or they were just too busy. Quite often they were simply not there. 'They say we can't see the Minister until we have official clearance. But how can we get clearance if we can't see the Minister?'

She had wondered whether her friend from the ministry, the one who had arranged her field trip, might help but, despite numerous attempts, she had failed to get through to him and her efforts to speak to Tripp's office had elicited the response that, yes, NADS *was* a part of the Bank's five-year rolling programme but, for funding purposes, all agriculture enquiries were handled by MODE through the High Commission. 'Try Dr Carruthers,' said the receptionist. 'He's the man for you.'

'Look, I'm with MODE, he's my colleague. Sort of anyway.'

'Well that's fine then.'

She had tried Googling academics and business journalists and come up with a name or two but none had yet replied to her emails. Now, though, with the new man on board, things *did* begin to move. He made an impression from the start. On his first day proper he had turned up, business-like and sharp, carrying a clipboard and a briefcase and a mobile phone, his hair neat, his shoes shiny, his suit black and appropriate. Setting off on a tour of government offices, appointments all properly made, Faith found it hard to hide her astonishment at the transformation. They sat together in the back of the vehicle and, as the car crawled through heavy traffic, she could feel herself excited by the presence of this serious and pensive young man. At one point in the day, as the car nudged along Yusuf Lule Drive, heading to a meeting he had arranged, they passed a colossal high-rise, the structure covered in cranes and scaffolding and spotlights, hundreds of workmen crawling over the superstructure like ants, twenty stories of glass, chrome and concrete.

'What is *that*?' she said, peering out from the car window, nervous, needing something to say, struggling to bear his silence.

'It's the NSSF.'

'What's that?'

'The National Social Security Fund.'

'Yes, but what does it *do*?'

'Built by Chinese.'

'To do what though?'

'You find everybody contributes one dollar per week from their salaries. It's a deduction.'

'But what for?'

'To construct that building for one.' His teeth were luminescent, pure white in the reflected fluorescent glare.

'What's a gofer?' she asked.

'Huh?

'A gofer? Do you know what that is?'

'Somebody who goes for things. Why?'

When Charlie Crisp came to collect her the next evening he was in a rusty old, rattletrap Land Rover, strips of canvas flapping from the windows, and he screeched it into the hotel at such a speed that the mass of lobbyists and conference delegates swarming around the hotel door seemed to think they had to jump for their lives. He pulled up next to a shiny new Prado, shiny Oxfam logo on the side panel.

'Are you Faith?'

She hauled herself into the battered passenger seat, just as the driver of the Prado, leather seats, leather steering wheel, console like a spaceship, opened his door: a uniformed chauffeur with a peaked hat.

'Hey you, move that *thing!*' Crisp shouted and, then, as the Prado edged forward to let them through, he roared out on to the main road, barging the vehicle into the torrent of traffic, the crazy flood of taxis, buses and *boda-boda* motorbikes.

'Oxfam!' said Crisp, a small wiry man in dark trousers, worn linen shirt, neat little Robespierre glasses. 'Who voted for them?'

Crisp was an independent researcher, he had said on the phone, or perhaps some kind of journalist, it depended who the client was. Faith tried to explain why she had emailed him. She'd read some of what he'd written about donors and the poor record of so many grand projects. She'd thought it might be helpful to talk to him, reckoned he might have a different view of what was happening at NADS. And, during her time at CARE, she had absorbed second-hand something of the thrill of hanging out with the 'journos', liked the attitude, the style. Maybe she could learn something.

'The cheek of these people,' he continued. 'NGOs. Nothing Going On.' He lent over to turn up the volume on the CD player and then fumbled for a partially smoked spliff that was lying in a tray under the dashboard.

She tried to laugh. 'I was with CARE you know and we really worked on…'

At that moment, a child pushing a wheelbarrow lurched into the road and he had to break hard to avoid a collision, the Land Rover slewing and skidding alarmingly on the gravel shoulder. 'Rule one,' he said, 'in this country, avoid road accidents.'

'Is that the voice of experience?'

'It most certainly is. And, if you do knock anyone, keep going, otherwise you'll be in trouble. The mob will drag you and beat you like a rat.'

She watched him draw on the joint. He held it long and deep, letting go an impressive lungful of thick smoke and eventually offered it to her.

'I don't think so,' she said, more severely than she meant.

He raised an inquisitive eyebrow.

'I don't like it,' she said. 'It makes me a little odd.'

'The only way to get by?'

She took it hesitantly.

'Go on, it's good for you. Support the local farmers.'

They edged their way down Lugard Road, dodging market stalls, potholes and pedestrians, trying to stay patient. 'Traffic's even worse than usual tonight,' said Crisp. 'This fucking conference. Why don't we just go to Emin Pasha? It's nearby.'

After twenty minutes of stop-starting they had smoked a second joint but barely travelled three hundred metres. By the time they eventually reached the car park it was dark and, as she jumped down from the vehicle, she realised she was wobbly and very weak in the knees and Crisp had to take her arm to steer her through the candlelit reception area, past the bar and into a large restaurant crowded with yakking dignitaries and aid industry *beau monde*. A band was playing lounge reggae by a startlingly luminescent pool.

The head waiter escorted them to the last free table, squeezing through little huddles of the development elect, the predominant blacks and greys of their designer suits here and there speckled with splashes of colour: reds and greens and dreamy peach, occasionally blue denim, little islands of activism.

'I still don't understand,' Faith heard a man say as they shuffled past his table. 'Why did the project fail? We did everything we could.'

'Peter Piper's Poverty Pyramid, Brian! You should've referred to that.' His colleague was the alternative type: longish blonde hair and wispy beard, collarless shirt. 'You should've got more background,' he added. 'You need to understand the history of this country. It's very complicated.'

'Easily said, Damien, but if we'd known the history we'd never have gone ahead.'

'Wow,' said Faith, looking around. It was the only reasonable response.

'Poverty Conferences,' said Crisp. 'Always good for the restaurant trade.'

The weed and the traffic had made her head spin and she felt a little nauseous. Bright lights along the walls, dizzy shadows. Crisp was saying something in her ear, maybe about a drink, but it wasn't really a question and in a moment the wine waiter was at her elbow filling a solitary glass.

'Aren't you having any?'

'Not allowed. But don't let that put you off. The wine here is the very best.'

She looked at the label.

He grinned. 'Trapiche Malbec, yes? The Villafane 2003 is outstanding. Extremely concentrated and a great body.'

She took a swig. It *was* nice. So many people, so much noise. Was the ceiling abnormally low or was it claustrophobia? She scanned the room. The place was crawling with goons. The stairs were covered by two men in army fatigues, mirror shades and pistol holsters. Outside on the veranda, a bespeckled corporal was tinkering with an AK-47. On the roof over the pool area, a hooded commando holding an RPG launcher.

'The security here is incredible. Is all this really necessary,' she said.

'Well, there *are* lots of bomb plots. And last year seventy odd people died in suicide bombings on World Cup Final night. In a restaurant not unlike this.'

'I read about it. But why would anyone want to blow up *this* place?'

'I know. What a thought. Oh my God. Imagine the tragedy. All these experts dead. It would put back African development by a generation. Productivity would fall into the abyss. The country would be hurled back into the stone age.'

She shuddered. It *was* too awful.

A waitress came to take their order, all silver high heels and six inch cleavage. 'Ah, Mr Charlie, my friend, how are you? *Lovely* to see you again.' In a uniform that was part Baganda grass skirt, part Cherokee headdress and part Thai hill-tribes smock, a bit of Las Vegas croupier thrown in for reassurance, she was clearly another player in the on-running Third World drama and she cooed over Crisp like a long-lost friend, two old troupers acknowledging recognition of their role in the production. 'Oh Mr Charlie, you never come to see me anymore.'

'Now,' said Crisp, when she eventually sashayed away, wobbling on her silver shoes, 'what was it you wanted?'

Faith had expected to meet in his office, she said, apologising, not in a place like this. 'I'm doing a review of NADS.'

'Agriculture?'

'Yes.'

'Is that your subject?'

'Sort of.'

He made a face. 'So, what about NADS?'

'Everyone says it's a great project...'

'Do they?'

'All the donor people do.'

'What is a great project?'

She shrugged. 'A project doing the things it was designed to do?'

'Which are?'

'Well, helping poor farmers, I suppose.' Wasn't that obvious?

At that moment, the band started an up-tempo number and a couple edged past their table heading for the dance floor. 'My paper,' said the woman, an elderly *begum* in an evening dress, an off duty professor perhaps or an ambassador's wife moonlighting in consultancy, 'is on the changing paradigm. Thirty years ago we all made a killing planning the nationalisation of the public utilities. Then we got a king's ransom to help privatise them all. Now they're thinking of renationalising them again. Isn't life a hoot?'

'Look,' said Crisp, seeming to relent, 'I don't know anything special about NADS. My stuff is broadly about holding people to account. Something I assume you, or the donors anyway, should be doing anyway.' He looked at Faith, as if taking her in for the first time. 'Right now I'm campaigning against this bloody conference.'

'The Poverty Conference? Really? Is it such a bad thing?'

'Workshops for fat cats. Papers that are never read. Cocktail parties. And those are the *good* things.'

Even though she had attended such events herself, albeit nothing so grandiose, she could think of no defence to offer. 'Networking? It's not so bad.'

'The country has spent two hundred million dollars or more for a long weekend. They built new terminal buildings at the airport, special parking for all the imported Benzes, extra road corridors for the Benzes and the fat cats to drive on. One hundred and fifty Benzes by the way, one each for the thirty-six cabinet ministers, do your math, also police cars and motorcycles, luxury buses and ambulances, it goes on and on. The budget shows emergency road repairs at over twenty million dollars, for a weekend remember, road rehabilitation, road maintenance, road beautification. They handed out money to unknown contractors, all party contributors, to build five new hotels, including your one. Most of them are nowhere near ready and are probably never going to open.'

'I heard there are some top people coming though.'

'Yes?'

'Even the Pope?'

'Perhaps we'll get to kiss his ring.'

When they eventually got up to dance, the floor was teeming, worse than the traffic outside and trying to move was like swimming in treacle, bumping against soft rocks. Within seconds she was wet in all the wrong places. She was still dizzy from the marijuana but she surrendered to the rhythm of the music and to the allure of Crisp's graceful dance steps.

'Everything here is about the budget, Faith. It's quite simple. It's not rocket salad. Although,' and he paused for effect, 'it may be that shortage of funds is not the real problem. In agriculture, public spending runs to a hundred and fifty million dollars a year, most of it paid by donors. That seems quite a lot to me. But it's only just enough to keep the staff in their offices or at the workshop merry-go-round that drives this country.' He looked at her as if to see how she was taking this startling news and seemed to lean in closer. 'Of the twenty per cent that *is* allocated for investment, maybe half is never actually spent and of the half that *is* spent maybe two thirds is wasted or pilfered. What does that leave? Five million dollars. And probably half of *that* goes for four-wheel drives. The ministry runs three hundred vehicles for Christ's sake. Some of them working as taxis in Mombasa by the way.'

'Supposing the...'

'Enough, really, it's a nice night, no more of this. Look at the sky.'

They were on the edge of the dance floor now, just steps away from the tropical garden, so thick and luxurious it looked like the primeval rainforest itself, sweeping up to their feet ready to swallow her up. And the sky *was* gorgeous, the Milky Way smeared across the heavens, the Southern Cross visible just above the horizon. But that wasn't what she was here for. 'Do you think...?'

'I tell you what, if you want to talk to someone on the inside, talk to Tripp. He's your man. Personally, I can't understand much of what he says but maybe you will.'

'It's all that economics,' she said, as if apologising for him.

'You've met him already?'

She nodded.

'You quick mover you. He speaks English as if it was his fourth language. You've heard of the quiet American?'

She hadn't but made a mental note to look it up and put on her most attentive face.

'Six silk suits and no personality,' added Crisp, as if that might help.

The evening rolled on. They danced and talked and she drank more and danced again. A couple of times they went out into the garden for more spliff. She did try to bring the conversation back to NADS but to no effect. She was spinning into the night, high and wild.

'One thing you need to understand,' they had wandered over to a bench by the swimming pool, Crisp's mouth was against her ear, 'is that if people seem to be hiding stuff, or reluctant to talk to you, or shy, it's not because they are trying to be difficult or because they are stupid, it's because they feel awkward and they don't want you to see that.'

'Why should they be awkward?'

'People *feel* awkward. Look around. Everything here is rubbish. Nothing works. The roads are broken, the drains are blocked, the power is off, the Internet's down, the shops are shit. Plastic crap from China that doesn't work, made especially for Africans. The phones don't work. The drugs are fake. The toytown politics would make you laugh if you weren't crying.

People know it's all rubbish and they think there is nothing they can do. They know you know it's rubbish. They know that you know that they know it's rubbish. That's where the passivity comes from, and powerlessness and feebleness. Of course it's awkward. Worse, it's humiliation.'

'So what can we do?'

'Who?'

'Us.

'Us?'

'Well, OK my team. Me. That's why I'm here.'

He laughed sourly. 'That's the whole point. Everything you do just makes it worse. *You* are the source of the humiliation. Me too, of course. It's hard for us to get it, I know, but how would you feel if a young girl from Africa, who knows nothing about you, suddenly waltzed into your comfy little Oxford life and announced she'd come to help and says you'd better co-operate or else?'

She could feel herself blushing.

'It's all right,' he said, his hand on her shoulder, guiding her back to their table, his tenor suggesting he was about to impart some particular words of wisdom. 'It'll be easy enough. You'll zip through it. Have some more wine.' It was the last of the bottle.

'How did you get to be doing this, to being a journalist?' she said, trying a different angle. 'What's your background?'

He looked reluctant to go there. 'What does it matter?'

'I'm interested in the psychology of development workers. Why people do what they do? Why do they work so intensely in someone else's country. Why do they all have such difficulty working in their own communities?'

He frowned. He clearly didn't think it was important.

They drove back with barely a word, the traffic virtually nothing now and the Land Rover negotiating one pothole after another, from occasional street light to occasional street light, Crisp focusing closely on the road. It seemed a long way. She was sure they had passed the sign for Malcolm X Drive already but there it was again. Finally, they pulled up in the driveway of a large white house partially hidden in trees and he was out of the car and walking up the path. He'd left the headlights on and she sat for a minute trying to focus on the cloud of lake fly swimming in the funnels of light, brushing against the windscreen, swarming inside.

The house was a beautiful old colonial bungalow, blanketed with creepers and vines, decorated with rattan furniture and drapes, Baganda headdresses, masks from Bundibugyo, Ankole drums. On a bookcase, a terracotta head with long hair and a kind of plug on the top.

'What's that?'

'Glad you noticed it. It's a copy of the Luzira Head.'

She'd never heard of it.

'It was uncovered by prisoners building the prison. In 1929. It's clay. It's a thousand years old. It's unique in the prehistoric art of Eastern Africa and it's been locked in a cupboard in a basement in the British Museum on the other side of the world since they took it there in 1931. No one here will know anything about it.'

She was impressed. 'And that?' she said, pointing to a stone shaft decorated with incised bands similar to those on the neck of the head.

'*That*,' he paused, and seemed as if to pout, 'is a lovingly handcrafted copy of my cock.'

She laughed nervously.

'Only kidding. That is the *Entebbe* figurine. Somebody else's cock. But quite handsome don't you think?'

She laughed. As confidently as she could manage.

'Were you expecting to fuck?' he asked, straight out but still pouting.

'Excuse me?'

'I thought perhaps you might...'

'I think I need a cab. Can you call one?'

'Oh come on. Don't get on a high horse. Let's have another joint.'

'It's getting late. I've got work to do.'

He seemed surprised, put out, as if this was not in the script at all. 'You don't have to...'

'I don't have to but I want to.'

He laughed.

'Are you a gentleman?'

'Of course.'

'Well, call the bloody cab. I'm not here on holiday, you know.'

EIGHT

April 13th 2011

"I don't want you to think in the statements I made that I'm being disrespectful towards you as white people. I'm being frank. And I think that my statements will give you a better insight on the mind of a black man than most statements you get from most people who call themselves Negroes, who usually tell you what they want you to hear with the hope... that will make them draw closer to you and create a better possibility of getting from you some of the crumbs that you might let fall from your table. Well, I'm not looking for crumbs so I'm not trying to delude you."
- Malcom X

'So what's *your* story, Bent?' It was a few days later. They were in the bar at the hotel and she was back on her psychology of development workers agenda, trying to reconcile the legend of the trade with the curiously diffident manifestation slouched in front of her. 'How did you first get into this game?'

It hadn't been hard to find him. Since arriving, he'd barely left the hotel. He'd adopted a tall stool at the far end of the basement bar and, in just a few days, he'd made it *his* seat. From there, from behind aviator shades, he seemed content to just watch the world go by although he *said* he was thinking about 'the strategic picture', working out in his head what the team should eventually conclude. He had a large bottle of beer in his hand when Faith sat down with him that afternoon, most of it already gone.

'You know what, Faith?' She knew already he was going to dodge the question. 'I have to admit. I'm tired. Jet lag, I suppose. At my age, it does take its toll.'

Jet lag! But he'd been here ten days. And wasn't jet lag supposed to be an east-west thing? Well if it *was* jet lag, perhaps it was the consequence of some new form of intergalactic travel. Still partly in charity shop gear, Baxter certainly looked as if he could have been time-warped in from another place. Or another epoch. His outfit today was embroidered waistcoat and loose cotton trousers, almost the Pathan hill tribe look. Then again, compared to the other people in the bar, he didn't particularly stand out. There were a few Chinese businessmen, a handful of ecotourists and one or two of those ubiquitous American missionaries but otherwise it was wall-to-wall NGO people, cheesecloth and sandals and headbands and woven string bags.

'Maybe you need more sleep?'

He took a mouthful of the beer and Faith wondered what could have befallen him. And when did it happen? Hilleard might have said he was one of HSC's top guys, a giant in the profession, but at this moment, all *she* could see was his unusual relationship to the space-time continuum.

'We are in a bit of a bind,' he said.

'I *had* started to worry...'

He sighed, painfully almost, a touch of exasperation. 'Nothing serious really but we've got ten days to do this assignment and it'll be a squeeze even just to tick the boxes they want. I'm afraid we'll have to lock ourselves in our rooms and just write like fuck, day and night.'

'I got the impression from Charlie Crisp that there might be some interesting political angles and that we could explore a new...'

'No, no. There's already enough here without inventing new angles, let's not complicate things. It'll be easy enough though if we...'

'But if we....'

'First: MODE wants the review to be positive so a new project can go ahead. They have a ton of money they have to get rid of. The government wants the project because of course they want the dosh.'

'So we just agree to give them what they want?'

'Do you want to give them something they don't want?' He was getting irritated now. 'Faith, as you have no doubt already surmised, the reasons the donors want the project and the reasons the government want the project are not entirely reconcilable. Everyone knows the reasons are different. The government knows we know the reasons are different and we know that they know that we know that the reasons are different. But nobody can admit this or even that we might all be prepared to live with the fact that the reasons *are* different. As long as nobody says so explicitly. And certainly as long as no one tells the popular press.'

'I'm not sure I follow.' This was beginning to remind her of Crisp's tortuous analysis.

'Nobody does,' smiled Baxter. 'But it will be no great problem if we agree to be explicit with the firm understanding that we won't be.'

The whisky, when it came, was a triple and the first one barely hit the side. After that Baxter seemed to have no desire to say anymore and he was halfway through his second before allowing any more questions.

'Back to the beginning then, Bent,' she tried again. 'How did you start in this work? What is it actually all about? Deep down.'

'What's what about?'

'Development. Africa. All that. Whatever you want to call it. How did you get started?'

He shrugged. 'The same way people get into anything.'

'Which is?'

'Well,' his voice slurred, as if he was having trouble finding the words, 'in my *special* case, I'd have to say it wasn't typical.'

As she thought about it later, she realised that, if there *was* a time machine, some contraption somewhere that could isolate the old Brighton teddy boys, with their drape jackets and winkle-picker shoes, the sixty year olds whose jeans were three sizes too tight, then quarantine them permanently in 1962, if there was such a machine, then Bent Baxter might have the one key to fit the ignition.

'My father,' said Baxter, 'found the Lord. He'd heard there were openings for missionaries in East Africa. Signed on for a Seventh-Day Adventist introductory course, in Tanzania. They put him in a village somewhere out in the bush and he saved souls for a couple of years. I went to visit him, 1968 it was. I loved it, I got the Africa bug. Missionaries and development workers, it's the same pathogen.'

Faith laughed.

'Later, after I'd returned to the UK, I was at a Deep Purple gig in Glasgow, standing at the urinal, when the fellow next to me, a little bloke with a cock like a horse, looks me up and down, says he likes my suntan. Got it in Tanzania, I tell him proudly. 'Really?' he says, clearly interested.'

At that moment, a gaggle of youngsters came bounding in, taking a table close by: black linen suits and sunglasses, men and women.

'Oh Christ,' said Baxter, wearily. 'This is the IMF team, the scouts. I saw them earlier. Did you hear? The top man, Dominique Strauss Kahn, is jetting in to address the Poverty Conference. We're very privileged but apparently he has a lot of, how should we say, 'special requirements' and all the riders have to be checked, very carefully, well in advance.'

Faith had heard something too. An IMF visit was a big deal at the best of times, testing for all concerned.

'Anyway,' said Baxter, picking up his narrative again, 'the wee man from Motherwell tells me he's looking for someone to do a job for him. You on the market? he asks. Depends, I say, on what you're offering. Two weeks in Brazil, he says.'

Could this story have any basis in reality? Faith couldn't tell. She was living in slow motion, it seemed. From a window on to the street, she watched a man trying to push a bicycle loaded with charcoal up the steep hill outside. Silhouetted in the fading light, he seemed sleepy, sluggish. It was as if the task was impossible and he was stuck in quicksand.

'Crocodile sandwich!' One of the IMF team was up close to the barman and shouting. He was a boy, hardly more than twenty, all ponytail and manicured nails. 'And please make it snappy.' Tough, rarefied, smart, she already knew IMF people are not your usual UN per diem chasers. They work hard and they play hard. Indeed, so she'd heard, the full-time staffers are so pin sharp they keep their watches on Washington time and demand all their contacts do the same. While ordinary folk are waking up, the IMF team are still taking dinner from the night before (or is it the day ahead? It's easy to get confused). While the regular Joes snuffle over their breakfasts, these kids are ordering evening cocktails. While the world goes out to work, the team will be settling down for some 'creative accounting' with the town's demi-monde. Faith had heard there were sometimes problems with the 'time zone strategy', as it is called, but that people got used to it and IMF missions only come two or three times a year. And African civil servants are an easy-going lot, so the word on the street had it at least, and they don't mind a change in their schedule from time to time, they might even welcome a break in their tedious routines, might even like being in their offices from ten at night until dawn. And, for Christ's sake, it's for a good cause, and those old hacks know they're privileged to be in such highbrow company. And if they do mind, well tough, the IMF can easily appoint somebody else.

'But, going back, long story short, the wee man gives me his card and tells me to call. His name was Zoo Adderbury, he said, and he was a departmental head at MODE.'

'Zoo Adderbury. He's the PS now! I heard he was making a presentation at the Conference.'

'Indeed, the very same. Well I went to his office and he fixed me up with a civil service ID and an itinerary to travel. They were great days. In my first six weeks I went to twelve countries, business class every one. I was an instant expert.'

'How to improve the lot of the impoverished native!'

'Precisely.'

Outside, the man was still struggling with his bike. He'd made little progress and seemed in danger of having the whole load collapse on top of him.

'You know,' Faith tried again, running a finger round the rim of her coffee cup. 'The thing I can't understand is why everything is so difficult. The people are poor, they want our money, we totally want to give it to them. Why can't we just hand it over?'

Baxter thought this was *very* funny. 'Just put the cheque in the mail? Yes, why has no one thought of that before?'

Was that so hilarious? Faith wondered if Baxter should hold back on the whisky.

'So how did I start?' he said, suddenly all serious. 'Or did I start? Actually I wonder more why I continue. Is it curiosity? Or fear? Push or pull? Am I motivated by a desire to see new places or is it that I just need to get away from the old ones?'

'You got a family?'

'That's not a question you ask in this business.'

But she had and Baxter was soon talking about his other life in Aylesbury or Amberley or Abingdon or whichever English village it was. He'd had several wives, it turned out, but the current one, Peta, who'd once been a choreographer in Chiang Mai, he said, in a puppet show, had lasted longest. Faith wasn't sure she wanted to know but Baxter was keen to tell her how dancers are part of a long and honoured tradition in Thailand, different, he insisted, from the girls that she might have heard of, out on a tiny stage in a pokey dive in Patpong, bare-arsed and howling into the void. There is a chasm, he insisted, of class, culture and folk tradition between the two. They'd had no kids but Peta, who could speak barely a word of English, had, Baxter contended, made up for that with her natural exuberance, her daily outpourings of pidgin gibberish charming all but the most resilient.

'I find as I've got older I spend a lot of time wondering why this and why that. Why did things pan out this way and not that? Why have I spent so much of my life on the run? Funny thing is I met Adderbury a couple of days ago and I realised it's all come round in a circle.'

By now the IMF team had lured across some girls, probably refugees from last night's disco, and Faith watched as a couple draped themselves across the proffered knees, all torn fishnet and ankle bracelets.

'A life on the run?' she said. 'Another variant of the same pathogen. Why stay at home with your family when you can get paid to hang out in bars with your hand between the legs of somebody you don't know?'

Baxter laughed. 'The invisible hand?'

She laughed too, realising this was a reference to something but not knowing what.

Outside, the bike had fallen on the man, the charcoal spilling all across the road. He was trying to gather it up but a gang of scavenging kids had come and were snatching it out of his hands.

The Ministry of Agriculture has offices on the nineteenth floor of Worker's House, one of the first of the multi-storey high-rises in Kampala. It's the home of numerous government offices and donor agencies and the only workers you're likely to meet there are waiters, porters and 'customer service' girls.

The lift was a transparent bubble which travelled with a diagonal trajectory across the outside of the building and as it accelerated, Faith took Baxter's arm and started counting. When the doors opened at the top she peeked between her fingers. It felt like she was suspended in space. She was inside the abyss but had yet to start to fall.

Two army officers, battledress fatigues too small, sub-machine guns too big, sat listless by a teak desk. One was fat and bovine, the other fat and malevolent. Baxter spoke to the bovine one who beckoned them to sit down. There was nothing to read and the officers stared without apology. Faith asked if she might have some water but they didn't seem to understand. Suddenly, and without apparent signal, the nasty one barked an order.

Baxter climbed to his feet, shuffled to the door and launched himself in. 'It's best,' he whispered as Faith and the two policemen followed, 'to observe the protocol.'

First they had to cross an anteroom perhaps sixty feet across. On benches along both walls sat some fifteen or twenty people, waiting as if expecting a church service. At the far end of the room, two steps led up to a more intimate space, almost a stage, where, under a wall light, a vast desk brooded over the proceedings and, behind that, hung the same old portrait of the President. Perhaps the desk had to be that big as Major-General Brigadier the Honourable Minister of Agriculture, sitting in what looked like a throne, was even more amplitudinous than his bodyguards.

'My friends,' said the Minister rising from his chair. 'So pleased you could come.' He wore an expensive pinstripe suit that was tailored to perfectly hide his girth. Expensive turtleshell spectacles were somehow marooned on the end of his nose and an expensive diver's watch encased his left wrist. It was the kind of watch advertised in magazines like Time, usually with copy boasting the piece would be waterproof to 400 metres. Which was about 399 metres deeper than the Minister was ever likely to go, at least without some concrete on his feet.

Baxter did some cursory introductions.

'Oh!' said the Minister, collapsing into his seat and, as he did so, petulantly pushing aside two of the four mobile phones carefully laid out before him like cards in a game of Solitaire. He was clearly disappointed to hear they were mere consultants. 'They told me you were from MODE', he said.

Baxter explained that they were *contracted* to MODE and the Minister seemed mollified when he grasped that the team was undertaking a review of NADS, seeming quickly to understand that they were expected to approve a new, and presumably substantial, tranche of funding for the project.

'NADS is very important for us,' said the Minister. 'Even the President has an agenda. And MODE, we are the best of friends.'

It was then that Faith became aware of another figure hidden in the shadows to the right of the window. The second man was in a regulation grey suit and tie but he had a toupee and it was somewhat askew. How had she missed him?

The Minister was friendly, even respectful. And this was good because none of them were, at that moment, a sight to inspire confidence. Faith had found Baxter in the sauna and had to harass him to get to the appointment on time. Now his shirt had come away from his trousers and was showing the large sweat marks occasioned by his exertion, front and back. Pale and hesitant, the poor man seemed, so Faith thought, somewhat reduced.

'NADS,' said the Minister, 'can you imagine? What a project! I've already had an EU team pushing to get in on it. This afternoon I have the Americans, tomorrow the African Development Bank. I gather the Papal Nuncio has been on the telephone, trying to arrange an audience. You are throwing me in at the deep end of the spotlight. IFAD were here for two whole days last week. Everyone wants to hurl money at NADS! What can I do? Even for me it is too much.'

'And I gather you've been putting my staff through their paces,' he continued, 'turning the place upside down, working us like blacks. That is fine, we're not as good as we think we are, I know that. And we have to prove it. Thanks to MODE we know we have to put square pegs in square holes, not the other way round.'

There followed muted applause from the audience in the anteroom.

'Madame,' the Minister peered at Faith over the top of his glasses, a searching look, up and down. 'Welcome. Are you the gender specialist?'

Carruthers stepped forward. 'Minister, Dr Cullimore is the sociologist on the team.'

The Minister bowed graciously and shook her hand, holding on just a little longer than necessary. 'It's only that we are very gender sensitive here.'

'We have one more on the team,' said Baxter. 'He's out in the field. Lord Pareto, from the COMPASSION head office.'

'*Lord?* Lord did you say?' The Minister was impressed. 'That is *very* good. MODE is serious I know. You see with some consultancies, let me be frank, we do get so many crooks.' He shook his head, ruefully. 'You see, Mr Barker we are sophisticated people here. We don't need volunteers and hippies, people's wives, that sort of thing. We will only have *true* experts.'

'Of course, Minister,' said Baxter, who was swaying so much Faith wondered if he might fall, and who, at that moment, looked the nearest thing to a true hippie the Minister was ever likely to meet.

'Take this one for instance,' said the Minister, brandishing what looked like a CV in the air. 'Imagine. This man came on a recent mission from Belgium. He was supposed to be advising us on fiscal policy, and, what else, Julian?'

'Budgeting, Minister,' said the malefic *aide-de-campe*, leaning down close to the Minister's ear.

'It says he is an economist,' the Minister went on. 'We were suspicious and when we looked, we found he was not.' To let them savour the true horror of this situation, the Minister let his words hang for a second in the air.

'As you say, Minister,' said Baxter, cautiously. 'There are so many cowboys in this business.'

'The London School of Economics,' bellowed the Minister, suddenly. 'We demanded his degree you know and he couldn't cope. Could not produce. *No!* Not even *that*. Not even that. Can you imagine? The London *School* of Economics!' He pronounced the words slowly, letting them run off his tongue, the better to emphasise the disgust and shame he felt at being so hoodwinked. 'I ask you? A school! Now I might want a quiet life but I am not turning a blind ear. I said to him do you think we don't have schools here? Do you want to open a can of worms? Do you think you can steal from us with impurity?'

The next few minutes were standard fare: a long speech from the Minister about the importance of their mission and the need for sensitivity; a discursive reply from Baxter, most of it a panegyric to NADS as related to him at his pre-mission briefing as well as grateful thankyous to the numerous people who he said had helped the team so far; and then the issuing of a letter of authorisation for each of the team, signed by the Minister himself, identifying the holders as *bona fide* consultants to the Ministry.

'This could be important,' said Carruthers, handing the letter to each of them in turn, an extra one for Pareto. 'Don't lose it. This will help open doors. Sometimes officers need a little persuasion.'

'You are of course welcome in our country,' continued the Minister. 'Once we have trapped a donor, so to say, we have to give them full co-operation. Now what about the facilitation?'

Baxter must have been elsewhere and, for a moment, did not reply. 'What facilitation is that, Minister?' he eventually asked.

'All this help we are giving, of course. I've spent half an hour with you already.'

When Baxter failed to respond to this, Faith stepped forward. 'But we are here to help *you*, Minister,' she said.

The Minister thought this was a terrific joke. 'Oh Madame, you *are* a MODE person I can see. They are always talking about efficiency and value for money. You are welcome to help, of course, and we are grateful, but we all need a slice of the gravy train. There is no such thing as a free lunch, Economics year one, that's something you *muzungus* have taught us.'

There was a pause while they all wondered what to say next.

'But,' said the Minister with a show of magnanimity, 'since you have come out clearly with all guns flying, perhaps we could consider a discount. An invitation to the Climate Change Roundtable in Bangkok perhaps? Or the next Poverty meeting in London?'

Carruthers said he would speak to MODE and the Minister agreed that was fine. 'As long as the outcome is what the outcome was at the end of it.'

At that moment, seeming as if to wake up suddenly, Baxter pulled himself to something near his full height and, fumbling for his notebook, abruptly blurted out, 'Minister, as you know, we have been most impressed with the ministry here and with the record at NADS but there are one or two matters which, unfortunately, as servants of the Crown, we are duty bound to bring up with you. Small things but we need to tick the boxes nonetheless.'

'Of course,' said the Minister. 'I would expect nothing else. I know you are professionals.'

'Faith is the one who's covering this,' said Baxter. 'Maybe I should hand over to her.'

'One thing, Minister,' said Faith, starting straight in, 'is that we hear there may be some intention to move away from the group focus of the existing approach... towards more focus on selected individuals...'

The Minister looked puzzled but she ploughed on. '...And that there may be a lessening commitment to working with the poor. We can't help noticing that there is no reference to poverty reduction in the documents we have been given.'

'Ah hah,' said the Minister, with the confidence of a man who has seen that one coming a mile off. 'You see, we don't like the word poverty reduction anymore. It sounds as if we are poor. We want to use the word wealth creating instead. It means the same thing.'

'Except,' said Faith, seizing her moment, 'that you *can* create a lot of wealth but if it all goes to very few people that would not be good development...'

There was quiet in the room, the Minister glancing at Carruthers, perhaps confused.

'…With no poverty reducing effect,' continued Faith. 'If you get my meaning…'

Baxter shuffled his feet, thumbed the pages of his notebook.

'We have seen things, Minister,' Faith hurried on, 'in the newspaper, about how party favourites have been doing well out of the project.'

The Minister wrinkled his brow. This time it was clearly a scowl.

But Faith had the floor and carried on. 'I even read that an enquiry is being held into corruption in the districts and that large sums of money are missing.'

At this point, Baxter, perhaps emboldened by the Minister's silence, came to her support. 'Our problem, Minister, is that if there are any outstanding issues, not that we think there will be, the donors may struggle to sign off on the new phase. This could delay the funding.'

'Delay?' Clearly bewildered now, the Minister looked again to Carruthers who smiled wanly. The Adviser had, Faith observed, a definite air about him, one of having lived for long periods in sealed air conditioning, like something that had learned to flourish in the dark.

'Delay, Mr Barker! I will not have. There are always bad eggs in the barrel of course but not delay. Everything is as it should be, on that I give my assistance.'

'Fine,' said Baxter, rather too quickly thought Faith. 'I appreciate your frankness, Minister. That's good to know.'

'And remember, poverty is a moveable feast. For me, a number of activities have passed through my mind.'

Baxter nodded.

'Now, in case you didn't get me right, you have to understand that we are all very busy. Have you heard about our Poverty Conference? Now, there is poverty. You cannot say we do not try. You will see. Mr Bonanza has thanked us. He is coming himself to …'

'Minister, eh…' Carruthers butted in. 'Remember, it's still embargoed.'

'Yes, yes, quite,' snapped the Minister, annoyed at being interrupted. 'Anyway, embargo or not, Mr Baker, all my officers are on extra duties. They are beavering. Time is flowing under the bridge.'

'One thing is we need the NADS work plans,' said Faith, not giving up. 'We need to know if expenditure matched the plans.'

'Well, if you say you need this, then you shall have it. Of course. We are building a database and it is already very rudimentary. We are pleased to assist.'

Faith smiled, this was progress. She had taken a risk and it had paid off. 'Minister,' she said, interrupting quickly. 'We also need to visit some more NADS sites...'

The Minister scowled again, real exasperation now. 'Sites? What's that got to do with anything? This is an easy assignment, Madame. Why are you making challenges? You've been to NADS already haven't you? I remember, I authorised it myself. You rode in my helicopter. Westland Gazelle SA 341. Special privilege for my MODE friends.'

'But only for two nights,' she said, realising quickly that she was on thin ice. 'We need to see more. I need to talk to more farmers. I need to do some participatory socio-economic enquiry.'

'No, no, no. Those *peesants* are not for participatory. There are other buttons you must switch.'

'But it's part of our assignment, part of our Terms of Reference. We need to know what the farmers think.'

'The farmers think!' The Minister was angry now, not used to being argued with. 'I must tell you, madam doctor, the farmers don't think. That is why they are farmers. They farm. Thinking is not for them. We do the thinking here. Meeting farmers would be making a wrong mistake.'

'But Minister...'

'*Madam*e!' The Minister stabbed his finger in the air. 'I am hammering this. Be careful you are at the precipice of a runaway train. Just do the work that you have been asked. Now, if you will excuse me, I have a visit from COMPLAINT wishing to give us a fish farming project.'

'COMPLIANT,' whispered Carruthers.

'Huh?'

'I think it's COMPLIANT, Minister,' he said again, slightly louder. 'It's an NGO.'

'So what are they complaining about?'

Carruthers saw them out and offered a few last words of advice. 'You must understand, Faith, we are all very proud of NADS and it *has* done a good job. No one's going to appreciate you swanning in here and telling them otherwise. And remember, like everywhere else, they have different ways here. When they're in our country, they have to do things our way, yah? But we're in Uganda now and we should do things the Ugandan way. It's a mark of respect.'

Of course. How could she argue with that?

But Carruthers wasn't finished. 'And, whatever the Minister says,' he dropped his voice, 'MODE likes participation and we'll need to see evidence of it in your report. We need to tick that box. You see we've learned how important it is that everyone participates *freely*. We want *everyone* involved.'

'We're all committed to participation,' said Baxter. 'I've even been on the course.'

'Good,' Carruthers continued. 'It's just that *some* people don't get it. NADS is a success and we need to keep it that way. Otherwise, we're all in the shit.' He ran his eye around the room and, as another smattering of applause rippled gently through the assembly, he took a tiny bow, like a great actor acknowledging an ovation for a star turn.

'And,' he whispered, 'I hope you've heard *this* time. The problem in the settlements is getting serious. Watch your backs and keep an eye on the security reports.' He made a sweeping gesture with his right hand and the two police officers rushed over, clicking their heels, forming an escort to left and right. Then, when poor Baxter stumbled on the carpet edge, they were able to catch him under his arms, maybe a little more tightly than strictly necessary, and frogmarch him to the door.

NINE

April 15th 2011

"He went to Africa full of bright ideas and great schemes and, in one way, he saw them all doomed to disappointment... so much so that earnest men are apt to find their ardour cooled and their courage gone."
- Mackay, 1899. The Story of Mackay of Uganda, by his Sister.

The pensioners' band was doing a turn in the bar, reaching culmination, the players slapping each other and shouting out a veritable frenzy of rinky-dink. Baxter was in his favourite seat, watching intently. He couldn't miss the uniformed clerk come in from reception, cordless phone in hand.

'For me? Are you sure?' Who could want him here?

'Bent, is that you? How are things in the Pearl of Africa?' It was Hilleard, the voice of authority, calling presumably from the other side of the world. 'You all right, old chap?'

'I wouldn't put it that strongly.' When you're talking to people on your own side, you don't need to hold fire, you can remove the rose tints, and Baxter started in on the long catalogue of confusion. It went on for a while. 'And, also, the Minister has banned us from more field visits. Can you believe it? I mean what is the fucking point?'

'Hang on, Bent, hang on. Stop right there.'

'No one's telling us the truth, no one is around when you want them, the project would seem to be wobbling...'

'Bent, Bent, Bent, hold on...' Hilleard clearly hadn't called to hear this. He was a big picture man, weren't they all these days, and he didn't want all this detail. Didn't want *any* detail.

'Bent, that's not why I'm calling. I've got a couple of housekeeping issues. I just need to make sure you're up to speed with recent developments.'

Hilleard was a good fellow of the old school, the kind of cove once common in the venerable institutions of City and Church, the sort who acts up to the part of lightweight and buffoon, presumably out of breeding and good manners, feeling no need to dramatise his real and, everyone assumes, substantial talent and intellect. The secret of his success was sometimes ascribed, by his less charitable colleagues anyway, to the confusion he sowed. He couldn't be the simpleton he seemed, therefore he must be a wise man, one of the rare few who had actually lifted off into the balmy region of higher consciousness. There *were* a few who had questioned the relationship between higher consciousness and cretinism but they were rarely with the company long.

'Company's restructuring, Bent. The new paradigm is imminent. I need to warn you. You need to be ready for it.'

Baxter waited. What could this mean?

'We're rebranding, I think that's the term. Right now we're working a deal with some international PR johnnies. Bosworth Bollinger, you've heard of them yeah? It's all hush-hush. They've got a consultancy business of their own, probably some kind of tax write-off if we're honest, but the thing is they want our expertise. We've got Skip Bifferty working on it and he's reeling the blighters in, Bent. Little by little. I'm talking loss-leaders, market segmentation, tax breaks, unique selling points, change management strategies, all that stuff...'

'Well...'

'And they're loving it. By the time they understand the reality, we'll have swallowed them whole.'

'Right.'

'But there is one small issue outstanding.'

'Yes?'

'The lawyers need to get it resolved before the signatories meet...'

'Yes.'

'That Aral Sea money.'

Long pause.

'We really need to get it back, Bent.'

Longer pause.

'That's why I'm calling. Our only hope, Bent, lies with the elusive Mr Macpherson and you, old chum, are the last person to have seen him. I know you have other things on your plate but all the other trails are dead.'

'Everything's on the file, Godfrey, we've been through this twice.'

Baxter could feel Hilleard's frustration across five thousand miles.

'Do the right thing, Bent. We're all depending on you. It'll be best in the long run.'

Baxter was struggling to think. 'Look, Godfrey, I'm trying to do some real work here. It's hard, are you hearing me? Your lordly friend from COMPASSION has gone completely AWOL and Faith is struggling with the workload. As usual MODE want the impossible but are no fucking help. The officer is a conniving toad. We've got no hope of finishing on time. And you know my health's been a bit wobbly recently, actually I'm worried that…'

'Your health?'

'Well, y'know…' But it was pointless to complain. The company never wanted bad news and it was a mistake to try to give it to them. Solutions not problems, that was HSC's motto.

'The other thing, Bent, is…' another weighted pause, 'there's been some confusion on your contract. MODE London's been harassing us. Seems the Contract Office got the inputs wrong, the budget upside down, the timing awry, the head up the arse, the knickers in a twist. It's the standard MODE snafu.'

Baxter waited to hear what this might imply.

'Brutal truth is we'll have to cut your input to, what was it, five weeks.'

'*Five weeks*! That means there's only six days left.'

'Is it?'

'But six days, it's ridiculous. Godfrey, we can't do anything *serious* in that time.'

'Serious, Bent? C'mon let's not get ideas.'

The taxi driver knew the place, Baxter didn't need his map. But when they got to the Clock Tower, there was gridlocked traffic and a gaggle of policemen waving them to a stop. As they waited, Baxter in the rear seat, the windows tightly closed to keep out the diesel fumes from the backed up *matatu* minibuses, more policeman appeared, some with truncheons. People were running. Baxter could see people carrying banners. 'Thieves OUT,' said one.

'What's going on?' said Baxter but the driver offered only a shrug.

Then, without warning, a small phalanx of demonstrators were haring towards them, shouting and screaming, one man banging his fist on the passenger door, police chasing, truncheons swinging. Baxter saw a woman getting clubbed on the head, blood down her shirt. 'Come on,' he shouted to the driver, 'let's get out of here.'

As the crowd surged, seemingly rushing *into* the fray, the driver mounted the curb and started up the oncoming carriageway, dodging some speeding *bodas* and a couple of cows that had run loose in the confusion. They were soon at a large roundabout where the car nipped across the lights, jumped the intersection, and left the trouble behind.

'What the hell was that? What was happening?'

'Troublemakers.'

'It looked bad. What was it about?'

The driver shrugged again, wasn't bothered, didn't care, it was just another obstruction on the highway, another moment in the incident-full day. 'Just in case, sir, we'll go by the Mukwano Road.'

They took a right into the industrial area and picked their way through the potholes and derelict buildings there before finding the relative familiarity and calm of Bugolobi. Baxter began to relax and, climbing Mbuya Hill, he could see Lake Victoria glistening in the distance, while, in front, a great gate loomed above them like the entrance to some comic-strip medieval castle, all battlements and razor wire, a sign for 'The Compound' hanging high above. The car was barred entrance and a uniformed officer with a machine gun motioned Baxter to get out and walk.

'Have you got a Lord Pareto staying here, would you know?'

'Number 46,' said the man, a pasty-looking runt with clipped moustache and sunglasses, NYPD-alike badge jutting from his cap. He snapped his heels and pointed with his gun, up the long avenue of manicured lawns.

The houses in The Compound were all much the same: ostentatious and affected, a contrast with the traditional colonial bungalows of the middle-class suburbs, not to speak of the settlement shacks that Baxter had seen all week from his car window: not for those poor sods The Compound's five metre satellite TV dish, the swimming pool, the Jacuzzi, the tennis court and the army of staff you need if you want to pick weeds from the lawn by hand.

Number 46. Baxter stopped, checked the number again and tentatively made his way up the path. On the veranda, his knock seemed to echo around the house as if it might be empty. There was a long pause then a noise inside, a television perhaps. At least somebody was *in*. He knocked again.

No reply.

'Hel-lo? Anyone in there?' He put his ear to the door.

Murmurs, strange whimpers. *Resonance*.

There was a small window into what seemed to be the kitchen but the glass was frosted and Baxter could see nothing.

He reached for the handle but, even as he touched it, the door fell open, swinging inwards. He took a step back, surprised. It may have been an Ideal Home from the outside but, inside, the place was a shambles, like it had been burgled and turned over, like a river in spate had run through it, wine bottles everywhere, paper, ashtrays, a scarf hanging from the light shade, scattered clothes, underwear.

A TV was on in the corner. A film. Porno. Three people having sex.

And there was Lord Pareto, Lord Pareto of Pangbourne.

At last.

But he was having sex too.

On a bed under the window, a fat girl in a bathrobe guzzling chips from a room service tray, eyes glued to the TV. On the floor, a younger girl, naked, on her knees, her backside to Baxter, brown, fleshy and tattooed, a plastic bracelet around her ankle.

For a moment, Baxter felt as if he'd been struck with an electric current and seemed to lurch backwards only to find his feet were somehow stuck to the floor. 'Oh, sorry,' he said, almost falling.

Mirrors had been placed judiciously around the room and the scene was reflected out to him in triplicate, quadruplicate, quintuplicate. A kaleidoscope of images, a vortex, a montage, and at its centre, Pareto, spread across the only armchair, hair askew, trouserless, legs apart, snacking off a large plate of meat and at that very moment being more than liberal with a bottle of Worcester sauce. The naked girl's head was in his groin. From the racket she was making, you might have thought she was drowning.

Pareto seemed indifferent to the interruption. 'Come in,' he said, as Baxter stood and gawped. 'Dr Baxter I presume?' His manner was jovial, welcoming even.

Baxter tried to look composed, felt momentarily overtaken by some atavistic sense of not wishing to spoil the party.

'This is Destiny,' said Pareto, stroking the girl's hair. 'But take the friend if you want. I paid for them both.'

Baxter turned to the fat girl but wasn't sure of the etiquette. She smiled and offered her plate of chips. He was tempted to take one but refrained. 'Eh, Lord Pareto?' he said, trying desperately to remember why he was here.

'You can call me Dickson.'

'I wondered if I might have a word.'

But it was the wrong time, he knew that. The kneeling girl was whining, annoyed at the commotion, working hard, trying to get a result.

Pareto grimaced and, chewing up another bit of steak, guided her head firmly *down*. 'Just hang on a minute,' he said.

'Look, I'll wait outside.'

But it was too late. Pareto was coming, a leaky, squeaky, noisy business that spoke more of pain than pleasure, more of triumph than surrender, and, he slid down in the chair, shivering like a man in the throes of a near terminal seizure, his eyes rolling up into his head.

'Oh fuck!'

And then the girl was bolting, coughing and spluttering, to the bathroom.

Pareto pulled himself to his feet and switched of the TV. Then, with the plate of meat in one hand, he shuffled into the ensuite kitchen. 'I tell you one thing, Dr Baxter,' he said, over his shoulder. 'The fillet in this country is second to none. Grass fed and *exceptional* value. But the blow jobs are rubbish. Christ, look at the bite marks on my dick!'

TEN

April 16th 2011

"...There are too many idiots in this world. And having said it, I have the burden of proving it."
- Frantz Fanon, Black Skin, White Masks

7pm and once again Kampala was gridlocked. Faith was seriously late by the time she had abandoned her taxi in the melee that is Luwum Street and exchanged it for a *boda-boda* and a roller-coaster slalom along Kampala Road. The bike dropped her at the Speke Hotel, a once historic haunt but now, with the expansion of the town, nothing more than a tatty old pile marooned in a traffic island.

With her rucksack on her back, she edged through the security detail at the door and tramped into the reception area with its faded wall hangings and drapes. Tripp was at a table in the corner, a bottle of French wine already open. He was in a white shirt, tanned, groomed, as gorgeous as ever.

'Something the matter?' he asked, rising from his chair. 'You look harassed.'

'I'm fine.'

'You have to learn some distance, Faith. Then it all gets *much* easier.'

She shrugged.

'Otherwise it'll kill you.'

She shrugged again.

The direction of conversation led inevitably to Baxter.

'He's absolutely no help,' she said. 'I don't know why.'

'And the work itself? How's *that* going?'

She told him about the meeting with the Minister. 'Everyone told us how good the guy is but he seemed a bit of a dag to me.'

'Really?'

'*You* said he was good.'

'I don't think that's the word I used.' He smiled, quite clear about that. 'I heard he'd banned you from any more field trips.'

'How do you know that?'

'We know everything. The guys… I told you…'

She took a deep breath. 'So why is he so uptight about it?'

'They don't like teams of foreigners running around the place digging into things they don't know. Who would? And it's probably a blessing in disguise. Going again will only confuse you. Take it from me. You shouldn't let things get too complicated.'

This was the kind of thing she was expecting.

'Look, Faith, I tell you, when I started at the Bank my line manager advised me not to leave my office unless I absolutely had to. Meeting people, going into villages, talking to farmers, she said, it'll unsettle you. The important thing, she was very clear, was that theory should dictate practice and not the other way round.'

She remembered what Crisp had said about Tripp speaking English as a fourth language.

'Might sound strange but she was right. She was a star economist.'

'Like accountants, I've heard, but without their animal allure.'

'One day, you'll understand.'

She needed another drink but the bottle was empty. In moments the waiter had brought another.

'So what *is* the theory then?'

'Finally! You're getting there. Very good. What is the theory? Well. What *is* the theory?' He leant back in his chair. 'When I was doing my PhD, that's always what the old *daktaris* used to ask. If you did a presentation, they would look at the ceiling and stroke their beards and say, that's all very well but what is the theory? So, when I was doing my viva, I really filled up on the theoretical stuff and span it out for half the presentation and, just when I thought I'd bored them all into submission, I started into the results, only to be interrupted by one of the senior professors half asleep at the back who had to cough for a minute before he could speak. I thought I knew what the question was going to be so I wasn't worried but you won't believe what he came up with. Tripp, he said, very good, you've given us your theory, and very interesting it is, but what is your theory of the theory?'

He *was* a bit dry, that was unavoidable, but in some curious way, Tripp reminded her of a dazzling park ranger she'd met one night a year or so before, on a brief visit back to New Zealand. She had drunk too much and, late at night, the two of them somehow contrived to climb a viewing platform over the empty landscape of Lake Timaru, not a soul for miles. They had humped themselves into exhaustion and, while he at least had his shirt on, she had still been stark naked, hung-over and groggy when the party of early-rising Japanese birdwatchers had emerged from the top of the ladder the next morning, like startled moles blinking in the light.

What was Tripp's home life? Was he married? Or would he have a local woman? She remembered the girls in the truck. No, the local women would surely frighten him. He had to be a family man, his living room at home, neat and tidy, American bourgeois, colour photos of cheerful wife and sporty kids generously displayed on mantelpiece and television top. And Tripp himself, the breadwinner, coming home from work each evening, so fired up about development and the prospects for growth that he needed diazepam, earplugs and a face mask to get to sleep and a mouthguard and a Silent Night electronic anti-snore nose clip to stop him choking himself to death when he finally did.

He was on to the Poverty Conference now. Very important in the strategic context and the preparations were going great. What a boost for the continent. Lots of exciting papers tabled, lots of international bigwigs coming in. Everyone was gearing up for the signing, some kind of whizz-bang treaty that would really put Africa on the map, commit all countries to ending world poverty by 2020, reinforce stability across the arc of instability.'

'The what?'

'Is that a new one for you? There's an arc of instability that stretches from Afghanistan through Pakistan to the Middle East and the Horn of Africa on to northern Nigeria and Mali. It passes about four hundred miles north of here. We need to stop it getting any closer. It's all part of the big picture.'

It seemed the conference communique wouldn't be binding but it would be a 'road map' to something that would lead to something that *would* be binding, although there might be some opt-outs. Now the Conference Committee was manoeuvring to get one of the very top development heavyweights to fly in and finish the whole thing with a grand gesture. Celebrations, parties, fireworks. This guy was a 'blue skies thinker', a 'player' and he would definitely get a ton of media attention. It was hush-hush still but the prospects were very good.

'Another star economist?'

'Sort of. Honorary.'

'Ah hah,' she said, realising she'd known the answer all along. 'Dominique Strauss Kahn.'

'Get out of it. Our guy is a real star.'

'Jeffrey Sachs?'

'Fuck Jeffrey Sachs!'

She must have looked impressed.

'Unfortunately he's so short of time he has to be helicoptered in. And they haven't got a landing pad big enough at the Serena. We're going to have to chop down those teak trees on the front lawn which is not good environment PR. We had to make a big contribution to COMPASSION and COMPLIANT just to keep them quiet.'

'Come on, tell me, who is it, the visitor?'

But he wouldn't.

So they had another bottle.

By the time they left the hotel, Faith was giggling and drunk and hardly felt the first drops of rain but, within moments, the sky had come undone and they were stumbling through sheets of water, puddles and spilling gutters. The traffic had reduced somewhat but the road was almost flooded and her cotton dress was wet through. By the time they found a taxi they were laughing fit to cry. The driver had to put the headlights on just to be able to see the road.

'I did consultancy once myself,' Tripp said, settling back into the soft seats of the taxi. 'Short term. Hit and run, y'know? Quick and dirty.'

'Right.'

'Quick and dirty. It had its attractions…'

She watched him from the corner of her eye.

'…but,' and he paused for effect, 'I prefer the world of strategic considerations.' That seemed to be his attempt at small talk.

The driver hooted and they swerved, narrowly avoiding a *boda*. Undeterred, the driver ploughed on, battling the rain and the giant potholes. He seemed to be trying to wrestle the car into submission.

'I have a boyfriend,' she said, feeling it better to get that in now.

'Me too,' said Tripp and they drove in silence for a while, nothing but the sound of the wipers slapping on the windscreen.

'NADS…' he hesitated.

'Yes?' She was watching the rain, losing concentration.

'Of course there are problems, Faith, I'll be honest, mission creep, elite capture, whatever you want to call it, moneys missing, all the usual stuff but it *has* to go ahead. It's a good project, really it is. And it's the only game in town.'

She felt a shiver of excitement. There's always a moment when the bridge is definitely crossed. They were buzzing along an open stretch now, up to second gear, and she had her eyes on the tarmac ahead.

'Government is insisting we move forward and Bank management is fully on board. We're all in too deep, got to go forward. And for me, I have to shift loans. We're a bank, remember, people forget that.'

'And you have to remember the strategic context.'

'Egg-zactly.'

The car pulled out to pass a broken-down lorry. She turned to watch the people on the street, only a few now, struggling along in the deluge.

Tripp came closer. 'I know how to celebrate.'

She could smell the wine on his quickening breath. The rest seemed to happen in the place where slow motion meets atomic time. And it was all over in a moment.

'Keep going, driver,' Tripp snapped, 'and face the front.' His suit trousers had a complicated double zip mechanism and it took him an age to get it running. He turned towards her and for a moment she had the impression he was wrestling with a snake, some translucent urban viper that had crawled into the car to avoid the rain. But why had he put his head on her shoulder?

She shifted her knees, moved her feet against the door.

'Jesus!'

'Fuck!'

'Je-sus!'

And then the hot fluid spurting on to her leg.

They drove two blocks in silence and he stopped the cab on Lumumba Avenue. As he was getting out he seemed to remember something. 'Did you hear about Charlie Crisp?'

From the window, she watched some marabou storks, wings up, shoulders hunched, sheltering themselves from the rain. They seemed to suggest old men in shabby tuxedos. Then a huge timber lorry, great tree trunks loaded to the top, edged alongside the car and blocked the view.

'They took him to a safe house.'

Safe house? What was he talking about?

'It's the usual euphemism deal. Safe houses are houses where you're not safe. They picked him at dawn, a bunch of 'em, black balaclavas, automatic weapons. He's lucky, not everyone who goes into the Kololo bunker comes out again so quickly. Fortunately, he'd already sent Bucky to his village.'

'Bucky?'

'His boyfriend.'

Faith must have looked surprised.

'You didn't know? Former DJ. Very chic. He was lucky too or they would have had him for lunch. Lucky Bucky.' With a flourish Tripp pulled a shiny black wallet from his jacket pocket and paid the fare. 'That was just what the doctor ordered, by the way.'

He left the driver a generous tip. Compensation, perhaps, for the spunk on the seat.

Baxter wasn't in his room. She walked to the bar but he wasn't on his favourite stool. She found him on a couch in the shadows by the back door, slumped down, arms outstretched, the TV on behind him. In a khaki kikoi with a scarf around his head, to cover a rash he said, he looked like the famous picture of Marat in his bath, alive maybe but only just. Then again he could have been a patient recovering from dental surgery or, in his now ever-present sunglasses, Greta Garbo two days after she died.

'Bent, I've been looking for you…' She had to shout over the din. Far from deterring the NGO reps, the night-time gun fire and the worsening troubles in the suburbs seemed only to have increased their ardour and they were thronging the place more avidly than ever, screaming for drinks and singing along with the karaoke jukebox. Some academics were in today too, probably waiting for their moment on the Poverty Conference big stage, *maîtres à penser* in sports jackets and cord trousers. With their black, ring-bound reports spread before them, the great men and women were yelling with the best of them, knocking back the booze as if there was no tomorrow. At a table next to Baxter's sofa, two bearded gentlemen and a woman in a leather skirt were doing justice to a bottle of Paul Cluver Viognier, arguing furiously about GDP per capita and the composition of the nation's Human Development Index.

'Bent,' she said, 'you're not going to like this but…'

'They found my suitcase,' he yelled back. 'It has arrived in-country but now they've lost it in the airport.'

She *had* wondered. The khaki gear was a new departure and she wouldn't have thought Tuareg terrorist chic was ever likely to be his forte. Then again, after a week of raiding its stores, maybe this was all the Lost Property office had left. Or perhaps he thought it might reassert the rudiments of his authority and, of course, it had the benefit that if you had to sleep in it, after a heavy night say, the fabric, the electric nylon, wouldn't show the creases in the morning.

'I've had a thought…'

'Too late, Faith, too late.'

'No, no, listen…'

Baxter was playing with his pen, watching the NGO crowd.

There was the guy with the CONCERN T-shirt that she'd seen before and a young woman wearing a pendant displaying the Luzira Head she'd seen at Crisp's place.

'Bent, are you listening?'

'Sure.'

'We must go back, find out more.'

'Sorry?'

'We should go back, find out more.'

He looked at her first like he had misheard and then as if she had made a scandalous suggestion, an expression of pure pain lighting up his face. She noticed he was emitting a curious odour, a delicate essence not unlike stale coffee or women's shoes.

'Find out more what?'

'Stuff about the project. Try to totally nail down what's going on.' She couldn't tell whether he was going to laugh or cry.

'C'mon, Faith, please, we're past all that. And I really need your support.'

'But we have to.'

'No, we don't have to. We're going to do what they expect consultants to do. What they want consultants to do. We're going to write a report. We're going to tell the client that the project is good.'

'But the client already knows this.'

'We'll tell him in a different way. That's what we're for, that's where we add the value.'

She made a face. 'Let me try to understand,' she started in, trying to be calm, all Commandante on the outside, 'we're here to give the go ahead for a new phase of NADS. Using MODE money, World Bank money, lots of other donor money. And bucket loads of it too.'

'You got it. Everyone loves the project, it's one of the few good ones around.'

'They're asking us to account for the money, to justify the...'

'There's been two *very* positive evaluations...'

She closed her eyes, took several deep breaths, counted to fifty. 'I just feel the ducks are too *obviously* in a row.' She was impressing *herself* now, her grasp of cliché improving by the day.

'Maybe, Faith, but it doesn't matter. Anyway, things are *never* as good as they say.' Baxter got to his feet, perhaps showing some small signs of life. 'Look, Faith, we're doing a review, signing off on a tiny dot in a tiny speck of the machinery. It's not a Greenpeace action. And there's no need to dramatise. You've done well so far. Nobody thinks you came here just to get a suntan.' He sighed. It was almost his default mode now but this time it sounded more like a million pebbles in the surf on Dover beach. Still, as he put his hand up to shade his eyes, she had a moment of sympathy, a sense of a man fading into his own private sunset.

'I think...'

'Faith. Just listen... we're going to write our report. No problem except we only have four days to do it in. So, we don't need to reinvent the wheel, we just pinch some paragraphs from the old reports, rephrase them here and there and push 'em back where we got 'em. You, you young person, can put in some nice graphics, if you want, some flow charts, some arrows pointing left and right, infographics, isn't that what they call it now? Up and down, round in circles. Sex it all up a bit.'

'But isn't that plagiarism?'

'The arrows?'

'No, the text.'

He thought that was *very* funny. 'No such thing as plagiarism in our business, love. But, if you insist, we will plagiarise the words of earlier consultants who plagiarised from those who plagiarised before them. Think 'out of the box' if you must, but get the fucking report written. We have to be out of here early next week.'

She knew she was in the right place because there was a man lying across the corridor, comatose in a puddle of blood and shit. She stepped over him and started up the stairs, noting, yet again, hanging over the stairwell, the portrait of the President, this one torn and tatty around the edges.

At the top of the stairs, a woman sat alone on a bench, shivering. From somewhere inside an old blanket, she was dripping blood on the floor. Faith squeezed cautiously round a trolley load of overflowing urine pans and past a consultation room with a faded 'Safe Sex with an Ebola Patient' poster on the door, its indelicate cartoon instructions educational even for a worldly girl like her. She turned into another corridor or was it actually a ward? Patients were lying on the floor, a foot or two apart, most of them without sheets or blankets. Many were elderly and seemed to be barely clinging to life. The place stank of piss and sweat. A man in a white coat was clutching a styrofoam bucket, selling sachets of *waragi,* the local gut-rot gin. Drinking spirits before six was a sign of loose morals, her mother had told her once, and it was only 5.30. Too bad, she thought, and bought four.

Further on there was a more obviously medical air: people in white coats bustling around, a lively matron in blood-stained crimplene, tiled floors, faecal brown walls, a whiff of chloroform. Crisp was in a secluded room at the end. Two guards jumped to attention as Faith approached. The patient had bandages around his head and a splint on each arm. The air conditioner was up so high it was like walking into a fridge.

'For Christ's sake, what are you doing in here? Why don't you go to the private hospital?'

'Solidarity with the masses,' he said, trying to laugh, his voice weak and reedy.

'You could die in here. The place is drenched with weird infections.'

'I'm always attacking ministers who go abroad for health care. They steal the money that should be used to build clinics here then go to London whenever they get a pain in their fat *asses,*' he said it in the American way. 'I thought I should practice what I preach.'

She could make out two tubes disappearing inside his pyjama top. He'd been out of intensive care, he said, only a few hours.

'But what happened?'

'Oh, the standard stuff.'

'Who did it?'

'Don't know. There are so many different intelligence agencies, different agendas.' He seemed to be finding it difficult to talk. 'I had a good story. I had names and dates.' He had to stop to cough. 'But to what do I owe the pleasure?'

'I just came to see you.' She put the sachets of *waragi* on the side table.

'Can't have that.'

'Oh.'

'I told you, I'm not allowed.'

'OK, well, at least I can say thank you for the nice evening the other night.'

'*I* enjoyed it.'

'I'm still chasing this NADS stuff of course.'

'Of course.' He began coughing again and she had to wait for him to finish.

'Tell me about Bucky.' Was that too abrupt?

'NADS, you said?'

'Or Bucky.'

He laughed. 'NADS is more complicated than people realise. It certainly started well but like lots of things it went off the rails. But there are too many careers dependent on its success. Everybody needs it to continue. The donors probably still think NADS is helping small farmers, through farmer's groups and grass-roots organisations and solidarity and all that. But, actually it's just another mechanism for handing out dosh to the President's supporters. It's the only institution that even half works in the countryside and the party wants to use it to strong-arm the people's vote when the election comes. NADS is not doing any real agriculture now, just organising handouts. If you vote for the party you'll get a packet of seeds, a hundred votes'll buy a goat, a thousand'll get you a tractor.'

'I'm going to go back.'

'Don't think it's not just the same in our country. You read the papers don't you? Bankers, journalists, police, politicians. Corruption, corruption, corruption, blah, blah, blah.' He was determined about that. 'The only difference is our people take more and are better at not getting caught. Go back where?'

She got up and walked to the window. Beyond the garden, she could see Lake Victoria, placid and blue. There were kids in a schoolyard playing football. 'If I went back on my own I might be able to find out something.'

'Back where? Find out what?'

'To Gulu, to the sites I went to before.'

'You think there are secrets to discover? There are no secrets.'

'I just want to ask better questions. Perhaps we could get civil society groups involved or NGOs?'

'NGOs! What for? Who do they represent? I told you. They're just a creation of the donors.' He started coughing again and reached for some tissues by the bed. 'Civil society! There are only two people in 'civil society' in this country and I'm one of them.' His smug grin was a little more than she could bear suddenly and she reminded him that he was lying on his back with rubber tubes in his gut and a suction pump in his bottom.

He smiled, a small measure of contrition, tried to extend it into a laugh but then had to stop as the laughter morphed into more deep coughing.

'By the way,' said Faith. 'Tripp. What a totally scummy man.'

'Really?'

'Yes.'

'He's been a long time 'out' as they say in the business. You get a bit removed from the real world.' He paused for what seemed like forever. 'The development industry is a cruel delusion, Faith. It develops nothing but the careers of the people who are drawn to the life, like flies to shit. If any true innocents get beyond the entrance gate they'll have their hearts broken pretty sharpish. There is nothing to see but a trail of disappointment.'

Perhaps she looked a little startled.

'And that's just the good stuff.'

She laughed.

'I've got to the stage,' he said, 'where I think if fifty per cent of the aid gets through everybody wins. '

'Everybody *cheats*, you mean.'

Out the window, another enormous timber truck, like the one she'd seen at lunchtime, lumbering up Mulago Hill, black smoke belching from a chimney atop the cabin. There were only three trees on it but they filled the wagon entirely. Each of them must have been twenty feet across at the cut.

'I think the villagers would turn out. They saw I was only there to help.'

'How would you get there? What would you see? Where would you sleep?'

'In the village.'

'Faith, this is not a game. Wandering around the bush is dangerous. Especially now, with all this trouble.'

126

'I'll take our gofer guy with me. He knows the place. He speaks the language.'

'He won't go. Why would he?'

'He will.'

'Not without his allowances, I bet.' And then, after a tantalising dramatic pause, holding his trump card for as long as was reasonable, 'You won't see our mystery celebrity you know?'

'Oh yes? And he or she is?'

'I'm not allowed to divulge. It's top secret.'

'Oh, come on.'

'No, I'm under strict orders.'

'Give me a clue.'

'Well…'

'Come *on.*'

'Ok, one word name. That's all you need to know. I'm saying nothing more.'

She laughed. 'Eh, Moby?'

'Who the hell is that?'

She paused to think. 'Adele?'

'No.'

'Cher?'

'No.'

'Lulu?'

'To open an international conference! Anyway, it's a man.'

'Meatloaf?'

'No.'

'God, I dunno. Ludacris?'

'Who?'

'Ludacris.'

'No, he's quite dignified actually. He's met George Bush and Nelson Mandela.'

'Posh Spice?'

'One name. Someone with a social conscience.'

'Eh… Donovan?'

He shook his head. 'At least I've heard of him.'

Then suddenly, 'Of course, Sting! I've even met him, you know, when I was at CARE. He was *so* nice.'

'No, not Sting. Anyway I shouldn't say more. It's heavily embargoed. But, just as an indication, in the pre-event scoring he came out ahead of the Pope. They realised this guy was much groovier.'

She was racking her brains. 'Ronaldo?'

'A *singer.* He's coming to see me personally! His people were harassing me for an appointment.'

'Slash?'

'Look, he's going to close the show, shake the hands of the signatories, tell them how history has been made. World poverty is to be abolished.'

'Vangelis?'

He shook his head.

Faith was baffled. Never mind, whoever it was they would surely be interested in the NADS story. Might even be an ally.

'And afterwards,' Crisp added, probably figuring he was on to a winner now. 'I thought I might take you to Mihingo Lodge. It's a lovely little place in Lake Mburo National Park. They've got some gorgeous *bandas* there. We could unwind, relax a bit. Take a couple of days off. I could show you a few local customs...'

She said nothing.

'Unless you objected to being with an old invalid of course?'

'Will Bucky come?'

He giggled uncharacteristically. 'He will if you let him. He does what he's told, I can assure you of that.'

Better not to react.

He rolled on his side. 'My legs seem to hurt more than my chest.'

'You have other *women*?'

'Sometimes.'

'Lots?'

'We're in Africa.'

'And Bucky?'

'Bucky is my friend.'

'He doesn't mind you taking little girlies to honeymoon cabins in the game park?'

'He doesn't know.'

'Everybody cheats?'

'Don't you?'

5am, no power in the room and no light, just another morning in the Imperial Hotel. She lit a candle and ran a bath and lay back in the water. She looked herself over in the mirror. She looked good. She was brown and healthy and her breasts were getting *better* with age. She washed her hair and shaved her legs. She was ready.

She pulled on her walking boots, stuffed a wad of twenty thousand shilling notes into a money belt around her waist then, with her rucksack over her shoulder, checked out of the hotel and, all by herself at last, staggered out into the early morning gloom.

A yellow taxi, darkened windows, side lights on, was waiting at the top of the street and it slid down the hill towards her. Somehow it put her in mind of a leopard stalking prey. The driver's window was open. He smiled.

'Thanks for coming,' she said. 'Next stop Gulu.' Just the name had an adventurous ring.

Part III

ELEVEN

April 17ᵗʰ 2011

The gofer guy was waiting, as he promised he would be, just before the flyover, near the Mandela stadium.

'How are you?' Faith asked as he climbed into the car.

'I'm good.'

From high on the flyover, she looked down on the carriageway below, pristine and pothole free and stretching in a straight line to the horizon. It was the best road she had seen in Uganda. 'But why are there no cars on it?' she asked.

'It's not open.'

'It looks all right.'

'That's the Northern Bypass. Our most famous road. It was planned in 1965, built with European Union money. They gave 75 million dollars to some Sicilian builders who ate the money and built the surface so thin it can't safely be used by trucks. No one can fail to be blamed but it is three years past its opening date.'

Faith had noticed how, as she had got to know him better, the gofer's confidence had started to grow. Now, with the preparations for this trip, he seemed to have moved up another gear. And, as they left the city, he seemed almost another man.

'What's your name again? Tell me exactly.'

'My names are Alphonse Remi Amase Nakut.'

'It's totally weird 'cos they told me your name was Lodi.'

'Also.'

'So shall I call you that?'

He shrugged. 'It has one benefit,' he said.

'What?'

'The problems with the road.'

'Yes?'

He laughed 'We get less lectures on corruption.'

And then she was once again on the great highway north, 3,000 miles, all the way to Cairo. Eventually. Two or three wars zones later, depending how you counted them. The first time around she had slept most of the journey but on this trip she took it all in. People and more people, bicycles, *bodas,* cars, vans, lorries, buses, container trucks. All driving like the end of the world was coming that afternoon.

And, somehow, the road itself was different. Where the first time it had been colourful and charming, it seemed now to project a more threatening air. She was more conscious of the hurtling juggernauts with their faulty brakes and drivers sustained for three days with nothing more than khat and dexedrine; of the buses, loaded to bursting point with primary schoolkids, being driven as if they were on the last lap at Le Mans; of the potholes that seemed to go most of the way to Australia; of the motorcyclists ducking and diving; of the air choking black with diesel smoke and lead. Another thing she hadn't noticed on the earlier trip was the army of women loitering in the fast lane, their backs to the traffic, sweeping the road with what looked like giant toothbrushes.

'What are *they* doing?

'Sweeping the road.'

'Why? What's the point of that?'

'Well, it gives them work, keeps them off the street.'

Little *dukas* and market stalls lined the highway but, behind them, there was nothing much. It was an urban strip, hardly more than one house deep, running for fifty miles. Every so often they went through what might be called a township, a bunch of houses: Luwero, Nakasongola, Karuma. People looked ragged, struggling to make a living, buzzing against their walls like flies in a bottle. Clusters of marabou storks. A few vultures circling. At one point, there was a troop of baboons trying to scavenge dog carcasses off the road, dancing on and off the tarmac as they tried to avoid the speeding trucks.

'This,' said the driver, proudly, his eyes fixed on the road ahead, 'is a dangerous road. It said so on the BBC. The *World Service*.'

'It's because of the trucks,' said Lodi. 'They're overloaded. Logs, charcoal, bricks, sand, coffins.' His opinions were getting stronger. It was as if self-assurance was coming to him in proportion to the distance they travelled from the town.

'Why don't they do something?'

'Who?'

'I dunno, the government?'

'They are, they are bringing prosperity.'

Lodi was still laughing as they swerved to avoid yet another gargantuan wagon, this one hurtling and sliding round the bend towards them, black smoke billowing from its exhaust funnel, its huge load of tree trunks swaying and crabbing. A moment of alarm and it was past. Finally they slowed down to turn off the main road and started up a narrow murram track.

'This is the same place I went to before?'

'Sure.'

'It's important, I need to triangulate the…'

'Yes, yes.'

'I'll be able to ask questions?'

'Of course.'

Eventually, they pulled into a little hamlet and people came running towards the car. Lodi got out and a crowd gathered round, men firing questions, children pulling at his sleeve. Close to some huts a larger group had gathered. They were watching Faith, clearly talking about her. A young girl in bare feet peeled away and approached her. She stood off, about six feet away, her thumb in her mouth, her head cocked, staring.

'I am Faith,' said Faith.

The girl didn't seem convinced.

'What is *your* name?'

'I am Fortunate.'

Faith smiled but the girl did not react. Maybe she didn't see the joke. Maybe she was shy.

Lodi returned. 'We'll walk from here. These boys will carry for us,' he said, gesturing to a group of youngsters unloading boxes from the car.

'Is this the same place I was before?' She didn't recognise it.

'We're reaching from a different direction.'

Lodi had insisted they bring rations and they had tins of sardines and corned beef, bags of rice, bread, soap, cooking oil, paraffin, several cartons of beer, packets of seeds. And there was a tent and some bedding too. He seemed to be ready to live out here for a month. She had wondered if they *really* needed it all but he had been quite determined. 'We'll hand the food out as gifts,' he said. 'And the seeds. The people expect it. If we are to get any co-operation it is essential.'

Fieldwork, the real thing, time with real people. This was what she was here for. She smiled and swung her pack on to her back. It wasn't just Lodi, she was more confident too. Making the decision to come, planning the trip, these had all helped her feel stronger, convince herself she was doing the right thing.

The walking was easy enough. The young boys took the lead and made a fast pace but she was fine with it. She knew how to skip along narrow paths, balance on logs and jump streams. She wondered if Lodi was surprised that a woman could keep up so well but he made no sign one way or another and they walked in silence. The boys handled their awkward loads without complaint, jogging along, apparently indifferent to the weight or the pain of the sharp corners as the boxes dug into their ribs.

'Lodi. Are you sure this is the right way?'

'We're coming from the back.'

She could hear birds in the nearby trees and from time to time she would catch a glimpse of colourful plumage, a crowned hornbill perhaps, swooping down to investigate the intruders below. Once, on the crest of a hill, they had a glimpse to the south and there was greenery and forest, green into green, into paler green, into the distant receding evening haze. She let her mind glide away, swimming among the drifting leaves of pale bamboo, floating across the delicate tapestry of moss. As it began to get dark and a light rain began to fall, they came to a collection of huts each one leaking smoke from the thatch on the roof.

'This is it. We can work in the morning.'

Children ran up the path to greet them, shielding themselves from the rain, great leaves held across their heads. 'Welcome,' they chanted, and they reached out to touch her.

She took two little girls by the hand and ran with them in among the huts to where some men and women were gathered. An old lady came forward, eased the bag from her shoulder and carried it off in the direction of a group of houses set back from the main body of the village. Lodi waved to her to go along and she trotted behind, into a hut in which was set a small bed and some rattan shelving.

She sat down on the bed. The mattress was thin, made from cheap foam rubber, but it felt wonderful after the long walk. She leant back on the pillow and considered the day. She had achieved a lot. She had made it back to 'the field'. She had met some villagers. Tomorrow she would ask some hard questions.

She woke about five as a family of goats began to snuffle around the hut and as the women began to stir, fetching wood and water, starting fires, loading up with kids, heading out to the gardens. She pulled on her muddy boots and went outside. Lodi had been up a while, it seemed, and he brought her a cup of tea. 'Some farmers are coming. I have arranged.'

'This is definitely the place I was before? I don't recognise it.'

'It's just that we've come on a different road.'

A little later, a group of women appeared, some in what might have been their best clothes: shoulder pads, voluminous skirts, scarves, lots of colour. When Faith tried to speak to them in well-enunciated, clearly-spoken English, they giggled and laughed, almost in unison. As always there were numerous and lengthy pleasantries but, through Lodi, they eventually agreed to answer her enquiries. She said she had come to ask questions about NADS. Did any of them remember her from her last visit?'

More giggles, some blank faces, uncertain conclusions.

Did they know the District NADS Co-ordinator? The man who had been with her before? What was his name? She couldn't remember.

They knew him but he had been replaced. 'He was a good man,' said one woman.

Reassured, Faith said she wanted to ask more questions.

That was fine.

According to the files she had seen, Faith said, there had been a 'sensitisation' exercise here. Ten trainings had been organised and twenty farmers groups sensitised. Some of them had even moved to the next stage of 'full empowerment'.

This was true, said a second woman.

Good. 'Were they empowered now?'

'Yes,' said a third woman 'But we are still poor.'

'But everything has stopped,' said a fourth.

Faith was puzzled. 'Why?'

'The government,' said a young woman at the back. 'They should provide us with what we need.'

'What is that?'

The woman wasn't sure.

'Water,' said the first woman eventually.

At that moment, a small group of men appeared further up the path. At their head was an elderly man wrapped in a blanket, carrying a stick. 'Madame, madame,' he shouted and began to stride purposely towards them.

'This is the village big man,' said Lodi. 'We must talk to him.'

'But let's finish with these ladies first.' She was determined not to be bullied, to give the women's story equal credence.

'No, no, we must talk to him first. Otherwise he will be offended.' Lodi beckoned to one of the carriers who produced a box full of rice.

The man took the box and passed it to one of his companions then launched into a long speech which Faith was unable to understand although she gathered that the essence was broadly of welcome. The first woman, the one who had been talking earlier, wasn't interested. She waited only to shout a few words of abuse at the man and then stalked away. Somebody laughed loudly but everyone else ignored her.

Lodi talked for a few minutes to the old man in what she presumed was the local language. People were smiling now, even laughing. Lodi said the madame would like to ask some questions. The old man nodded and beckoned for her to sit on the ground. A number of other men came forward and crouched down, a little removed from the main group. It was a gathering of thirty or so now, men and women.

'I was here before.' She looked to Lodi and he translated. The old man and his entourage were staring at her with a look somewhere between bewilderment and confusion.

'Is that OK? Can I ask some questions?'

The old man thought for a moment, paused, then replied with some gravitas, in English. 'I am the model farmer here. The President has appointed me. I have one thousand dollars and I will make modern agriculture.'

'Great. Can I ask you about that?'

He seemed to agree.

'Are you in a group?'

'Why should I be in a group?'

'NADS?'

The man looked puzzled.

'NADS,' Faith said. 'It's trying to build groups and bring good things for all.'

'I am the leader.'

'Leader of the group?'

'Leader of all.'

'Is it helpful?'

'What?'

'The group.'

'Madame, good things are good but groups are not always good. The President wants progressive farmers. We must modernise.'

'What will happen to the group here? They have been doing trainings and working together.'

'The President doesn't want *peesants* anymore.'

She wrote that in her notebook. 'Can I ask what background you have in farming?'

The old man wrinkled his brow like he was trying to remember something. 'We are all farmers in this country. Everyone is a farmer, even me a retired army officer. Army people do what they can. That is our training. That is my house.' He pointed to a large bungalow within a low-walled compound.

Faith could see a satellite TV dish, an internet antenna, and a black four-wheel drive in the front yard.

'Did you get money from NADS?'

'Well, I picked houses for my pigs and bought an improved boar.'

'How much did that cost?'

'They gave it to me.'

Another voice from the back of the gathering, a young man this time. He had a wild look but he wore a smart jacket and his English was good. 'The President says we must grow everything we need and add value on the value chain.'

'Great but how will you do that?'

'But who are you?' interrupted the old man, bewildered and querulous, adding, before she could reply. 'Why are you asking us questions?'

She was thrown by his tone. 'I want to tell my people what is happening, what is being done with their money.'

'What has it got to do with *you?*' said the young man in the jacket, jumping back into the conversation. 'This is our country.'

'Yes,' said Faith, rather more stiffly than she meant, 'but the British government is paying for it. We want to know that the money is well spent.'

'And how will you know that?' said the young man, angrily.

'We will make calculations.'

The lad wasn't convinced. He was educated, he said, had a diploma from the business studies college. 'NADS was a good project,' he started in. 'Productivity was improving. That's all you need to know isn't it?'

Faith was unsure of herself now. She didn't know anything about the technical aspects of agriculture: yields, out-turns, by-products or whatever. 'Was? Why do you say was? Is NADS having problems now?'

'Don't you know? It's all been stopped.'

'Stopped? But this is what I'm trying to find out about. Why has it been stopped?'

'The NADS office was demolished.'

'Demolished?' She wrote that in her book, excited. 'What happened?'

The man in the jacket looked around the others in the crowd, seemed puzzled. Perhaps he was reluctant to talk about a sensitive matter. 'People came,' he mumbled. 'It's all gone.'

'People came?' She was almost shouting. 'Was that something these "people" did? Demolish the office? You don't have an office now? What people?'

'Yes.'

'Who was it? How did they do it? Was it government people? Soldiers or something? This is *very* interesting.' She made another note in her book.

'It happened about two weeks ago,' started the young man.

'Go on, go on,' she said, writing furiously now.

'*Muzungus*,' said the older man, the model farmer, 'some *muzungus* came in a helicopter and crashed all the buildings down.'

TWELVE

April 19th 2011

"Broad brushstrokes throughout are good. Avoid having the African characters laugh, or struggle to educate their kids, or just make do in mundane circumstances. African characters should be colourful, exotic, larger than life—but empty inside, with no dialogue, no conflicts or resolutions in their stories ... Taboo subjects: ordinary domestic scenes, references to African writers or intellectuals, mention of school-going children who are not suffering from yaws or Ebola fever... You'll also need a nightclub called Tropicana, where mercenaries, evil nouveau riche Africans and prostitutes and guerrillas and expats hang out."
- Binyavanga Wainaina, How to Write About Africa, Granta 92, 2005

'The thing is, Dr Baxter, it's a *private* place.' It was a couple of days later and the two consultants were at The Compound pool, stretched out on the sunbeds, 'testing' some of the high-grade marijuana that Pareto had strong-armed the obliging volunteers at COMPASSION to deliver to him at his Shangri-La on the hill. 'The thing is you can do what you like here. The authorities are not allowed in. It's part of the agreement with government. The policy here is, "Fuck you, we're rich".'

It was an unusual place, Baxter could see. 'Absolutely no missionaries under any circumstances,' said Pareto, 'and aid people only if they are vetted by the management.' At this time of day it was mostly women, mainly air stewardess types, reading, sleeping, doing lengths, chit-chatting through the familiar stories of childbirth, supermarkets, adultery. Later there would be government ministers in designer suits and sunglasses, Hummers and Benzes three-deep in the car park for the sauna and the massage rooms.

'How can you stay in that hotel, Baxter? What a nerve to put us in there! I'm told the smallest vibration could bring it down. Just moving your bed on the ninth floor might be all it took. The butterfly effect, what! Mind you that Chinese reflexologist was quite a find. All I wanted was a back rub and the next thing she's produced the biggest strap-on I've ever seen. Very enterprising.'

A leathery woman in a string bikini lay down on a sunbed opposite. From behind his sunglasses, Baxter followed the thin cotton of her thong as it disappeared into the cracks.

'And,' Pareto went on, 'we get paid for it. What more could one ask? It's a kind of paradise.'

Baxter smiled. It was hard to disagree.

'Do you know the story about Speke at the Kabaka's palace?' Pareto had clearly read up on his Ugandan history. 'He claimed he'd been held against his will but actually, it came out later, he'd had the run of the Kabaka's harem. The women were kept together in the dark and fed on nothing but goat's cheese. They were so fat they couldn't walk and their skin was clammy like whipped cream. It was a flesh factory. Speke spent three months in there, just drowning in cunt. Mind you, it unsettled his delicate Victorian mind and later he took a shotgun and blew his brains out.'

Another woman sashaying past, tinier bikini, impossible red stilettos.

'We get a lot of UN staff,' Pareto went on. 'With all this trouble now, they're scared to go out. Even the shopping malls are off limits. Most of them just sit around drinking and looking for...' He let the sentence tail away as if elaborating would involve a wholly unacceptable breach in time-honoured standards of taste.

Baxter's mind was wandering but he knew he had to throw out an anchor. He might have been in paradise but he still had to pay attention. He was a professional and he still wanted to do the right thing. Despite what Faith had tried to suggest, he did have principles and it would be wrong not to finish the job. He had to get back to work, do the writing she had so disdained, and her share too. He might even manage to fit in one or two more meetings. Whatever was necessary.

What would MODE be making of all this? Was it possible London wouldn't yet have noticed that the team had fallen off the radar? Might the unrest in town have distracted them? Or might the wheels within wheels already be grinding into action? Whatever the timing, he knew that, at some point, a message would come: Where are the consultants? Where is the report?

But, up at The Compound, just as Pareto had said, the air was clear, the alcohol untaxed and the varied charms of the ladies of leisure difficult to resist. And, perhaps unexpectedly, Pareto had been a brick. He'd smuggled Baxter and some carrier bags of old clothes through the gate, assigned him a room in the house he'd rented with his COMPASSION Amex card, even gone to the airport on his own to chase up and recover some of the lost luggage. 'Stay for a day or two, Baxter,' he'd said. 'You need a breather, a change of air. Get out of that dreadful hotel.'

So Baxter had his own clothes again. And his meds. Even a razor. From now on things could only get better. He and Pareto might even become mates.

'How does a chap like you get into this game, Dickson?' Baxter hadn't smoked a joint in months. He realised that was a curiously intimate question but it seemed at that moment as if there would never be a better time to put it. They were both goggle-eyed and legless anyway.

'All those bleeding hearts you mean?' Pareto exhaled a prodigious cloud of smoke, the lemony aroma spreading across the whole pool area in a clammy toxic mist. 'It's a fifty-fifty arrangement,' he said, 'it works out well. They scratch my conscience and I drive their Land Cruiser V8. COMPASSION is a good gig for a fellow like me. I don't ask for much, just the occasional mission. As you are no doubt aware, my friend, there comes a time in every man's life when he will not see tits like those on Destiny unless he is prepared to *pay*. Frankly, if COMPASSION will put up the moolah that's fine with me.'

They spent the afternoon on the sunloungers, like teenagers dodging school, most of the time in catatonic silence, the rest in hopeless laughter. From time to time they heard the howl of police sirens drifting up from the traffic smog in Bugolobi and they could see small phalanxes of military vehicles and officers on foot moving around the settlements.

'What do you think about Faith?' Baxter asked at one point.

Pareto seemed to be asleep at that moment but managed a dozy grunt. 'What about it?'

'Faith, our colleague.'

'Oh, her. I haven't been following I'm afraid. What's the issue?'

'Why do you think she went off like that?'

Pareto was genuinely perplexed, seemed to have no notion of what Baxter was getting at.

'She said she wanted to collect more empirical data,' said Baxter.

'Imperial what?'

'You know, *field* work.'

Pareto sighed. 'What is it with these modern girls, Baxter? They're so *serious*. I tried to get her to calm down a bit but she wasn't having it. I've been with COMPASSION five years now and my experience suggests you can go a long way in the development world with a nice arse and a pair of high heels. There's no need for any of that Mother Theresa stuff.'

Baxter nodded, hesitant, unsure of his pastoral responsibilities here.

'Still, if I was you, Baxter, I would write it all down, the whole sorry story. Put it on paper.' He paused as if to think. 'It's something I've learned. Writing gives you a measure of protection. If the worst comes to the worst, you can flog the story to the Daily Telegraph. Y'know, waste of public money, send a gunboat, that kind of angle.' Pareto was buttoning his shirt now, putting on his sandals. 'The thing is you'll need some backup, some evidence, they don't like to publish *complete* fiction. At least, not by an unknown.'

In the evening there was shouting and a few rounds of automatic fire somewhere in the town below and they could see a house burning, maybe a mini-riot or a lynching. Baxter didn't like to think about it and, by and large, he didn't.

The first day of the Poverty Conference consisted of a multi-venue, multi-function, multi-purpose all-day knees-up, spread over the entire town: twenty plus events, from the modest passion fruit and biscuits working breakfast at the Church of the Heart of our Saviour Lord Jesus to the IMF's fin de siècle masked ball in honour of the all-too-fleeting visit of Dominique Strauss Kahn. All the delegates needed was a valid conference 'passport' around their neck and the block of taxi vouchers provided in their folder and they would be whisked around town from fun happening to educational occasion. The only problem that evening was the gridlocked traffic. After twenty minutes playing with his fingers, Baxter gave up waiting, swallowed a couple of Madame Mao's kit kats then got out of the taxi to walk.

He had worked out an itinerary that he reckoned ought to cover the prevailing priorities in the poverty world. It would take him from the bottom to the top, or the other way around, depending on how you looked at it. He was going to start at MishMash, an Internet caff and NGO hang-out on Acacia Avenue, check his mail and see what was going down on the hair shirt scene, mug up on whatever dark conspiracies the NGO types were conjuring around the circus that had come to town. From there he would walk up the road to O'Leary's Tropicana Bar, a haunt for commercial sector types and the growing Ugandan middle class. He would take in the Private Sector Exhibition they were putting on there then flag down a *boda* to the Serena for the diplomatic stuff and the high-end speeches. He might be able to meet up with Adderbury there, perhaps get an introduction to DSK, as everybody around town was by now calling their patron and good mate.

MishMash was a pleasure. It was still early in the evening and the place was less than half full. He drifted through a big garden and a gallery with African artwork, mostly carvings with unfeasibly large penises. As he tried to decide on a table, a pack of waitresses rushed him, clucking and cooing and batting their eyelashes and then, when they saw the conference 'passport' around his neck, more or less handing him the key to the bar. Why he did it he later could not say but he took a whole tray of pre-prepared wine glasses from the counter and headed outside, brushing as he did a white woman alone at a table against the side wall. She was tall, in her late forties, with *de rigueur*, steel-rimmed glasses and a striking shock of auburn hair tied up in a red bandana, somehow calling to mind old Soviet posters celebrating the five-year plan.

'You look a bit unsteady,' she said, barely looking up.

Baxter tried to smile. He intended a gracious gesture but it came out more like an impression of a Bundibugyo death mask. 'Tired, that's all.'

'They say,' she said, 'that a man who's tired of London is tired of life but a man who's tired of Kampala must have been here twenty minutes.' And then she turned to shout at a passing waiter, 'Oi, come on, bring the bloody gin. How many times have I got to ask?' She looked like she might have had a few already. 'Wanna join me?'

'Why not? But have a glass of wine.' And he offered her the tray.

'No, no. You shouldn't take things just because they're free. Martini's the only drink for me.'

So he watched her polish off a large Martini, generously measured and carefully shaken, salt around the rim, and they got into exchanging notes about what they were doing here, two lost souls washed up on the development beach. The weirdos one falls in with, he thought: Pareto, Carruthers, Adderbury, Tripp. Development workers overseas, they have little in common other than that they are exiles together, dysfunctionals to the last.

Her name was Martha. She had come for the conference. Of course. Night flight from Washington. Last minute decision so forced to stay in a lousy hotel miles out of town. Giving a paper the next day on, 'The culture of political economy and the political economy of culture.'

'Sounds impressive.'

'I wrote it on the plane. The problem is I'm on at nine and the venue I'm speaking at doesn't exist. There *is* a sign up and some rusty cranes but the place hasn't been built yet, just a big hole in the ground.'

He told her about the NADS work. 'I wasn't planning to go to the conference. It's just that the whole town has been taken over and we can't do anything else. We've been here two weeks and achieved nothing, my team has evaporated and the budget is gone.'

'Plus ca change. Who's paying for it?'

'MODE.'

She nodded. 'I worked there once.'

'Everyone does. At some time or another.'

'In Head Office. Victoria. You know it?'

'I worked on the third floor. I'm just a consultant now.'

'On the one hand, like everybody says, it's the best agency in the world.'

'And on the other?'

'It's like Kafka. *In the Penal Colony*. You know that one? It's a re-education camp, really. In reverse. They run an active deskilling programme for the staff and give you a tattoo when it's over. After eighteen months I came out knowing less than when I went in. I could paraphrase every leader of every Economist back to when I started but I'd forgotten who Virginia Wolf was.'

In this kind of situation, Baxter usually reckoned silence was the best course but he had no option now. His mind seemed to have floated off somewhere and was refusing to tell him what to do. Lights were flashing at the back of his eyes and his feet and hands were strangely numb and cold. The last thing he wanted was any kind of lecture. 'They say a man, or woman, who fears corruption fears life itself,' he suddenly found himself saying, thinking himself rather clever.

'Do they?' she said, evidently unimpressed. 'Do they indeed?'

There was a period of silence and she pulled a book out of her bag, some sort of textbook, with graphs and charts. Then she ordered another Martini.

Baxter turned in his seat to watch the other customers, waves of energy rolling in now, an intimation of colour, foaming spray seeming to float away like mist.

'My only friend in the whole place,' said the woman just as the waiter approached with the drinks, 'was this bloke, God, what was his name? He was in the Clerkenwell Road office. I wonder if you knew him.' She was rummaging through her memory bank. 'Worked with the disabilities programme, a lovely guy, what *was* his name?'

'Dr Horse.' Where did that come from? One minute he was sinking into some kind of semi-catatonic state, the next he was bringing up memories from half a lifetime ago.

'That's it. That's him. *He* was one of the good guys.'

Dr Horse's real name was Bill Dogget but for reasons never specified he had changed his name. Officially. By deed poll. He wanted to be a Red Indian chief, he said. It was under an earlier government, during a particularly bad time for MODE, when the horror stories from some earlier conflict had got briefly in the papers and polls showed the popularity of aid to be plummeting. Innocent personnel had been harassed, sometimes even set upon in the street, by human rights activists and development fundamentalists embittered at the way water projects and waterboarding had become confused in the public mind. The union had insisted on the right of anonymity for all its members and staff had been allowed to use pseudonyms. Dr Dogget had become Crazy Horse. Then *that* got in the tabloids and management refused to let him use the full name on official documents so he became plain C. Horse Esq. But that was a problem too because everyone thought it was Seahorse, those little mermaidy things. In the end, he was just Dr Horse, Research Officer, Basic Needs.

'You'd get these announcements,' Martha remembered, 'over the intercom. "Would Dr Horse please come to reception, there is a visitor". They were the highlight of my day.'

Could all this be true? Baxter was hanging on to the idea that they were both in town for some purpose related to alleviating poverty in the developing world. So what *was* this woman talking about?

'Turned out, actually, that he had a rare condition,' she went on. 'The last I heard it had mutated with such ferocity he had to wear a jaw clamp 24/7.'

'Really, what for?'

'Officially, to stop him grinding his teeth. But there had been a number of complaints. He tried to bite some visiting dignitaries.'

O'Leary's Tropicana Bar was an Oirish pub, noisy and crammed with deloigthful Oirish fiddle players and pensive literary types who looked like James Joyce. Not.

As Baxter pushed his way to the bar he could see it was mostly South African telephone engineers and their fiancées, beer bellies and pumpkin heads, most of them in tailored shorts, and that included the women. Not too many handwringers though, not too much angst, and that was good. There would be plenty of that to come.

Baxter ordered a beer.

'Development enclaves,' said the barman, a cheeky northerner with a nice smile and some scarring on his cheek, 'the only places left where sixty-year-old men in discos are not thought ridiculous.'

But before Baxter could slap the little fucker down, the band had started up like an F1-11 at take-off. This was not the industrial white noise event you might get in the avant-garde nightclubs of the western world though. This was just that the speakers were completely knackered.

There was a small dance floor where three suits were frug-frug-frugging together, struggling to muster the rhythmic finesse of a moth trying to beat its way out of a plastic lampshade. They were probably UN reps from Geneva or New York, multicultural, international, groomed, their faces as bland as the South African wine they were drinking and as hard and plastic as the conference IDs flapping round their necks.

Along the far wall, a handful of local girls in soft seats. Lots of lurex and satin and everywhere more leg than skirt. The one who came for him was tall and jet black and had a pink ribbon in her hair.

On the dance floor, she whirled and twirled and gyrated and thrust with the enthusiasm of the young, all legs and hips and tight bum. Her thin cotton frock rode up her thighs. Bright red lipstick emphasised her mouth and under the strobe lights Baxter could see the outline of her knickers.

'You like?' said the girl, pressing herself up against him.

He considered the proposal for a moment but close up he could see blotches on her face, an open sore or two. And she was too thin, not much more than a skeleton and, in this country that was not good.

'Buy me a drink.'

'What?' He could hardly hear her.

'Buy me a drink.'

He hesitated. Only for a moment but it was long enough for her to suck her teeth and walk away.

Had he handled that badly? Never mind. It was better to avoid temptations.

He walked back to the bar from where he soon learned to ignore the bottles that flew periodically across the room, a white man in a rugby shirt falling, twice, from the second-floor balcony, the UN secretarial girls singing Abba songs in the men's lavatory, a backpacker or a trainee PA perhaps, out on the veranda being sick into a plastic bag. Soon the reassuring fug of beer, sweat and vomit had enveloped them all as if it was seeping up from the floor below. He liked places where he knew only strangers and he was starting to enjoy himself.

Later, quite a lot later, without him quite realising when or where, he drifted down some steps and walked around the side of the building. He wasn't sure why but he made his way along the road, down the hill, the music from the bar fading as he walked. Better pass on a *boda*. Climbing on a motorbike was not a good idea in his sorry state. He walked on, ten minutes, twenty, just about keeping the presence of mind not to fall down any of the manholes that were open all along Nakasero Road. The lights of the Serena were visible now, reeling him in, and, after a few more minutes, he was at the back gate, where the guards airily waved the *muzungu* through.

Once in the grounds, there was lots of activity: people, cars, marquees, gift shops. Then party lights, a bigger marquee, gold fixtures lit by spotlights, a sign proclaiming the Pearl of Africa Restaurant, a gaggle of uniformed doormen, one rushing forward to take his arm, to ease him up steps.

'Poverty Conference, sir?'

'Huh?'

'You have ID? Yes you have. This way, please.'

The lights seemed perilously bright. There was the suggestion of a rainbow at the edge of his vision but he suddenly had an urge to be a passenger in first class, alone with the drinks trolley and the ingratiating cabin crew. The only problem, he realised, as soon as he'd crossed the threshold, more coloured lights dancing across his retina, was that he was flying faster than the aircraft and there was nowhere to land.

It was a place of romance and good taste, he could see that, sumptuous purple candles, brilliant paintings of red parrots on all the walls, a vast silver chandelier cascading over the middle of the room.

But something wasn't right.

There was an overturned table, broken glass on the floor, puddles of spilled wine. Not that many people.

'Sorry, sir,' said some kind of maître d', a beaming bumpkin in a green lamé suit who lurched suddenly out of the kitchen and was fussing around him like a gigantic tsetse fly. 'But, please sir, don't worry. We'll find you a secluded spot.'

Before he could resist he was being led by the arm, through the few remaining celebrants, bottles on the floor, more puddles, food on the floor, food on the *walls*.

'Jesus, what happened?'

'Private party, sir,' smiled the maître d', still gripping Baxter's arm, urging him forward. 'Although I think it was a dog.'

Baxter wondered if he had misheard but he let the man steer him to a little alcove offset behind a pillar where he had to bend down to squeeze in. A mirror hung on the wall to his left and, reflected in it, Baxter could see most of the near empty room: a few stragglers only, the most obvious being a young couple grappling on a chaise longue by the window, the woman drunk, her blouse open to the waist and, under a palm tree near the kitchen, facing away, a man alone at a big table, slumped forward, his head lolling on the place mat.

Baxter felt strangely reassured. He hadn't realised MODE still had these kinds of parties. He had assumed they would be frowned upon under the new paradigm. Anyway, whatever had happened here, it seemed the worst had passed. All that was left was for the staff to clear up.

The bumpkin brought him a bottle of the Conference Special wine, a surprising Château Valandraud Saint-Emilion, and he was well into the second glass, taking it perfectly slowly, savouring the sensory nuance, when he saw, from the corner of his eye, the man at the far table begin to stir, lift his huge hydrocephalic bonce and shake himself down. 'Hey, sonny,' he heard the man say to a passing waiter, 'c'mon, sit doon here and hae one wi' me.'

The lad seemed to hesitate. Baxter could see the boy's face in the mirror, distracted, nervous, not sure what to expect, aware that except in special circumstances, waiters in flash joints like this do not drink with the customers.

'Ah tell ye boy, Ah'm right beat.' The accent was stronger now, the effect of the drink, and the words ringing out, slurred and sour, all across the room. 'Right broosled actually. Y'know ah've worked in this game for forty years, given my life, I've run symposiums and workshops in aw the countries o' the wurrrld, every miserable shithole, from Azerbaijan to Zimbabwe, and ah tell ye this,' he paused for so long that, straining to hear, Baxter thought he'd lost his train of thought. 'Ah tell ye this, this one takes the fucking biscuit.'

The waiter looked round, trying to find support, rescue even.

Baxter's first instinct was to slip away when he had the chance. But perhaps it was wiser to hide, stay safe behind the arras. The last thing he wanted was to meet Adderbury now.

'Ah've been in plane crashes,' there was a trembling in the old man's voice now, almost as if he might cry, 'car crashes, bike crashes, fuckin' roller skate crashes. Ah've risked illness, many of 'em I may say. I've lived in scummy hotels, long lonely nights, trying my best to bring some light into this pitiful darkness. Workshops, boy, they're harder than they look. I'm not talking about signing petitions y'know, or writing to the fucking paper. Ah'm talking about putting my arse on the line, you know what I'm saying, son? Are you *getting* me?' This was a maudlin, self-pitying whine, very different from the avuncular tendencies Baxter had been treated to that day at the pool and the rising volume made the waiter back away. The two on the chaise longue were watching uneasily. The woman had fastened her shirt.

Then the maître d', back from the kitchen, alert, by the table, edging out the waiter, the light reflecting on his extraordinary suit. 'Can I be of assistance, sir?'

Adderbury had a small bottle of something in his pocket and, extracting it carefully, he began to wave it in the air.

The maître d' smiled awkwardly.

'Try a wee nippy o' this, Jimmy. Talisker a hundred and five, the best money can buy.'

The maître d' looked at the ceiling for a very long moment, almost as if praying for help.

'Take a drink man. I've just blown thirty fucking grand. Ah'm the guy who signed the fucking cheque. Are you no going to drink wi me?'

Nervous, realising his predicament, catching himself, the maître d' took the bottle and poured a small measure into one of the wine glasses still on the table.

'Here's to it then, eh? Every man for himself and God against all.'

They drank, the maître d' taking a cautious sip, Adderbury most of the contents of his bottle.

Another silence, Adderbury glaring around the room, a long, searching, only partially-focused stare. Baxter lowered his head, desperate to avoid detection.

'Y'know, tonight shoulda been the high point, the summit...'

The maître d' began to sidle away, perhaps hoping to shout for support. But Adderbury was too quick. He reached out, grabbed the unfortunate fellow, locking a hand tight around his wrist.

'Shoulda been the summit, Ah said,' softer this time but with more menace. But, at the same time, it was as if Adderbury realised there was nothing to be gained with this guy and so had resolved to push on himself. 'Instead, here Ah am, all alone, everybody gone, and some cunt in a shiny green suit's harassing me for poppy.'

The maître d' was like a rabbit caught in the full beams of a speeding car.

'Is there some lesson to be learned there do ye think? Some awareness that could be raised, some low hanging fruit that could be picked, if ye catch my fucking gist?'

The maître d' nodded enthusiastically. Of course, there most certainly was.

A car horn outside.

Baxter looked up, risked a glance, saw Adderbury once again trying to climb to his feet. The old man was staring around the room, a manic glare of concentrated fury. Baxter ducked down, slid half under the table, feigned an avid study of the flower arrangements.

The horn again.

'I can see you Baxter, you stupid fuck. Ye think I didn't know you were there? I saw you coming in. Why are ye hiding?'

The horn for a third time.

'Your limousine's here sir.' The maître d' took Adderbury's arm and tried to pull him forward. 'Let me get your coat.'

'Where's ma fucking bill?' He was shouting again, blind with exasperation and rage, half-crazy now.

'You signed already, sir. The cheque, yes. For the damages, we can invoice MODE directly.'

Silence.

'For all your many kindnesses, sir, we would take it as an honour if you would be so kind as to let us settle some gratuities on your delightful driver?'

Further silence. Adderbury seemed to be wondering if this was the moment. It was now or never. Back down or go nuclear. 'There's no understanding,' he said, more a mumble than anything even remotely assertive and with that he bowed his head. It was all over in a moment, a tiny gesture, a little sigh, a recognition that he was not the grand panjandrum of old, no longer capable of the monstrous action the situation so clearly demanded.

Carefully, the maître d' took the old man's arm and began to lead him to the door. From his seat, through a window to his right, Baxter could see the car outside, a colossal black Mercedes, customised tail fins, dark windows, CD plates, the chauffeur in sunglasses and full MODE Ruritanian ensemble.

Adderbury was halfway there, stumbling across the car park, when he turned and shouted back. 'C'mon Bent, let's go. The night is young.' And before he knew it, Baxter was on Adderbury's arm, helping him on his final steps to the car, the maitre d' simpering quietly alongside.

'The wurst thing, Bent... Ah put on a party, stretch the budget to burstin' point, champagne and the best dancing girls, and Strauss Kahn doesn't even show. Ah take it as a personal slight.'

Reaching the car, Adderbury unzipped and unleashed an impressive torrent of piss, the maitre d' retreating quickly, several security guards standing off at a safe distance. 'But who *does* come?' he grunted. 'Ah tell you who. Pugh and that fucking dog. Yowlin' brain cracked, totally fucking mangit. It was un-fucking-believable. Man's worst friend. He says it was not its fault, it was kidnapped and held in a box in Helmand for two weeks. Is that my fucking problem? Christ, Bent, where do we go? I tell you what, I need a ride.'

Baxter hesitated. Another pastoral delineation problem. What were his responsibilities here? It probably wasn't a good idea to go back to O'Leary's Tropicana Bar. Those Afrikaner secretaries would require more social skill than Adderbury could manage. Baxter wondered about the 50 cent cubicles along Bombo Road. That would be quicker and cheaper and he'd heard you could get free condoms from the missionaries that were always creeping around outside.

'Fine wi me, Bent. Who cares? NADS is chicken feed by the way. Everything is meaningless.' Adderbury was now propped against the car, trying to focus, feeling for the door. 'We are mocked and our aspirations revealed as pointless and foul. We have to learn to live in the moment, Bent. John Hanning Speke, he's nothing but the name of a hotel group now.'

Suddenly he seemed to lurch back as if heading again towards the restaurant. 'The greatest joy,' he shouted, seeming to want to address the small crowd of staff who had gathered to watch the great man go, 'the greatest joy a man can know...' then he paused, seeming to rack his memory, trying to drag up the words, 'is to conquer his enemies and to drive them before him. To ride their horses and steal their possessions; to see their faces bedewed wi' tears and to come on the white bellies of their wives and hoors. You know who said that, Bent?'

It had to be a Scotsman. 'Adam Smith? Livingstone perhaps?'

Adderbury narrowed his eyes, perhaps wondering whether that was meant to be a joke. 'Genghis Khan.'

The engine purred into life and the two men struggled into the car. In the front, Baxter turned to look at Adderbury. The old man's face was pale and distant in the glow of the neon security lights, a ghost almost. Baxter was hit by a giant wave of nausea. The kit kats were roaring now and he'd drunk too much too fast. 'I can't be too late tonight,' he said.

'Ye wha'?'

'I've got to work on my report tomorrow.'

Adderbury slapped his knees and laughed, a glance back at his other more genial self. 'Don't be daft, Bent. There'll be no work done in this town for many days. Sit back and enjoy the night.'

The car shot the junction at Kisamente, narrowly missing a cow walking in the road, and gathered speed. That was it, Baxter felt, he'd crossed a line, was by himself now, just another consultant on the nipple, another sucker suspended somehow in a faraway place not his own. He put his head between his legs and took several deep breaths. He opened the window to get more air. He leaned his head on the frame, the dark tarmac racing by below. This had happened before. In fact, sometimes it seemed as if his whole life consisted of going home with people he didn't want to, watching the road tear past before his eyes.

After a while, the only sound was the soothing hum of the engine and the whirr of tyres on road. He'd arrived in town, Baxter reflected, shoved up against the broken passenger door of an old Toyota taxi, its tyres down to the canvas and its number plate obscured by mud. Within a few days he had graduated to the rear seat of a brand new Mercedes CL65-AMG, six gears, V12 engine, added armour plating, inbuilt GPS radio security alert system, the CD plates and bulletproof windows polished that morning by the number one security driver at the British High Commission. He *had* to be going up in the world.

THIRTEEN

April 21ˢᵗ 2011

"You have been fighting but you did not have the expertise. You are like that unprofessional cook who cooks malakwang but now we said come here and become better cooks, if you have been quack doctors, we have trained you and made you professional doctors."
- Yoweri Museveni

It was muggy and very warm.

Baxter opened an eye.

He seemed to be lying face down, his nose in a thick-pile carpet.

It was dark.

The atmosphere was foetid and he could detect the different aromas of vomit, tobacco smoke and old man's stink. He lifted his head.

He could see a settee and, standing stiffly upright, close to the wall, a young Ugandan woman in a khaki uniform. She was standing to attention it seemed.

He dropped his face back into the carpet.

After a while he tried again.

The woman hadn't moved. She was still at attention, as if on parade. Was she a guard of some kind? She had a kindly enough face but her expression now was not encouraging. It was an uncertain mix of curiosity and apprehension. She looked as if she thought she might be in the presence of somebody carrying a contagious illness. Ebola perhaps? He'd heard there'd been a few cases in town.

A movement to his left drew Baxter's eye to a large mirror and there, in reflection, through a door, Adderbury, naked to the waist, trousers around his ankles, heaving himself off a lavatory.

'Ma kecks,' exclaimed Adderbury, holding up some baggy grey boxers, a small label pinned to the waistband. 'Our Laundry,' he read in a loud voice, as if he was talking to an idiot, 'regrets it is unable to guarantee the integrity of this garment.' He flushed the toilet, a violent jerk of his arm.

'Why's everybody sae worried about integrity aw of a sudden?' He buckled his trousers and shuffled into the room.

Strange hands had bundled him in here, Baxter remembered now. But when and why? It seemed like weeks ago. How long had he been here? 'Eh, where are we exactly?'

'Serena,' said Adderbury. 'Penthouse suite.'

Baxter tried to look around. The place did have a certain style, a degree of generic *Swahili* elegance. Memories stuttering back, the service lift up, the doorman helping him to the room.

'It took some arm twisting to get it, let me tell you. There are a lot o' big names in town this week and some o' them are quite, how should Ah say, willing to *pay*. Robert Mugabe wanted the whole fucking floor.'

Baxter was watching the girl. She hadn't moved a muscle.

'First off, I thought I should say,' Adderbury continued, his voice dropping to a confidential purr, 'I mebbe said some things last night that Ah shouldnae have. Maybe I'd too much swally and sometimes I do get a bit gloomy. But I love development, Bent, have no doubts on that score. I've given my life to it. It's our human obligation, you know what Ah'm saying?'

Baxter blinked, swallowed and nodded. Only too happy to agree.

'No hard feelings then? You probably got what happened. It was a brute o' a day. We were sure we'd get the signatures, like. Then, at the last minute, the whole deal goes tits up.' And, with that, the great man retreated once more to the bathroom, this time shutting the door behind him.

If Baxter was embarrassed by Adderbury's language in front of the girl, she seemed unmoved and continued to stare straight ahead, barely any expression at all.

When the old man returned he was still on the same subject. 'DSK was just the last straw really. It started wi' the Pope crying off. He claimed he was double-booked. I mean for fuck's sake.'

There was a knock and a scrabbling at the main door which was then flung back with a momentous crash. The dog appeared first, loping in like some mythic beast of the mire, then Pugh dragging along behind, his splendid golden locks sinuous like the Pre-Raphaelite vision he otherwise was not.

'Ah Dr Pugh, long time no talky talky, nice of you to drop in, like.'

'Where've you been?' grunted the blind man, grumpy and unapologetic. He was in his trademark pork-pie hat and dark glasses, clutching his ever-present white stick. 'I've been looking everywhere for days.'

'We've been networking,' said Adderbury, primly. 'And you know very well, Pugh, that time flies when you're oot on fieldwork.'

It was curious fieldwork. Nightclubs, backrooms, roadside cubicles, it seemed the car had driven them around every lowlife establishment in town. 'I don't know why,' Adderbury had tried to explain to Baxter at one point late in the evening, 'but, as I've got older, I've found it's the only thing that still works. The more sordid the occasion the more sparkle it seems to hold.' As he had delivered this speech, Adderbury had been sitting on a stool in Al's Bar, a naked girl, painted in gold, draped arse-up across his knee. His melancholy musings had then developed into a longer and more wide-ranging exposition on the general fading of the light and then into a rambling, even tearful, account of his long life and his engagement with the British aid programme, three generations of success, although mostly failure. It was the ur-history of MODE itself.

'Ma traineeship was on the Groundnut Project. You've heard of that eh? The biggest, most ambitious, most innovative project of its time. An apprenticeship for so many of ma generation. When it collapsed, they moved me to Kenya. It was Mau Mau, 1956. I was mainly mopping up: burning files and working on cost benefit models. Now I'm finishing, covering up for Blair, burning files and working on value-for-money models.'

Adderbury seemed about to weep, so terrible was his despair. 'In the sixties Ah got a post in the Economics Department at Aberdeen, as Ah'm sure you know, one of the great establishments of learning.' The only problem had been that, far from endearing himself to those distant descendants of Macbeth, it seemed, reading between the lines, that Adderbury's ambition, ruthlessness and capacity for late-night machinations, had set all the little troglodytes against him. A secondment to Makerere, the leading African university in those first days of the postcolonial dawn, had seemed a sound solution and, there, he was able to work hard and play hard, all the while cultivating his cronies in the emerging development establishment back home. 'Those were the days, Bent, and the winds of change were blowing hard, if you get ma gist.' He paused to adjust the girl on his knee, perhaps her weight was getting too much, and continued, the narrative dwelling on the Thatcher years and the high-office postings he had held in all the desirable stations of the world. As he told it, it was a rocket right to the top of the Whitehall apparatus, the speed of his meteoric ascent just another *decollage* to his extraordinary personal mythology.

'Before I forget, Bent, you know they caught Macpherson?'

Interrupted from his reveries on the night before, his thinking still not working straight, one eye on Pugh's dog which was chewing its way through the embroidered gold curtains, Baxter could do no more than frown.

'Aye, seems his first wife ratted on him. Seems he wuz in Moscow all the time, wi' a suitcase o' antique Kazakh silver stashed under the bed. The Russian polis're trying to extract a statement outta him.'

Baxter tried to make a silly joke, show he wasn't worried, didn't take it seriously. 'They say,' he ventured, perhaps a little too hesitantly, 'that if all the experts who visited the Aral Sea had brought a bucket of water, the sea would still be there.'

Adderbury growled. If jokes *had* to be told, he would be the one to tell them. 'The water was runnin' oot,' he insisted, 'faster than it was runnin' in.'

There was a long moment of silence while all parties seemed to wonder what to say next.

'If,' said Pugh, abruptly but almost in a whisper, a tone of barely suppressed fury, 'you've finished telling us about Kazakhstan, Dr Baxter, perhaps I could get a word in and tell you something about Uganda. Something *everyone* might want to know.'

'Fire away, Pugh, nae bother, aye,' Adderbury chuckled.

'We got the signatures.'

'What's that? I cannae hear ye. That dog is making so much fucking clatter.'

'We got the signatures. Every one.'

It took a few moments for this to sink in. 'The Pope?'

'He sent his deputy, the Nuncio.'

'Really?'

'Four in the morning. He was dead on his feet. Couldn't hold out another minute. I had to put the pen in his hand.'

'Strauss Kahn?'

'Well...'

'Yeah, yeah, tell me.'

'They couldn't find him at the key moment.' Pugh tapped the side of his nose in a strangely suggestive manner. 'No sense of protocol.'

'What a cunt.'

Baxter looked at the girl in the uniform. She was still as a statue, apparently oblivious to the others in the room. If anything, she looked bored.

'Well that's fantastic news, Pugh,' said Adderbury, 'well done. I tell you what, I've still a wee bit of bevy. Shouldn't we celebrate? C'mon, guys, let's have a nippy. We'll take one now while Pugh gives us all the detail. After that we'll get lunch at the pool. Big splash up. Go on, Bent, you go first, take a dram.'

Whisky at 10.30 in the morning was something Baxter thought he'd left behind, especially in the state he was in now and, anxious as to how to navigate the ritual of the drinks cupboard, he hesitated before rising.

'Go on, Bent. There's ice in the cooler.'

So Baxter got to his feet and made his way across the room, to the table where Adderbury's bottle stood. There was a weighty silence as he poured an inch of the special edition Talisker into a tall glass and set off back to his seat. Adderbury's next question and the dog issued forth more or less simultaneously.

'By the by, Bent, how's the NADS report going?'

And then he was on the floor, the glass flung to the wind, the creature tearing at his lower leg, his new jeans torn, his foot in the savage vice of its mouth, the air filled with screams and vicious growling. The whisky was all across his shirt.

'Ginger ?' said Pugh uncertainly. 'Is that you?' It was an uncharacteristic cautiousness on Pugh's part, as if perchance there might be *another* crazed brute running amok in the room. 'Get it off me,' howled Baxter as, all the while, the fearsome jaws ripped into the tendon behind his ankle.

Adderbury rolled up his newspaper and shuffled over to the fray. Deliberately and with some thoroughness, as if he might be experienced in the mechanics of such full-frontal assault, he began to belabour the animal about the head, thumping it with quite some force.

The girl tried to help too, grappling with the animal's collar. But it was all to no avail, Ginger's teeth were locked tight on Baxter's calf.

'Get him off,' yelled Baxter, but this seemed only to incense the dog further. It growled and tore and shook his leg with renewed vigour, blood spurting across the carpet.

Adderbury was beating hard now as if trying to hammer in a fence post. Everyone was yelling at once and the dog's snarling and fevered yelps continued apace.

'Stop hitting him,' shouted Pugh, 'it's not his fault.' And turning to the dog, 'C'mon Ginger, now, be a good boy.'

But Ginger could not be restrained. He was shaking Baxter's leg as if he had found a rat under the bed, the blood in his mouth seeming only to stimulate him into a renewed frenzy of growling and caterwauling. Baxter could feel consciousness slipping away when, suddenly, without warning and without any apparent signal, Ginger came to his senses. He released his grip and looked around, seemed to wonder where he was, seemed to reconsider his position, saw his own reassuring reflection in Pugh's shades, seemed then to relax. Without any sign of remorse or regret, he let go then slouched meekly over to the corner, lying down and closing his eyes. On the floor, Baxter was mewling in pain and shock.

'Jesus fuck,' said Adderbury, bending over to examine the wound. There were four deep puncture holes either side of the calf, all running red. The flesh was badly torn, bruising showing already right across the lower leg. Baxter was shivery and tearful and he could see his trousers were ruined.

'Pugh,' said Adderbury. 'Must we allow this monster to disrupt *every* occasion?'

'It's not his fault,' said Pugh plaintively, and turning to Baxter, 'He was tortured by the Taliban you know.'

There was no answer to this and Adderbury began to gather up some things, muttering to himself all the while. 'Change of plan, Bent. We'll need to get your leg fixed. Let's you and me go see that Chinese friend o' yours. She'll sort ye. Then we can lie on the sunbeds, get our breath back, catch a few rays.' As they left the room, he took a wad of notes from his wallet and wordlessly passed them to the girl in the uniform who palmed them effortlessly into the top pocket of her uniform.

'Who's that girl?' said Baxter, as he limped along the corridor, shivering, Adderbury next to him with his signature shuffle.

'Don't know. Comes with the room I think. Good though eh?'

Baxter was frightened to look down. There was probably a trail of blood stretched out behind, bubbling and rabid.

'Pugh's out of line,' said Adderbury, suddenly, smiling the wise man's smile. 'More trouble than he's worth. That's the problem with civil servants. Ye give them a contract for life but they never show any.'

Baxter was touched that Adderbury had confided in him. The old coot seemed to have genuinely unburdened something.

'The problem, at least for our mission,' said Baxter as they reached the lift, knowing only too well that their mission barely featured on Adderbury's radar but taking his chance, testing the old man's apparent good will, 'is that small farmers are not a priority for the government. You can see why Faith was worried. She thought the government was not only *not* interested in the poor, she thought it was *deliberately* exploiting them.'

'Deliberately?' said Adderbury, as if such a quaint view had never occurred to him before.

'I had to remind her,' Baxter continued, 'several times, that MODE's policy explicitly emphasises poverty reduction, sustainable development, good governance, democracy, human rights and the empowerment of women and that the British government *only* works with partners who share our enthusiasm for these causes.'

'Good for you,' said Adderbury gravely, 'couldnae have put it better myself.' Then, as the lift doors opened at the ground floor, 'By the by, it may be some small consolation, Bent, but the High Commission's having a knees-up tonight. For a very, *very* select few. On behalf of our mystery superstar. You could come as my guest.'

Baxter didn't follow. Who or what was our mystery superstar?

'You haven't heard? Where have you fuckin' been man? Pissy eyes, thinks he's an expert, never fuckin' shaves. One is the only number... or something.'

Baxter thought he might be about to cry. 'I haven't got the right clothes.'

'Ah, we'll find something, Bent. Dinnae worry, there's always spare duds, a tux or two, at the High Commission.'

FOURTEEN

April 23rd 2011

"One morning around ten, Amin drove into Kampala's main car park in his Citroen. He was accompanied by some of his ministers and bodyguards. He entered one of the shops that surrounded the car park and found a group of men playing ajua. Amin requested that he join in the game and a crowd gathered to watch. It was soon apparent that Amin was a good player, as he beat one man after another. Now in the middle of the jubilation, there came into the crowd a crippled man by the name of Wandera Maskini. He was very well known in Kampala. Wandera pushed his way through the crowd with his crutches and collapsed in front of Amin. He started to call the President names and told him that he should not have sent away the Asians because the common man was suffering. "We don't have commodities in the shops yet you call yourself a President. Son of a bitch! Kill me if you want," said Wandera Maskini.

Amin quietly got to his feet and left the crowd. That same evening, Radio Uganda announced that anybody who was lame, blind, had no hands, and was so poor and disabled that he needed help, should report to the nearest police station: the government would offer them jobs and free food. The following morning thousands of cripples and other disabled turned up in Kampala's police stations. They were loaded onto military trucks and driven to Jinja. Those who could not hold on fell into the river, while those who had hands and held on were shot and they too fell into the river."
- The Rise and Fall of Idi Amin, Drum Magazine, 1994.

'How did you get into this, Lodi? How did you come to be here?'
    'Huh?'
    They were on a hill behind the village, having spent the day trying in vain to find a farmers' group.
    'How did you get to being hired as a gofer for me?'
    He didn't know what she meant.

She explained as diplomatically as she could. She wanted to know why he would come and work, essentially for her, doing work like this.

'Because the muzungus pay well,' he said.

There was no arguing with that.

'Tell me about your parents then,' she tried, surprising herself by the intimacy suggested by the question. 'Where are they? What do they do?'

'Do? They are both dead.'

She hadn't expected that.

'Killed.'

This was already further than she wanted to go.

'At the Conference Centre.'

'What do you mean?' Faith couldn't suppress a laugh. 'At the Serena?'

'Sure. Before. In the Obote time. It wasn't a hotel then. My father got what they called the hammer treatment.'

She realised she had blundered into something it would have been better to avoid.

'They sledge-hammered him. For many days. It was just a conference centre then, then a torture house. Obote had his rooms here, even Amin before that. They liked to be near the action.'

'In the hotel?'

'In Obote's time it was rooms 211 and 217.'

'Still the same rooms?'

'Why not?'

She wasn't sure what to say.

'Prime Minister Gordon Brown stayed there. Robert Mugabe is there now, for the Poverty Conference.'

'What did your parents *do*?'

'My father was a doctor.'

'But what did he do *wrong*?'

'No one knows. They picked them both, him and my mother, during the night. We were at our place in Gulu. I was very small, I had to go to my aunt. They were taken here. We don't know what happened.'

'No conferences in those days I suppose?' It was meant to be a joke.

'Oh yes, many. In this country nothing can stop a good conference. It's how we live, haven't you noticed? Workshops, seminars. It's how we get our allowances. It was always like that. World Bank people, consultants like you, they came, they like allowances too. Most of the killing was done away from visitors, but sometimes people heard screams in the night. They tortured at their leisure. I think about my mother. Did soldiers rape her? Did they push things into her? My father had bricks on his testicles.'

'You know this for sure?'

'The men who did it are still around. They talk, they laugh, some have learned to forget. When they were driven out, they left electric wires, nail-studded shoes, hammers, clubs, lots of things. I met a man who said he was there. He told me that after three days of hammering someone shouted *awuwa yeyea*, kill him, and then they threw my father out the window. My mother I don't know, there was no body to pick. Probably dropped her in the lake. Like lots of others.'

'Dr Cullimore?'

They must have been some distance off but she'd heard the click of the megaphone just moments before.

'Dr Cullimore, this is me, your friend, from the ministry, you remember? Come out please, you should not be here.'

She froze as the words echoed around the valley.

'Keep still,' whispered Lodi.

'Dr Cullimore, I find you are here without authority. You seem not to have a license. You must come out. The ministry has asked that I come and talk to you.' The voice sounded plaintive, even hurt, as if the owner was talking to an errant child. She knew it was definitely her friend.

The sun glinted on something metal. Faith saw a jeep moving, about half a mile off, police or soldiers on the back. Then another jeep. Green uniforms. Was that a rifle? Surely not. Faith could feel Lodi by her side, his body warm against her.

'Lodi, what should I do?' With her finger, she traced the pattern of the little New Zealand flag embroidered on the back of her rucksack. To give up now would be too humiliating. In six days, they had managed to talk to *some* farmers but she needed

169

to show Lodi that all this effort had been worthwhile. 'Is there somewhere else we can go?'

Lodi frowned.

'Somewhere we could do more interviews?'

'*Dr Cullimore?*' Her friend again, the tone sharper, the words amplified and resonant. 'You are endangering yourself and your what? Your colleagues.'

Lodi's eyes were closed.

'Dr Cullimore, there will be problems for everyone.'

Lodi moved closer, to whisper in her ear. 'We could go north.'

'Is it close?' asked Faith.

'Well…'

'Which way is it?'

Another pause then she took Lodi's arm and they started to scramble up the hillside behind, keeping low, ducking under bushes, starting to run. She watched Lodi's easy motion as he again took the lead. There was definitely something different about him now. On his terrain, away from the office and the development world, he had become another man. They were beyond the end of the tarred road, they had crossed some sort of frontier. On one side was the Uganda of consultants and workshops, luxury hotels and swimming pools, helicopters and Land Cruisers. On the other, it was footpaths and a thousand miles of bush.

But what about their deadline? What was Baxter going to say? How would HSC react if she messed up her first real assignment? Surely the company would understand? Hilleard was a serious man and it had to be important to get the truth. And she had done so well getting as far as she had.

She turned to look back. Down below, she could see forest, stretching away to the horizon and far beyond, the Nile, brown, slow, ancient, set in a pale wash of faded blue. Running fast, she was soon out of breath. Her feet were blistered and her face cut ragged by the brush they had beaten their way through, Lodi going first with a machete, his arms strong and gleaming like gunmetal. She could smell his sweat. He was master now, of the gathering darkness and the dripping liana. When the rain came, as Lodi had promised it would, they forced on. He hardly spoke but, as the light faded, they stopped.

'We need to camp,' said Lodi. 'We can't walk in the dark.'

'Can't we find a village or something?'

'The police will be looking.'

She helped him gather branches and together they built a refuge, not much more than a lean-to, then Lodi started a fire. He collected some straw and leaves for them to sleep on. They had to get out of the cold that would come after nightfall at this altitude. They didn't speak but stared into the flames. Lodi opened a tin of mackerel and passed it to her. Then he broke some bread. Exhausted, she ate a little and handed the rest back to him.

'Why is it such a big deal that we want to ask a few questions?'

He shrugged, didn't seem to have a view.

'I just don't understand.'

'I'm not getting you.'

'We've come to talk to NADS groups and there hardly seem to be any. There are supposed to be hundreds.'

'If they don't get facilitated, they give up.'

'But why has the support stopped?'

'The party only promotes its own people. They can be model farmers even if they've never farmed before.'

'But government can't spend all that money on a handful of model farmers!'

'Six per parish. Maybe five hundred parishes. What's that?'

'Sixty million divided by five hundred divided by six? That's twenty thousand per farmer. Is that right?'

Lodi began poking in the fire with a stick. As he placed more logs on the flames she studied the back of his head and his neck, almost golden in the red light. She thought about her little house in Oxford with its garden and its airy front room and her cat asleep in the easy chair.

'What does that sort of money buy?'

'Four-wheel drives, rice mills, dairy cows, goats, milk coolers, tractors, nothing startling.'

'What about the others? The ones who are not model farmers? Don't they object?'

'They know what the deal is.' He turned and, without looking at her, began to unfasten his shirt. He was wearing a choker wrapped twice around his neck. As he bent to remove his trousers, she saw the muscles on his arms. He dropped to his knees and pulled at her belt.

'Oi!'

At another time she might have been alarmed at the suddenness and the urgency but somehow it was fine. Lodi might have been a new man and felt that this was his reward, expecting her to get down in the straw with him, big, heavy and strong, but she wasn't having it. He tried pushing her on her back, his shadow shimmering high on the shelter wall behind, looming over her like some giant bull.

'For God's sake, Lodi, get off!'

And then he was lurching away, scrabbling for his trousers, trying to cover himself. He was a good Catholic boy. She'd sensed that all along.

'I've been thinking,' she said, after only the shortest of pauses for breath, back on her feet and standing straight. 'I should probably get back.'

He looked a little sheepish. 'Where to?'

'To Kampala.'

He scowled, started fumbling with his shoes.

'I've got to write my report, get this stuff out.'

He looked sad now.

'Which way do you suggest, Lodi?'

'Which way?'

'How do I get out of here? Where's the road?'

He pointed back the way they had come.

'But isn't the main road north of here?'

'That is north.'

She wasn't at all sure and he stared in challenge. It was pitch dark, no moon, and she couldn't see the horizon. Why had they not brought a compass?

They shared a biscuit and then started back along the path, only the moonlight to guide them through long grass and old dead trees. She watched her feet. She placed one foot in front of the other. She noticed her trousers were torn at the knee.

They trudged along a muddy path, heading down into a valley, to a group of abandoned huts at the bottom of a deep ravine. The path continued to the horizon, winding up the next hillside like a coil of rope. For an hour they kept up a strong pace and settled into a rhythm. For a while she forgot about time.

Finally, they stopped and drank from the water bottle that Lodi had been carrying.

'Right,' he said.

'What?'

'We are here.'

She didn't understand.

'I've brought you here.'

She looked around but could see nothing. She looked at her watch. It was just after eleven o'clock.

'Over there.' He pointed.

What was he was saying? There was a rustling in the trees and the noise of frogs. Nothing else.

She listened again but there was only silence.

And then there *was* a sound. People singing. It sounded like a choir. What on earth was that? It was far away, on the other side of the valley.

"*...row the boat ashore.*
Hallelujah
Michael, row the boat ashore."

The singing was coming in their direction. It was moving.

"*Hallelu – ooh – ooh – jah*
Michael, row the boat ashore..."

'A church?'

'Listen.'

Over the singing, she could hear the hum of an engine. It was a vehicle and it was getting closer, the singing louder.

'Must be a bus,' he said.

"*Michael, row the boat ashore.*
Hallelu – OOH – OOH – JAH."

As she listened, Lodi squatted on his heels. 'What will I do?' he said.

'What?'

'Where will I go?'

She was irritated when she realised what he meant. 'Can't you go back to the village?'

'There are quite many police.'

'It doesn't matter. You haven't done anything.'

'But…'

'Tell them it was my fault.'

He didn't seem convinced.

'Tell them I was the one who got you into this.'

She realised he was anxious but she was in a hurry to get on and she could see lights now and the bus itself, rolling up the hill towards them, headlights on full beam.

FIFTEEN

April 21st 2011

"Every empire tells itself and the world that it is unlike all other empires, that its mission is not to plunder and control but to educate and liberate."
- Edward W. Said. Los Angeles Times, July 20, 2003

'Carruthers said it was the best extension project in the world.'

'Why would he lie?' grunted Adderbury.

Baxter had agreed to take a cocktail with the old man before the party, while they waited for the cab. In his new evening wear, he had limped to Adderbury's room, picking his way cautiously, like a stricken bird, careful not to disturb the wound on his leg so carefully dressed by Madame Mao only hours before.

'He also said we had to see it in the correct light, approach it in the Ugandan way.'

'These advisers eh?' chortled Adderbury. 'They start to believe their own publicity, start to think they're experts or something. The Ugandan way? Sounds like a Roman Road. The Ugandan Way! Is there a Ugandan way to fly an aeroplane?'

Baxter smiled, as he was clearly required to do. 'But you're an economist, Zoo, you know the figures don't add up'

'Flattery, flattery, Bent, that's nice of you, but I'm not a *real* economist.' Was that a boast or a confession? 'Ah've always lacked that instinctive feel. Aw thae equations and the Greek symbols and aw. Ah never knew how tae pronounce them. Elastic and inelastic, that was always a predicament. Ah couldnae remember the difference. It's like east and west or left and right. If somebody shouts, left here, Ah get confused. A doctor once told me I had spatial dyslexia. That's where my problem lies. Short run, long run, I never know which is which. Black and white, light and dark, it's aw the same to me.'

It was early evening and the air was clear and cool and, from the balcony of Adderbury's penthouse suite, Baxter could see right across the city to the great lake, maybe five miles to the south. A colossal derrick was glowing in the security lights, a blue metallic sheen, startlingly alien in the balmy tropical night.

'But the money lost, *wasted*. It's hard not to wonder if...'

'C'mon, Bent, you havtae put things in perspective.' And that was all he seemed to want to say. That seemed to be broadly that. Finito. Everything seemed to be fine.

Baxter gazed out over the city below. The light was fading to a dark blue, the night rolling in. Behind them, the room was bare, nothing to show but the trappings of a travelling man: two small framed photographs, one a young Thai woman in a Scottish Highland landscape, Skye perhaps, another of children on bicycles. On the spare bed a large suitcase.

The old man looked good in the dark. He was wearing a well-tailored white linen DJ with a red carnation in the lapel. 'Some o' thae activist people....' he mused, almost talking to himself now, 'like yer friend Crisp, Ah hear he believes that half the budget gets snaffled and so therefore we should cut aid to Uganda. But Ah say, well, OK, if half gets snaffled, that means half gets through. I mean that's not *so* bad is it? Half of 70 million. What's that? Fifty million quid a year. Thirty million people. Two quid each. That's nae something to sniff at is it?'

One Beano comic each. An ice cream. Five cigarettes. Baxter wondered if perhaps there was something here he had failed to understand. The complexities of this man, of MODE and its attendant culture, they were almost beyond the ken of a working stiff like him.

'I was in Cairo for a while, Bent. In the old days.' Adderbury lit a cigar and, in a well-practised manoeuvre, released a cloud of dark smoke into the air. 'It was much easier then, of course, nae mullahs or what have you. Ye had a regular slot. It was civilised. None of the anxieties o' today.'

A ferry was tracking the bay at Luzira. The wash was visible a mile or more behind it.

'Ye could take a couple o' hours, a couple o' girls, a quick rattle maybe, and be back in the office by four.'

Adderbury saw no significance in the newspaper reports of worsening riots, even incipient revolt, and now a Kampala-wide curfew at midnight. 'C'mon Bent,' he said, 'there's always rioting in shanty towns. That's what they're there for.'

And so they chatted on, two men with a mission, Baxter revelling in Adderbury's Talisker, the faded crystalline hum of yesterday's ketamine and the familiar downy caress of sweet mammy tammy. When reception rang to tell them the taxi was waiting, Adderbury paused to relight his cigar and laughed. 'In the long run we're aw deid, though. That's one thing I *can* remember.'

And the party was a killer too, everything it was billed to be, although hardly the select occasion for the very, *very* select that Adderbury had earlier been touting.

'It's out at Munyonyo,' said the old man, cheerfully, as they got into the cab. This was the spiv's village on the lake, built, it was said, from the proceeds of diamond mining in the Congo, where the Heads of State had been sequestered for days now. 'It's so big you cannae see the perimeter even with binoculars. But never mind that, tonight most people will be so full of MODE bevy they won't even see their hands.'

And vast as the place was, it was packed to the last rafter. Three thousand tickets had been given out, with forgeries hitting the streets within hours. For most of the night there were queues of the disappointed snaking round the block outside and four-wheel drives idling two lanes thick halfway up the mile-long drive. Celebrities were everywhere, UN ambassadors for every known cause. Was that Richard Branson in the foyer? And Spicy Spice? Was that George Clooney? Or was it Wayne Rooney? Baxter wasn't sure. There was Sting and Roger Moore.

'Is that Mia Farrow?'

'No, ye eejut, that's Annie Lennox. And that there's Her Serene Princess Stephanie of Monaco, UN AIDS ambassador. And there's Dionne Warwick and there's Her Highness Sheikha Fatima bint Mubarak Al Ketbi, agriculture expert and ambassador extraordinaire for UN food. You should know *her* at least. C'mon, son, you've got tae know yer celebrities if you wannae come to gigs like this.'

Adderbury's party had arrived late, all the better to make a splendid entrance. Baxter was in the back of the car, the High Commission Merc, with the girl from the room, last seen in parade ground uniform, now buffed up no end and in a sumptuous fur coat. 'Borrowed from the High Commissioner's wife,' whispered Adderbury as she oozed out of the car. 'And, let me tell you, not a stitch on under it. Christ, look over there. That's Celine Dion.'

'Really?'

'She's the UN agriculture envoy.'

Baxter knew the deal. This was MODE and its extraordinary culture again, the consequence of the high-pressure environment in which dedicated staff have to work. The problem for outsiders lies in judging just how to read the situation, in assessing where the dividing line should fall: between the standard autism cases that are the bedrock of civil service recruitment policy and behaviour of a genuinely more aberrant nature.

As they pulled up with a screech, gloved doormen helped them from their seats while other still lower caste serviles grovelled round their feet. Adderbury, in the front seat, was almost dragged from the vehicle by a group of young girls with garlands and confetti. He seemed bemused but took it in good heart. Everyone was thrilled the MODE PS had come all this way. Such an occasion.

The Uganda aid industry was proudly out in force, indeed the faithful had been clawing at each other's throats for accreditation passes. Baxter had met most of the movers and shakers in the course of his rounds and he mentally ticked off the 'Res Reps' from UNICEF and UNEP, WFP, the ILO, the FAO, the World Bank, the IWGIA, UNESCO, USAID, IFAD, UNDP, SIDA and CIDA, DIF and DIDGE. Recognisable in their jeans and sandals, there was a full turnout too from the NGO bosses, glowering young men in T-shirts and baseball caps and elegant women in saris and black suits, their logos prominently displayed on carrier bags and briefcases: CARE, CONCERN, COMPASSION, CONSIDERATION, COMPLIANT (or was it COMPLAINT? Baxter still wasn't sure). These were offset by a sprinkling of the key ambassadors, all formal in their evening wear and medals, their flunkeys tucked in close behind, just in case any technical questions had to be fielded. Tactfully, a few government ministers had been wheeled in but the Ugandans were mostly represented by an army of waiters from the American Club who were doing a splendid job handing out the champagne and canapés.

As they walked up the great staircase to the first floor, Adderbury first, then the girl, then Baxter limping to keep up, they could see all the familiar faces. There was Charlie Crisp, signature orange juice in hand, his neck in a cast, a local lad, maybe a nurse, helping him at every painful step. And there was Mr and Mrs McNaughton-Balls, she, in startlingly low-cut mini dress, breasts bursting out like spilled buttermilk, he, a tight-arsed beach boy in a sarong and red basketball shoes. There was Pareto lounging on a sofa with a startlingly muscled two metre transsexual and, to his left, the minister, seemingly settled at the bar. He was shouting something to the venue staff, several menials fluttering round him like bats on a fig tree.

And here was Carruthers pushing his way through the melee, still in his trademark black shirt but with a purple tie this time, like a gangster or a DJ, his toupee so green it could have been mouldy. Or radioactive. 'Dr Baxter! You've got a nerve. Decamping to The Compound is one thing. Gate-crashing our function is quite another. When are we going to see your report?'

'I'm here with Dr Adderbury,' said Baxter stiffly. 'On his personal invitation. Queries of a work nature can be put to me tomorrow.'

Carruthers looked poorly. His skin was sicklier than ever, almost matching his toupee now, emphasising the air of comic-book villain, the sinister foreign conspirator. His eyes were yellow like those of a distempered cat. Before he could say any more, however, Adderbury had barrelled over.

'Wonderful to see you, sir,' simpered Carruthers. 'What an event!' And then turning to a passing waiter. 'Bring the Alfred Gratien, back of the bar, chop-chop.' Then addressing Adderbury again: 'The Minister's been telling me you taught him as an undergraduate, sir. He says he's still got the notes!'

'Get me some proper swally,' grunted Adderbury who, as everyone should have known, was from that generation of Scotsmen who think champagne is a soft drink for women and babies. 'And where's DSK? I still haven't seen the fucker.'

'Couldn't make it apparently,' said Carruthers, nonchalantly. 'Something came up.'

Adderbury looked like someone had stood on his foot.

'I gather Pugh was busy too,' tried Carruthers, venturing a different tack.

'Pugh,' barked Adderbury, strangely red in the face. 'Are you mad? That fuckin' bam? You think we would let him into a place like this? He's got no idea how to behave.'

'Pity. I was hoping to exchange notes with him on our times in Baghdad. The Hercules landings at Bagram, the curtain of flares as you came hurtling in, IEDs on the airport road, clear objectives, happy days...'

'He's crazier than his fucking dog,' barked Adderbury.

Carruthers blinked. 'And Lord Pareto? I did see *him* I think.'

Adderbury scowled, said nothing.

'How about Faith,' said Carruthers persevering, and turning to Baxter, 'Still out in the bush is she?'

Baxter nodded but knew it wise to keep silent.

'We're so short of single women here.' Carruthers again, seeming to sense the mood and beginning to jabber. 'Hardship postings eh! It's the uncertainty that puts 'em off ...'

And then, suddenly, the Minister and his crew, bursting into the conversation.

'Zoo, my old friend, even me I must congratulate you. Imagine. What an occasion! Poverty in our time! Economics, the dismal science, you used to say. Carlyle. But now you have made a famous success. We are almost at the new paradigm.'

Adderbury dipped his head, a gracious acknowledgement. 'Always pleased to help, Minister. I think you've met my good friend, Dr Bent Baxter? A colleague over many years, an assiduous worker at the coalface of development.'

The Minister took a step backwards, to get a better look. 'Of course, but Dr Baker! So sorry, I didn't recognise you. We tried to call you once, you know, but you were not picking. But what's happened? You look, eh... different!'

It was true. Baxter had lost a lot of weight since the meeting in the Minister's office, and the bite on his leg was probably gangrenous. He was, at that moment, sweating profusely but the Minister didn't seem to want an explanation and was talking to Adderbury again. 'So very nice to see you, Zoo. I hope these protesters haven't been a nuisance?'

'Protesters?' said Adderbury. 'I hadn't even noticed. What are they protesting about?'

'They say the government doesn't listen,' said the Minister. 'Have you ever heard anything so ridiculous? All stirred up by outsiders, of course, but it has whipped the people into a frenzy. We are looking into it with a fine-tooth comb. It seems we may have taken our finger off the boil but now we are running quicker than our legs can go.'

'Good fer you,' said Adderbury. 'You know, Minister, that London has always regarded the government here, and you yourself too, with the utmost respect.'

'But,' said the Minister, noticing Baxter again and trying on his sincerest smile, 'I need also to thank the Doctor here. Everybody in the industry was expressing ignorance, Dr Barker, but your work has improved our knowledge. You started with what I already learned but you finished where I am now. Can we look forward to a quick approval on NADS Two? None of us here have the brains to remain a professional fool. I tell you, this will be the easiest decision I ever have to make but also the most difficult.'

Uneasy laughter rippled through the group and a man from the Minister's entourage took a step nearer, the better to study Baxter's reaction. Baxter felt his head spin. Was something going on here he hadn't understood? 'Well, since you ask, Minister,' he said, 'I'm sure it will all be fine in the end but our team *has* been struggling a little with the details. It has been more complicated than we thought.'

The Minister frowned.

'It may be, sir, that some of the senior officers have been, how should I put it, trading in a wider band.'

Was the Minister taking this in? Baxter wasn't sure so he raised his voice. 'We understood this was supposed to be a project to help small farmers but it seems to have been rather submerged under the President's model farmer programme.'

'Come on, Bent,' Adderbury interrupted. 'The Minister doesn't want to hear this now. We're at a party, here to have a nice time. Don't worry, Minister, Dr Baxter is an excellent technician but, as you know, sometimes these fellows...'

But the Minister wasn't interested in what he must have thought was internal MODE business. 'Oh, Mr Zoo,' he said, 'London, when I was a student, Soho, the nightlife... imagine... we spent two whole days just...'

'We're moving to Docklands now,' interrupted Adderbury, stiffly. 'It's an indication of the emerging consensus, Minister, MODE's commitment to the future. Have you heard?'

'Gerard Street,' interrupted the Minister. 'That was the place, remember...'

'We've a new team now Minister. We're no longer an aid *agency*. Did you hear that? We're to be a 'Department of Development'. It's wholly new thinking. I believe I can genuinely say we're at the cutting edge.' And with that, Adderbury was into his standard MODE speech for foreign dignitaries and anyone else who could be backed into a corner. 'As you know, we hardly do projects anymore, Minister, we prefer the long term, growing support modalities for those with a like-minded vision. This NADS thing is a bit of a special case.'

'I assume it has all been approved by now.'

'Not quite, Minister,' said Adderbury, uncharacteristically uneasy. 'But we're down to the formalities.'

'We will be green-lighted. Isn't that what you say?' said the Minister, 'And then Dr Julian can work out the specifics.'

Carruthers had been standing somewhat outside the group and now took another of his trademark theatrical bows.

'Julian and I,' continued the Minister. 'We're glove in hand, we're thick as thieves, isn't that what you say? He will do it all sooner than possible.'

Baxter may have felt poorly but, as he surveyed the Minister, he could see that the big man wasn't well either: red-eyed, overweight, and with a drinker's skin, matt and patchy, hanging on him like mildew. He was also curiously breathless. Was that an indicator of his perilous health or was it just over-excitement at the memory of fine times with Zoo? Heroic days when the old place was at its zenith and Raymond's Revue Bar was only five minutes away by taxi.

'Certain persons may tell you, Zoo, that there is something improper in my relationship with Julian. Imagine! They say I should not be having a white man for an adviser.'

'In this day and age? Surely not.'

'But they have made the wrong mistake. I tell my colleagues in Cabinet that he may have hair that is green and a skin that is white, but his heart is just as black as mine.'

Carruthers smiled and acknowledged the compliment. 'People always knew I would go places,' he said, 'but no one guessed how dodgy those places would be.' This was obviously a well-tested joke but before anyone could reflect on its unsuitability for this occasion, the main door was flung open and a rush of people came bursting through, at the head of them and very much making the running, a little man in battle fatigues, green army-style cap and olive sunglasses. For a moment, Baxter wondered if there had been an incident of some kind, perhaps a palace coup. Maybe, he thought, troops were securing the premises, but no one seemed to be alarmed and the little man began to rush around the room, quite the centre of attention, shaking hands pell-mell and kissing cheeks as he went. When he reached their little group, he took Adderbury by the hand. 'Sir Zoo! The forum in Boston, remember? How are ye, ye old devil? Give 'em hell. Fantastic!' And turning to the Minister, 'Honourable, how are ye, nice to see ye again.' But before the Minister could even reply, the whirlwind had passed.

Baxter was impressed. He had not thought to see Adderbury bested on his own territory but the old man had been quite overawed. No contest in the charisma stakes. And then the little tornado was on the stage without even an introduction, unheard of in the aid circus where no meeting could ever start without forty minutes of bumbling preamble.

'Hello there, Khartoum, great to be here *(cue: matey Oirish accent)*.'

Silence, bemusement. If it was a joke it was lost on this lot. The man's shirt was none too well ironed. Maybe the airline had lost *his* luggage too.

'I wasn't expecting to make a speech. I haven't prepared anything. Actually there's no time for a speech and I'm only saying fifty words. It's just that they insisted I say something.'

A tremble of applause.

'Last week I was talking with Bill and Melinda about ways to save the world; two days ago I sang for a TV audience of 130 million. Now I'm here in the Pearl of Africa. Not a bad week.'

A little laughter, more polite applause.

'And now we have your signatures.'

A voice from the back. 'Your fifty words are up.'

'Good one, good one but bear with me just a moment. Look, there's been no time for diplomatic necessities, there's been a cock-up with the timing, I hear. Bob Geldof would have had a word for it but in this company I'll pass. So I'm not saying much but I do need to tell ye a couple of things. I need to get to some uncomfortable truths. The thing you have to understand is, contrary to what you might have heard, I'm not about charity, I'm about *justice*.'

Baxter could see the faces turned towards the stage, expectant, excited. This audience was not used to this kind of talk. Even the High Commissioner was paying attention.

'I was at flower farm today. They're growing for the European market, nine thousand miles away. This is globalisation at its best and I'm supporting it. Loud and clear. I know it's not so romantic, I know it's not an emotive issue, but I have learned one thing. It's about what we were taught by the people that we met. On this trip, and I was in the Congo two weeks ago, I have met people that have changed my life in a way that I will not easily forget. I have met all kinds of people as I have gone along and I will carry them in my heart. But where does this trip go from here? You know I'm not talking just about emotions here. You have got to be tough-minded. We need to actually transform the lives of these people, and we can, and I believe if we can convince the Americans that the money won't go to corrupt regimes, and money won't be wasted on bureaucracy, I believe we can get whatever it costs, probably a half a cent on the dollar, and you can transform the lives of people.'

He was speaking fast and with passion and the crowd was listening. 'The people I represent, the activists from my community, have to learn, and I think they will, to take a very, very different tack in the next few years if everything is to continue. Of course we have to be ready to continue the campaigns and more. Civil disobedience if necessary. We have to get very noisy and bang a lot of dustbin lids. This issue is the defining issue of our time and some of us are ready to really work on it. There's no way we can look at this, the world bursting into flames while we stand around with watering cans, and if we're honest, conclude that it would ever be allowed to happen anywhere else.'

At the side of the stage, Baxter spotted Tripp sliding in behind a gaggle of PR groupies, nestling in with the IMF suits and ponytails. He was tapping something into his iPhone. Perhaps he was taking notes, recording a ringing phrase or two. The little fireball was now enthusing about what appeared to be called Sabbath Economics and Tripp was indulging him with a wry smile.

'The idea is that every seven days you stop consumption and exploitation, and every forty-nine years you write off debts and free slaves. It's the opposite of globalisation.'

At this the Minister, still standing close to Baxter, clapped very loudly. He wanted everyone to know he was fully on board for this.

And then suddenly the fifty words had finished and the High Commissioner, tactfully and modestly, with hardly a word, had asked for questions.

A young woman on the other side of the stage, white COMPASSION T-shirt: 'Which part of the agenda,' she asked, 'do you think we should focus on? Dropping the debt, making trade rules fairer or getting more funding for AIDS drugs and health care? And what about terrorism and the new paradigm?'

'Too many issues,' said the little man, hardly pausing to think, probably giving his stock answer. 'That's how we blew it before. Let's keep it manageable. Let's face it, I mean the Americans don't even know where Uganda is. If they do, they think Idi Amin is still the President.'

A little frisson rippled round the room. This was not the way the High Commissioner would have put it.

'Trade is some very sophisticated politics. You have to particularise the drama for them. You've got to have a melody line.'

'Hear hear,' said a deep voice from close to the bar.

'The man at the back?'

185

'Can we close the gap between dreaming and doing?'

The little man smiled, this was more his area. 'Does news have to look like an action movie these days to exist in the front half of our brain? Look, this stuff isn't even on the news. We should be careful not to devote more attention to things we cannot prevent.'

'Exactly,' said the questioner.

'*And*, we have to be careful not to offend the intellectual rigour of the people in this room.'

Firm applause from all assembled.

Then, a man in a dark shirt, up on the stage, taking the microphone, probably the senior PR guy. 'Look, we need a photo for the trip diary. Anyone who wants to be in the group pic, come outside. We're going to release some butterflies for the backdrop.'

'Keep up the good work,' shouted the little man over the ensuing hubbub. And then he was gone, swallowed up by the crowd, surrounded by well-wishers, one more pass through the room, one more bout of handshaking.

The whole show had lasted five minutes. There was a feeling of 'had it really happened?' But that didn't last and the good mood of the party just gathered strength. In the corner, Baxter could see Mr McNaughton-Balls, newly converted to the merits of Sabbath Economics, extolling the virtues of Christian forgiveness, while, by the huge marble fireplace, under the ubiquitous portrait of the President this time displayed next to a photograph of the famous Luzira Head, the IMF people were gathered intently round a fervent Tripp. 'The problem,' the World Bank man was declaiming, almost as if addressing a political rally, 'is the disconnect between the political economy and the reality on the ground. Our challenge is that the situation is not analogous to a social welfare function because the analogous conditions are not appropriate constraints on a well-being function.'

Huddled near the stage, the Minister and his entourage were hustling the Res Reps from DIDGE and DODGE, pleading for a challenge fund perhaps or a turnkey irrigation scheme, while Adderbury had retired to a recess under one of the big windows where, with the girl in the fur coat looking sultry on his left arm, he had cornered Mrs McNaughton-Balls. Wide-eyed and simpering, breathing heavily, at times almost fighting for air, the MODE receptionist was pressed up against the old man, her ear bent to catch his whispers, her matchless breasts heaving and resplendent, putting Baxter in mind of great ships of the line embarking on yet another imperial adventure. As radiant as a schoolgirl on a first date, she was clearly spellbound, thrilled to have witnessed the famous rock star in his prime, flattered by the pursuit of the notorious Permanent Secretary, almost delirious at the prospect of the delights hidden under that magnificent fur coat.

Baxter was excited too. Perhaps it was the cocktail of pills, perhaps it was Adderbury's protective embrace, perhaps it was the poison festering in his leg, perhaps it was the we're-all-in-this-together-and-you're-one-of-us camaraderie, or perhaps it was just a bottle and a half of best High Commission champagne, but, for a few moments, he forgot the troubles that were multiplying around him now, like flies on a shit heap.

He walked out on to the balcony from where he could observe the crowd. He'd palmed a few of Pareto's duty-free Marlboros the previous night and he lit one now, feeling the warm reassuring glow as the nicotine went to his head. It came to him suddenly, with all the weight of a sudden, blinding truth that actually, at the last, everything was going to come out fine. These people would help him. He was OK, he was on the inside. He was on the right road.

Part IV

SIXTEEN

April 22nd 2011

"There is yet some work to perform in Africa and if we old African hands retire who shall do it?"
- Emin Pasha, Bagamoyo April 2nd 1890

'Baxter? Wake up. *Wake up*!'

He was home. He was dreaming. Good dreams, warm dreams, dreams of school, old friends from long ago.

'Baxter? Wake *up*.'

'Huh?'

He was not at home. He was at Pareto's pad in The Compound. Pareto was shaking his shoulder. Hard.

'Hey, what?'

'Change of plan, Bent, shake a leg.'

'What?'

'Come on, get up. I have to get out of here.'

'What?'

'COMPASSION's insurance people have been on the blower. Apparently my policy doesn't include countries with a threat of insurrection. I'm only covered for the cocktails 'n' conference circuit.'

'What are you talking about? There's no threat of insurrection here.'

'What are *you* talking about, Bent? Where have you been? The whole town's in flames. Julian says roadblocks are going up everywhere. We've got to run. Hit, git and split.'

Baxter sat up. 'It's two o'clock in the morning.'

'Now, Bent, *now*!'

'But where, go where?'

'The airport, for fuck's sake. Come on. Wake *up*!'

'Why do I have to come?' Baxter's head was all in a spin.

'There are no taxis for love or money. Julian offered his vehicle but the chauffeur has buggered off. You'll have to drive.'

Then, somehow, they were in a strange car, heaps of luggage, Baxter at the wheel, heading to the Imperial where Pareto said he had left some of his camera gear.

'It can't be that bad, Dickson. I was talking to the Minister just last night.'

'Who?'

'The Minister. Of Agriculture. At the reception. You were there weren't you? He was quite relaxed. Look, you can see, the streets are quiet.'

'Bent, I saw it on CNN. The demonstrators are going crazy. Burning tyres, burning cars. One guy on a motorcycle got beaten to death. They've got some Asians trapped out on Highway 9. They've tried to burn the mosque near Shoprite. Teargas and water cannons can't stop them, it's way beyond that. The Minister knows nothing. Anyway, most of his colleagues have already fled the country. What do you think he wants that helicopter for?'

They parked outside the hotel and, while Pareto ran upstairs, Baxter took a stroll round the lobby. The place was empty and felt decidedly strange. Was it the lighting? Maybe, maybe not. Everything was oddly crystalline, iridescent. The pattern in the wallpaper was charged, electric, moving like a pulsating current. Was this a flashback or something new? Was that time without his meds starting to take its toll?

'Evening, and how is sir tonight?'

Baxter jumped in alarm and would have fallen sideways if the man yelling in his ear had not reached out to catch him. Was he yelling? Why would he yell? He was the Customer Relations Manager, a kindly old gent with whom Baxter had only yesterday discussed the changing weather and the current fortunes of Ugandan athletics. Perhaps he'd only appeared to be yelling.

'Fine, fine,' said Baxter, in a voice that even to him sounded strangled and unconvincing.

'I hope you are not going out, sir?'

'I have to go to the airport. My colleague has to leave immediately.'

'Be very, very careful then. The rioters mean business. Go the Katwe side, there's a curfew there.' The man had a loose top lip that looked to Baxter like a species of sea slug. Why hadn't he noticed that before? He was Kenyan, apparently, yet another washed-up foreigner. The cooks in the hotel were Danish, the front-of-house clerks Filipino, the accountant described himself as a Rhodesian and the man who supervised the toilet crew was a Serb. In six weeks Baxter had barely met a Ugandan. Who were the Ugandans anyway?

And here was Pareto suddenly, running along the corridor.

Baxter was transfixed, first by the sheer quantity of gear and then by the way the patterns on the multi-coloured bags reflected in the plate glass windows and seemed to set up dark vortices before his eyes. There were three bags in all as well as a set of golf clubs.

'I'll tell you one thing,' Pareto was shouting, 'if this is the way MODE runs all its missions, if this is the new paradigm, we're all fucked. Our reputation will be ruined.'

Baxter scanned the lobby but there was no one there to hear. And anyway scenes like this were common in hotels of this sort, part of the DNA of the building, consultants falling off into the void, the existential howling of yet another development worker stripped of all illusions.

Outside, they tried to load the car but Pareto couldn't find space for his golf clubs and seemed to be losing his equilibrium. 'You're supposed to be the team leader, Bent. Help me, for fuck's sake. Is this how *professionals* behave?'

Baxter wondered for a moment if he could administer sedatives. This might be the only solution. Tie his wrists, bind him to the seat, stuff the last of the tammies down his throat: better still, a brace of brutal injections in the bum, then bundle him into the boot to cool off.

A young girl was suddenly apparent, hovering in the shadows, white shirt, blue skirt, faux school uniform. Where had she come from? She had a bracelet on her ankle and was sucking a lollipop. She came forward, nervously, eyes down and climbed into the back of the car. Baxter realised he'd seen that ankle bracelet before. The two girls, that first day at The Compound. She was younger than he remembered but ageless nonetheless, or perhaps some age there had never been. In the weird fluorescent light there was something strange about her arms. Curious marks. Perhaps she'd had measles as a child or maybe a friend who liked doing nasty things with cigarette butts.

More nausea. He had to fight to keep it down. 'Dickson, what's happening? Where did she come from? If this is a MODE vehicle we can't take...'

But Pareto was in no mood to compromise. 'Come on, get this show on the road. Let's go. Move it.'

Then Baxter was driving again and the car was purring through the deserted streets, bright lights from somewhere refracting into his dazzled eyes. For a moment, he thought the dashboard had begun to swim away from the chassis. Everything seemed to be moving by itself.

At the Clock Tower there was a crowd, lots of banners, several people shouting through megaphones. Baxter read the placards. One said "Uganda for Ugandans" and another "Poverty Out". On wasteland to the left, men in suits on a podium were speaking to the crowd while a large phalanx of riot police banged truncheons on shields in a gloomy rhythm all their own. Other officers could be seen with rifles and water cannon.

The car moved up the hill towards Kibuye and Baxter could see a burnt out sugar truck smouldering on the hard shoulder, soldiers in armoured cars idly standing by. After that, the road was quieter, less people. By the time they reached Kajjansi, they reckoned they were probably through the worst. If they were lucky, the journey from here would take less than an hour.

And that's how it was. Once at the airport though, the concourse was packed with anxious travellers, tourists and diplomats all jostling for the last seats, so much pushing and shoving Baxter had to go round twice to find a place to stop.

As they began to unload the luggage on to the pavement, a rabble of kids swarmed around like ants on spilt jam. Pareto tried to guard the growing pile from skirmishes on all fronts but one of the boys grabbed one of the suitcases then dropped it, the latches bursting open, the multi-coloured innards spilling out on to the tarmac. In Baxter's storm-tossed state they seemed like the guts of some giant worm spurting out on to the highway. He could hear voices in his head now, strange echoes, some familiar, others not.

At the entrance to the terminal, another milling throng, and a young man with a uniform and a machine gun. 'Ticket,' he said. 'Only passengers may enter.'

'I *am* a passenger,' said Pareto and he waved a wad of tickets in front of the guard. 'Depart twenty hundred, April twenty-second, that's today, OK? Yeah? Got it?'

The guard scowled.

'So I need to go through, yes? Through this door. The one that says "Passengers". Yes?' The sarcasm was palpable. To Baxter's surprise the guard let him pass. But when the girl tried to follow, the guard stepped in, rifle to the fore.

'It's alright officer, she's coming too.' Pareto brandished the tickets again.

The guard took them, leafed through them, more thoroughly this time, then slowly, menacingly, looked Pareto up and down. 'Wait here,' he said.

'Typical,' said Pareto after the guard had locked the gate and wandered off, apparently in search of a superior.

'For God's sake, just say goodbye now,' said Baxter. 'It'll be much easier.'

'We're not saying goodbye. She's coming with me.'

'With you?'

'We're going to Mauritius.'

'Mauritius!'

'Why not? After all this bollocks I deserve some time on the beach.'

The guard reappeared, this time with a sergeant at his elbow and a small group of onlookers in his wake. They were all laughing and joking, enjoying the *muzungu's* discomfort.

'I need a clarification,' said the sergeant. 'Why are you taking the chicken?'

'She is my friend.'

A woman at the front of the crowd hooted and slapped her legs with her hands. 'Chicken, chicken,' she shouted, occasioning especial mirth from an elderly man over by Security. The crowd began to make clucking noises like a barn full of hens.

The sergeant looked carefully at Pareto, a cold calculated stare that seemed to consider how much intimidation this man might bear. There must have been something in the transparent imbecility of Pareto's luminous horse face that encouraged attack because the sergeant made a sharp signal with his hand and another two guards rushed over. One of them, a large northerner with scars on his cheek, made a lewd gesture at the girl. 'There is logical overlap,' he said. 'There is an emergency now. You are not with him. You can be *my* wife.'

'Wait a minute, wait a minute, we have two tickets, we are perfectly entitled...' Pareto was putting up a fair display but it was the fake bluster of a man who has just begun to appreciate the seriousness of his predicament.

'You are an old man. Why do you pick chickens?' The sergeant put a hand on the girl's breast and she laughed nervously.

'Listen here...' said Pareto, his voice jumping an octave and a half. But then, just as it appeared he was about to lose it all, he seemed suddenly to remember something. He rummaged in his bag, eventually pulling out a battered wallet. 'I think you'll find, officer,' he extracted a sheet of folded paper, 'that *this* may suffice.' Straightening the paper carefully, he looked it over, then, with something of a flourish, sensing he was making a critical move, handed it across to the now attentive sergeant. 'You should know that I am not a man without friends.'

The sergeant had to read the page twice to get an understanding of it. He read it a third time then paused. He looked down, smiled, as if all was now clear, and handed the paper back. 'Check-in's over there, *Sah*,' he barked, clicking his heels in an exaggerated show of deference. 'This way, *Sah*.'

Pareto grinned, confident, it seemed, that this was the end of the matter, and began to walk away, beckoning the girl to follow. 'Come away my little chickadee,' he laughed, rolling his tongue lewdly along his top lip.

Baxter, who had no ticket, was ready to turn back at the door but the sergeant waved him through. 'Very sorry sir,' he said, his tone serious now and entirely subservient. 'The Conference has tested us to the limit. We have not been issued guidelines.'

Baxter trailed at a distance. 'Chancing your luck there,' he said, as the three of them reached the check-in desk. 'What's in that paper?'

'Fortune favours the brave, Dr Baxter. Your problem is your instinctive timidity.' Pareto waved the paper in the air. 'This is full authorisation from the Minister himself. Remember? You got the letter too. It's quite clear. We are to be given all the assistance we need.'

'It wasn't intended to cover this situation.'

'On the contrary, Dr Baxter, I think you'll find it's quite explicit. There's plenty of precedent and these lackeys know it well. Insurrection or not, we have the right to fuck who we want just exactly when and where we please. *Droit de seigneur*, it's part of the Structural Adjustment process.'

If Destiny understood, she wasn't letting on. In fact she was grinning from ear to ear. Maybe she approved of structural adjustment, perhaps she was a paid-up supporter of NADS. Just then, the plane swept in, its rows of windows like the lights of some great city in the sky. Pareto grabbed the girl's arm and pushed his way to the top of the queue. It was a manner suggestive of a march down the catwalk at Cannes and not a word of goodbye.

Baxter watched them for a moment before limping out on to the concourse. Dizzy and weak, tiny lights were exploding in his head like fireworks on a distant horizon, dry lightning. He staggered to the car and, as he reached it, heard a crackle on the tannoy, a strangled voice, faint and far away: 'Urgent, urgent. Would Dr Pareto, passenger to Mauritius, and his accompanying friend, please report to the security desk at the back of the hall. Urgent, urgent, without delay.' What could that mean? Baxter hesitated for a moment then walked on. He'd been hearing voices all day and, anyway, it was no longer his business.

Fifteen minutes out of the airport, on the way back, and he was overtaken by a police car, sirens blaring. Although it was foggy and drizzling, he could smell smoke in the air. A little later there were bonfires off to the right. But there was no reason to worry. He'd heard the curfew had been brought forward to 11pm but there was still plenty of time to get back.

Approaching Kajjansi again, there were suddenly vehicles in every direction: blue lights and red, green and yellow reflections off the wet road, oncoming jeeps driving too fast, another screaming police siren. Then a large convoy of army trucks travelling at speed. The rain was heavy now, and, with no lights, the lorries seemed swallowed up in the darkness, soldiers sitting on the roof of one truck, soaked through and shiny. More coloured lights. It seemed they might be in the sky, but Baxter couldn't make out where. Flashes, tracers maybe. He heard a rumble. Was it thunder? Gunfire?

At Kibuye a group of men were silhouetted against a large bonfire waving sticks and shouting. At Katwe, the first barricade: he pulled over and some figures appeared from a little hut below the bank, kids mostly, uniforms too small, guns too big. They were in camouflage and dirty and some of them had painted their faces. Baxter knew well enough that when you're approached by a fourteen-year-old wearing a white leather greatcoat, purple motorcycle boots and a headdress sculpted from a bird's wing, it's best to be cautious. He knew that one's first instinct might be to take the boy with a pinch of salt but he also knew that, when one is only just the right side of the curfew, when the kid is agitated and probably whacked out on aviation fuel, when his Kalashnikov is oiled and missing a safety catch, it's better to let your second instinct do the talking. 'Evening officer,' he said, as the boy approached the window. 'And how are you tonight?'

'Those people, what do they want?' said the boy, tetchily. 'For me, I get mystified.' He snatched Baxter's passport and flicked it open.

'I'm a tourist,' said Baxter, with as much ingratiation as he could manage. 'And I love your wonderful country.'

The boy began to amble away, then turned. 'Come,' he snapped.

Baxter got out of the car and limped to a small hut by the barrier. As he made to step inside he noticed a man in a leopard-skin pillbox hat sitting at a desk rubbing at a mark on his shirt. At that moment, a flash and simultaneously a terrific explosion, the whole countryside lit up, the frightened faces of the soldiers, frozen for a second, an entire eternity, held still for all the world to see. And then everyone running.

The man in the leopard-skin hat burst from the hut, colliding with Baxter, knocking him to the ground. There was another series of bangs, close and loud, shouting, the clatter of boots on tar, shots. Then he was on his feet, scampering towards the car. Another flash and he was in the door, moving away, around the barricade, and on down the road.

He reached the town centre in a few minutes, his heart beating like a jungle drum, only to find another encampment, another roadblock, this time a troop carrier full of soldiers in red berets. He was instructed to wind down his window.

'How is here?' said a man, a northerner in a corporal's uniform.

Baxter didn't know.

'We have reports of disturbances.'

The way the corporal was talking it seemed to Baxter as if he was moving in slow motion, in some kind of treaclescape. Baxter wondered if he himself might be in shock. Or maybe a dream state. Then again maybe the others were in it too. 'There are lights in the sky,' said the corporal. 'Luminations.'

'Yes,' said Baxter. 'I saw them.'

'Signs from God.'

'You think so?'

'Witches have been reported, near Kajjansi,' said the corporal.

'I met them,' said Baxter. 'Look, I have the bites to show it,' and, before he could stop himself, he had opened the door and pulled up his trouser leg.

The corporal saw the bandages, stooped to lift an edge, peeked at the festering wound. From his expression it was clear he was impressed but a couple of youngsters who had slouched over from the troop carrier were not so easily fooled. 'Ah, there are no witches here,' one of them said. 'Not anymore. These are modern times.'

There seemed to be fires on Mbuya hill and Baxter thought it wiser to go back to the hotel. He managed the rest of the journey without incident, the only unusual thing being a thick cloud of lake fly at the beginning of the town swamp, millions of insects ploughing into the windscreen in a mosaic of crushed blood and fibre. As he emerged from that, he could see more flames, this time high up on Naguru hill, burning scrubland or torched houses, it wasn't clear, and the night sky seemed oddly yellow.

The Imperial was much as he'd left it although the Customer Relations Manager had now vanished. Baxter took his key from the unmanned reception desk, hobbled up the back stairs and collapsed on to the bed. In a moment he was dead to the world.

SEVENTEEN

April 23rd 2011

"The king was giving appointments, plantations, and women, according to merit, to his officers. As one officer, to whom only one woman was given, asked for more, the king called him an ingrate, and ordered him to be cut to pieces on the spot; and the sentence was carried into effect - not with knives, for they are prohibited - but with snips of sharp-edged grass, after the executioners had first dislocated his neck by a blow delivered behind the head."
- John Hanning Speke. Journal of the Discovery of the Source of the Nile. Edinburgh: William Blackwood. 1863, 1st ed.

This time his dreams were not so good.

He was back in Kazakhstan. Specifically Aralsk, that cold, wind-blown, chemical-infested, misery-inducing nowheresville, somewhere on the lost shores of the Aral Sea, chickentown on the steppes. Back in the *dacha* bathroom, picking glass out of his face. Outside, the horizon was lost among dark clouds of salt and chemical dust while, all around, were the abandoned warehouses and broken cranes of the old fishing port. Huddled groups in ragged clothes struggled along the foreshore, children picking their way among the shit and scum littering the vanished seafront. And there was their Land Rover, black and shiny, diplomatic plates, on its side, engine racing.

And then the phone, screeching and yawping, and his arm out and fumbling and his old mate Hilleard, shouting again in his ear.

'Bent, we've been worried.'

All he wanted, Hilleard said, was to know that Baxter was OK. 'Have you seen the news? They're saying the whole country is on the brink.'

Baxter was puzzled. It was rare for HSC to be solicitous in any way.

'Godfrey, it's the middle of the night...'

'Bent, you OK? You sound strange.'

'I'm fine. I was asleep.'

'And the situation there?'

'Everyone says it'll pass. The army will handle it.'

'We were wondering whether you shouldn't be coming home?'

'No, no, there is still work to do.'

'Really?'

'Absolutely.'

'Well, if you're sure...'

There was a pause. Hilleard seemed to be waiting for something. 'But look, Bent, I thought I should tell you...'

'Yes?'

'We've got some news at this end.'

Baxter closed his eyes.

'The takeover, Bent. I warned you didn't I? It was all very sudden. Bosworth Bollinger, you remember?'

Baxter said he did.

'I think I told you we were looking for partners, well, we thought we were entering a partnership but they've swallowed us whole.'

What did this mean?

'They're one of those companies with a finger in every pie. PR, engineering, food manufacture, leisure activities. They made us an offer we couldn't refuse.' Hilleard rattled on, a bewildering tale of betrayal and bad faith. By this account, development consultancy, once a business based on idealism and philanthropy, had suddenly been deluged with shysters and crooks. 'They've given me *one* day to write the Press Release. Some puff about how we can climb every mountain, no problems only solutions, you know the kind of bollocks. I mean, for God's sake...'

Baxter tried to commiserate but Hilleard couldn't be stopped. 'Of course we laid out your splendid record, Bent. We emphasised the exceptional circumstances, the dreadful stress, anti-depressants, that sort of thing.'

Baxter knew what was coming.

'The Kazakhs are pressing charges. And they want punitive damages.'

So that was it.

'They claim we should have known about Macpherson.'

'Known what?'

'His convictions.' Hilleard's tone was muted, measured, formal, as if he was attempting to distance himself from the import of what he was saying.

Baxter had been over this so often he was beginning to wonder whether his story had ever been true. It was starting to feel like something that had happened to someone else. 'A man with convictions,' he said. 'Always a novelty in our business.'

'And then, just at the key moment, we've been banned from all World Bank tenders.'

Baxter was finding this narrative hard to follow.

'It seems our recent Yemen proposal contained a few CVs that were out of order. It was an honest mistake but their response has been quite disproportionate.'

This was no surprise. Massaging CVs had been going on for years. The competition did it too. In tendering for large assignments, firms would assemble teams so demonstrably expert and perfect for the job in hand that they could only have been custom-built for the occasion. As indeed they usually were. Whether staff were available to go to the Yemen for five years or were willing to go, or even whether they were qualified as they claimed, was rarely material. The important thing was that the paperwork should be just the ticket. A CV was needed and a CV would be found. If the CV needed a little manipulation, well, that was all in the game.

'There was a problem with Jimmy Pettigrew,' said Hilleard. 'He was to be team leader. He had all that opium experience. He was a shoo-in.'

'I thought he was dead.'

'So did I. I rang his number a month ago and his wife *told* me he was dead. But it turns out he's working with Arthur Anderson, seconded to some hush-hush Middle East unit at MODE, planning invasion scenarios apparently. Iraq, Iran, Syria. It's all part of the new paradigm.'

This was all too familiar and there was certainly nothing startling in any of the rest of Hilleard's story. When HSC won a tender as, to everyone's surprise, they occasionally did, they would simply declare that in the weeks and months during which the competition had dragged on, as it always did, their man had taken a job elsewhere. Or had died, if a more dramatic get-out seemed to be called for. They were then invariably allowed to substitute someone else and no one would ever check or be much concerned if the substitute was not, as he or she never could be, as good as the identikit first candidate. Indeed the substitutes were almost always people who could never win such a competition with their own *real* CVs. They would be those who were willing to go, inevitably the unemployed and unemployable, the unqualified and the deranged. And of course the living as opposed to the dead, although it was sometimes difficult to know the difference. But if HSC occasionally substituted a dead expert with a living deadbeat, the competitors would not object because they did it too. It was all too easy. The problem was in getting caught.

'And as a consequence...' Hilleard was still talking.

Christ, what was coming next? Could the directors - Hilleard and Crooks - be required to face enquiries? And where would that lead? Prison sentences? They were, everyone knew, lucky to have evaded justice for so long.

'We've had to cut staff. Skip Bifferty? Remember him? I had to let him go.'

Baxter was shocked. He hadn't realised things were *that* bad. Bifferty was the star of the company.

Hilleard sounded almost tearful. 'The instructions from Bosworth Bollinger,' he went on, 'were that if the man was ever seen on the premises again we should call the police.' Hilleard was fighting for breath, as if he might be about to have an asthma attack or even as if he was on the edge of a rare kind of rapture. 'And now, he's published an article in the Guardian alleging development is a corrupting force and a total waste of time. Calls us "the new imperialists".'

'The new what?'

'Waits till he's safely out of here first, of course. I hadn't realised but the man's clearly a fanatic.'

Baxter was drifting, losing focus.

'Sorry, Bent, I know I'm rambling,' added Hilleard, dreamily, almost an afterthought, 'but, look, the point of the call is that we had a visit from some Russian gentlemen.' He spoke as if, while his words might be real, their essence was still floating across the surface of the ancient Kazakh water. 'They wanted to talk to you. They wanted to know where you were. They weren't polite. Their speciality, they said, was pulling out a fellow's teeth when there was nothing wrong with them.'

It was mid-afternoon before he was able to finally lever himself out of bed. He put on some shorts and his flip-flops and limped along the corridor. The lift was out of order so he made his way down the fire escape, through the storeroom on the fourth floor and the Chinese restaurant on the third. The arcade was closed and some of the plate glass windows boarded up. Even Madame Mao had shut up shop. The pool was green with algae and leaves and a couple of marabou storks were standing on the diving board, eyeing him beadily as he passed.

In the bar, it was gloomy and dark, no one there but a melancholic waiter drying glasses with a hand towel.

He eased on to his favourite stool and opened a newspaper that was lying on the counter. There was only one story, the rapidly deteriorating security situation. The government was teetering on the brink and the aid agencies were saying they could no longer guarantee the safety of their staff. Expatriates were being airlifted out. It seemed that once the celebrities had gone, all resolve had melted. The place was collapsing like a house of cards.

'Pearl of Africa, eh, Bent?'

Baxter turned to see Charlie Crisp signalling to him from the corner booth. He was with a local lad in white shirt and jeans. They'd been hidden somewhere in the darkness. Even though he still had on the neck brace, the renowned journalist looked much healthier than when Baxter had seen him at the party a couple of nights before.

'Should you not be running to the airport,' said Crisp. 'Like all your donor friends?'

Baxter walked over. 'It *does* sound bad,' he said. 'The paper says the army has been called in.'

Crisp was having trouble turning his head and the scars on his face were still livid. 'There's no doubt the country is heading for hell in a handcart but not yet. This is nothing special. By the way,' he added, indicating the boy, 'this is my friend, Bucky. You must have heard about him. He's doing his best to keep me going.'

Bucky smiled and offered his hand for Baxter to shake. 'How do you do?' he said, lowering his eyes.

'These situations,' said Crisp, almost apologetically, 'bring out the worst in all of us. The only time Bucky and I get to go out in public is when everyone else is hiding in their foxholes.'

Baxter sympathised. 'But why is all this happening now?'

'Well, the President has to maintain a delicate balancing act. And sometimes it wobbles a bit. He's got family and friends on one side, he calls them his investors, the people that feel the country is their own personal bank. On the other side, you've got the *wananchi,* the people, largely passive, credulous and powerless but occasionally given to disorder and high spirits. The *wananchi* are unpredictable, that's a side effect of powerlessness. Who was it said the defining characteristic of oppressed people is that they fight among themselves?'

Baxter had no idea. Another hustler from the past no doubt.

'Anyway, when the genie's out of the bottle, it's sometimes difficult to put it back. But the President will manage, this time anyway. In the prevailing international situation, baton charges and tear gas usually come good in the end.'

Baxter had another look at Bucky. He was wearing dabs of cheap rouge, deathlike against his black skin.

'The donors won't like it.'

Crisp laughed. 'Too bad. When storm troopers kidnapped the Leader of the Opposition from the high court, the donors said they would suspend aid. They didn't. When the government rigged the last election they suspended for a month and then started up again. When some ministers stole millions from the health budget, they ignored it. Why would they suspend now?'

'Live ammunition, bodies in the street. It doesn't look good.'

'Look mate, bottom line. The War on Terror. There are 7,000 battle-hardened, US-trained Ugandan troops in Mogadishu and others in Mali, South Sudan, Yemen. There are still thousands of Ugandan security guards in Iraq. The donors need Uganda much more than the other way around. The President knows, the Americans know. The only people who don't seem to know are the working stiffs. I suppose it's difficult to get a man to understand something when his salary depends on his not understanding it. Who said *that*?'

Again Baxter didn't know. His head was spinning. Something circular was happening here. A whirlpool, some karmic force, he realised, was sucking him deep into its sway. As he watched, Crisp's fingernail was idly tracing patterns on the inside of Bucky's thigh. 'There's still my report,' he said. 'What if I refuse to support the NADS' second phase?'

'The Department of Economic *History*, Bent. It's all too late. Too much is wrapped up in this. Too many careers. Private planes, Bent, champagne like water. It's very persuasive. These development types live on public contracts: agriculture projects, roads, airports, irrigation schemes. They don't let salarymen like you turn them down.'

Baxter had lost his sense of place, felt himself swept up in this moment of execration. He wondered if he was losing his wits. 'But you can't build a country like this,' he said.

Was Crisp laughing or was he crying? It wasn't obvious. 'This is not a *country*, Bent, you know that. It's a theme park and not even a good one. The magic lake's been poisoned, the deep dark wood's been chopped for charcoal, the cute gorillas are dying, the rhinos are all dead. The only thing to do now is privatise the place and flog it to the investors for a song. You think the Serena Group might be interested?'

Never mind Crisp. Even by industry standards that level of cynicism and despair was unacceptable. Baxter had forty years' experience in development and he knew you had to trust the big picture, had to believe that every journey starts with a first step, and all the other stuff that practitioners spout, the butterfly effect, the low-hanging fruits and all that. He knew that reports *do* sometimes change things. He himself had written reports which had changed things. Hadn't he? Now he would write the best report of his life. Tell the truth, that's what the man had said. If he told the truth, people would listen, Adderbury would listen. He was going to write *the* report.

What to say though? NADS was no good, that was the first point. It had been infiltrated. It had been good once but it had been captured and the money siphoned off to support the political apparatus. Inescapably the whole enterprise was a loser, a waste of money, a misconceived nonsense, an exercise in cynicism, a colossal conceit, a total fucking dog. How diplomatically could he put it?

All afternoon and most of the night, he sat at his laptop, stopping and starting sentences, reformulating, making graphs and tables. He imagined the pages spewing out, as faster and faster, he chuntered on. Occasionally he became confused and wondered whether things were in the right order but, never mind, he could fix that in a second draft.

The throbbing in his leg was really bothering him now but more painkillers and the sheer urgency of his situation drove him on. MODE had to be warned. NADS was undermining the farmers groups and all the work that had gone into building them. Funds were being redirected to the President's cronies and the party faithful, stolen really, just as Crisp had said. This was terrible. It was his duty to draw a line under the whole fiasco. Right *now*.

As he wrote on into the night he came to understand that this was to be his masterpiece. It was a model of clear thinking and erudition. Even Adderbury, when he heard of it, would be impressed. Perhaps the old man would offer him a job. That would certainly have its attractions. After all, he couldn't keep this life up much longer. He needed to settle down. A management job, at MODE, that would be the solution. It wouldn't have to be anything too grand, maybe a part-time academic gig. Then again, there might be some High Commission sinecure on which he could see out his days far away from the unwanted attentions of any Kazakhstan enquiry.

Just before dawn, around four, he broke open the whisky. Experience had taught him how to come down from a writing high, to know just how much of what was needed to ensure decent sleep would come later, to avoid the long frozen hours of gibbering nerves and grinding teeth that would otherwise follow. Later, when he thought he must be reaching a conclusion, he carried the bottle out on to the balcony and sat down to watch the sun rise over the lake.

Eventually, he went back to write the summary 'The project is a total *disaster*,' he saw somewhere on the screen, the spirit of the Conference urging him on, 'it's a disgrace. No one but a cynic or a fool would find anything worthwhile in it.' He was drop-dead tired, nauseous, his vision breaking up, pixels dancing across his eyes. But he was OK, a sense of achievement was washing over him. He had, he felt, broken the back of it.

He was suddenly aware of the air conditioner screeching like a Mig fighter at take-off. Perhaps that was the roar that obscured the banging on the door or maybe it was just the howling in his head. At any rate, it suddenly seemed the banging, the *hammering* on the door, had been going on for some time, maybe at first just an insistent pitter-patter then the louder thump of fists on plywood.

'Police,' said a voice. 'Dr Baxter?'

He looked but, for some reason, he couldn't *read* his watch.

'Police,' said the voice again. Louder this time.

He dragged himself to the door and peered through the spyhole. He asked for ID and a tatty purple card was pushed under the door. "Constable", it said, just the one word. Was that his name or his rank?

'What do you want?'

'We need to talk to Dr Baxter,' said the voice. 'To help with what? Enquiries.'

Unsettled notions floated through his mind. Dreams, confusion. But, like dreamers do, he opened the door.

The first punch caught him below the left eye, sending him reeling, two men lunging forward as he tried to slam the door. Too late to keep them out, he trapped one man's foot, heard a pained screech.

But they were on him, tearing at his shirt, beating him round the head with a club of some kind.

He was babbling. He could hardly understand the words coming from his own mouth. 'What do you want? I've done nothing. I've done *nothing.*'

The next blow was a kick to the groin and he went down, gagging, spitting, burning tears in his eyes. And then a boot to the teeth, a crunch and blood on the carpet. And the men standing back a bit to view their handiwork.

'What's that smell?' said the second man, a tall guy, Rasta dreadlocks and cut marks on his cheek.

Baxter found himself pausing for a moment, seeming to scan the room for a source of the bad odour. There was indeed a bit of a whiff. It crossed his mind that some dreadful slime might be oozing its way out of the swamp that was his leg, out of the swaddling of lint and bandages and cotton wool, leaking on to the floor.

The rasta looked to his accomplice, still trying to locate the contagion, to explain the rancid stench that had suddenly become all too apparent.

'I can't smell anything,' mumbled Baxter.

Then the first man, and again the club. Baxter saw it swinging, felt it come down somewhere on his body, couldn't have said where. He curled up and covered his face. Someone grabbed his arm, trying to pull him towards the bathroom but he feigned dead, an old trick made more convincing by exhaustion, the effects of chemical overload and blind panic. He could feel more clag now, welling up in his trousers, in his shoe. It really was. Seeping, oozing, slurping. The carefully wrapped bandages on his leg must have come away. The dam had broken. The whole construction was in ruins. Savage kicks to the stomach and groin, a couple on his leg, more clubbing round the head.

'I don't deserve this.'

'Beat him.'

'Blows till you're blind.'

'What do you want?'

'You must answer some questions.'

'Why are you beating me?'

'We are police,' said the rasta, with some emphasis.

'If you are police why are you not in uniform?'

'We don't want the criminals to recognise us.'

And then more kicks to the head, more dogged, more determined, more vicious, more *sustained*. They beat him with a special relish, a singular attention. They beat him as if it was personal. Blows till you're blind. Kicks to the choicest, softest spots.

And then he was gone, the pain stopped, his receptors receiving only some weak internal signal: clips, footage of someone else getting beaten, in silence, on a tiny TV on the other side of the room, in black and white, the light dim and dimmer.

'Kill him.'

'*Awuwa yeyea.*'

More kicks, fluid, spit, urine, semen, whatever, running down his face.

Immobility, coldness, quiet.

Then the men zipping up and ambling up the corridor, away to the stairs, taking their time.

Silence, except for a distant fire alarm, a thin electric bell.

His shirt. Could it be repaired? Would he need to go back to left luggage? And so close to the end of the mission. A vision of Pareto. A man sleeping under a tree. Was he hurt? How could he be? He couldn't feel any pain.

A face above him, looking down. An old woman, hotel staff, a cleaner perhaps. She must have heard the noise. 'Are you all right, sir?' she said, peering into his bleeding, broken face.

'The horror,' he mumbled, the words toppling from his mouth in a stream of teeth and bloody drool.

'Yes,' she said. 'You can say that again.'

EIGHTEEN

April 24th 2011

"This music's plaint forgives, redeems
The deafness of the world. Night turns
Homewards, sheathed in notes of solace, pleats
The broken silence of the heart."
- Wole Soyinka, In The Small Hours

A few minutes after midnight, just at the same time as Baxter was getting his licks, some two hundred miles away, on the outskirts of Barogal, a small town in the north of Uganda, a white Toyota Hiace minibus was struggling slowly over a particularly deep set of potholes, making its tortuous way down that section of the long road from the Sudan that reaches to where the Nile meets its Okole River tributary. Inside the bus, a group of white Americans, most of them on the wrong side of sixty were working their way slowly through Liturgical Hymns Old and New: Melody/Guitar Edition, singing with real gusto considering they'd already been on the road for eight hours, had been rejoicing for most of that time and had had nothing to eat but bananas for two days. The driver was in rather better trim than the rest of his colleagues, dapper in blue overalls and heavy boots, wiry with rugged, leather-brown skin. In the passenger seat next to him was a white woman in her late twenties, a small rucksack by her feet.

'You were lucky I came along,' said the man, in some kind of good ol' boy accent. 'You shouldn't have been out there so late. Who knows what might have happened. It's not safe out here, ma'am.'

Faith was hardly listening, was still savouring her moment of decisiveness. She was tired but happy, sore from her long walk, excited about the journey ahead and wiser, much, much wiser. As she stared into the oncoming headlights she wondered how she could ever have been so dim.

'Have I not seen you before?' the driver said.

Surely not.

'On the plane? Three weeks back?'

She tried to think. It seemed so long ago.

'At London Heathrow.' He pronounced it with the emphasis on the "Heath". 'We was queuing together at departure.'

The missionaries, of course. She turned and scanned the congregation behind. It was the fatties in the green shirts and baseball caps. Some of them didn't look quite so fat now. Had they been fed on a constant diet of *matoke* and maybe lost their appetites?

'What are you doing out here?' Wasn't it a bit incongruous, she wondered, all these hillbillies, on a bus, in the middle of Africa, on a highly dangerous road, at night?

'In congress? What's that?'

She smiled. 'Sorry, I'm just asking what you're all doing out here?'

'Didn't I tell you? We're bringing the word of the Lord, the power of the holy spirit.'

'Oh yeah,' she said. 'I remember.'

'We're on a crusade.' He pronounced it with the emphasis on "crew".

'And what does that involve again?'

'Some orphanage work, ma'am, but mostly Bible studies, bringing the good news. We're touring the country, making connections with pastors, meeting local people.'

'You've got a local partner?'

'Sure, many. We got our own TV channel.'

'Really?'

'Sure.'

She must have looked surprised.

'We met the President. And his wife.'

If she looked surprised it was because she was surprised. Was this guy for real?

'They were thrilled to see us. We got in at the top. We met the entire Cabinet, they were shaking our hands.'

'How did you manage that?' Keep talking, that was probably the wisest course. She was thinking about how hard it had been for her to meet *any* Ugandans. It had seemed like donor people, the bearers of the multi-million dollar contracts on which the country ran, had to sweat blood just to see a doofus like the Minister of Agriculture.

'It's the power of prayer, girl. In three weeks we've baptised four hundred people in the Holy Spirit. How about that? The President's wife cried when she heard. Done a bunch of medical work too. Doc Kincaid, in the back there, he done look at a bunch of crossed-eyed kids. Also some damaged brainers. That's his special area.'

The vehicle was moving a little quicker now.

'And that's only *this* month. In twelve years, we've saved thousands of souls.'

'Twelve years? You've been here twelve years?'

'You bet, ma'am.' He laughed. 'Twelve *short* years.'

'You must know the country well.'

'I guess. Just 'cos I'm saved don't mean I don't see what's goin' on in the material world, don't mean I ain't interested in the world outside. Name's Bill, by the way. Big Bill.'

She remembered now. 'I'm Faith,' she said.

'Fine name, ma'am,' he said. 'And what are *you* doing out here?'

'Well...' Where to start? 'I'm working on a big agriculture project for donor support.'

'Out here?'

'All over the country actually.'

'Uh huh.'

'Everyone thinks it's a great project but I have found out that it's got problems.'

'Is that so?'

'Totally.'

Was this guy an airhead or what? She couldn't tell. 'You know about NADS?' she said.

'Only what I see in the newspapers.'

'And what do they say?'

215

'That it's rotten with corruption.'

'There you go then.' And, with that, they lapsed into another silence.

'Tell me,' said Bill, after a few minutes, 'you talk to the people. Do you believe they know what is really happening? Are they good judges of the situation? Would you expect them to know all the facts?'

She didn't have to think. 'I'm sure,' she said confidently, remembering the textbooks, knowing at least the answer to that one and happy for this one clear, blinding, moment, 'I'm sure there's nothing in the world, nothing the philosophers could devise, which these people don't already know.'

Bill nodded, seeming to mull this over. 'Our church don't believe in government aid,' he said. 'All respect, ma'am but, once government puts its dinky in, you're always on the slippery slope and I tell you *that* for free.' He laughed with genuine amusement.

'But what else to do?'

'Pray for the great missionary force. Simple.'

They navigated a village, the traffic slowing up. Twice they had to swerve to avoid a child crossing the road. They stopped talking and the community singers behind started into *Amazing Grace*. In Faith's head a voice was shouting the headlines at home: inefficiencies in NADS, indolence, smugness. And those were the good ones. With a bit of a push the hacks might rise to exploitation, dispossession and impoverishment. Surely there had to be questions. The activists would be furious. MODE in foreign aid fiasco. The culprits would be named and shamed. MODE would be forced into retreat. Their calumnies would be exposed for all to see. Apologies would be required. The traduced people of Uganda would be compensated. She would be lauded, a whistle-blower, a hero.

Another village and they slowed for some speed bumps. Even at this late hour, there were crowds, food vendors with barrows, market stalls.

'So many people,' she said.

'Lost people,' said Bill.

It was her turn to laugh but it came out as a strange cackle that sounded a little desperate even to her.

'The fate of the godless and the savage, missy.' He was serious. 'End times are coming, however you want to look at it. On earth as it is in heaven. You know about the rapture? Never mind that. You've heard about the Greenland Norse, the Maya, the Great Zimbabwe? You know these stories?'

She nodded, not entirely persuasively.

'Where are these people now? Easter Island? You must know that one. They had no god. Forests and parrots and beautiful women and all manner of earthly things but no time for the good Lord. They cut the forest. The wise men warned, but the people needed the wood, or so they thought. And they cut and they cut and they cut. And eventually there was nothing left but desert and silence. By the halfway point it was too late. No government action could have saved them.'

A third village, more people on bicycles, the road tumbling into the headlights' beam, the crew in the back still singing their guts out, the first flickers of dawn visible to the east. Faith would persuade Baxter to hold their report until he had digested the full import of her new material. She would stay well clear of Tripp and Carruthers and their squalid cynicism. She would call Charlie Crisp and get him to write something in the Guardian, alert the local pressure groups, get an online petition going, make a *serious* fuss.

'And I heard, Faith, as it were, the noise of thunder, one of the four beasts saying: Come and see. And I saw. And behold, a white horse.'

This was getting weird. What was he saying?

'The prophets say that all the Uganda biomass will be gone in a hundred years and the lake will be dry. The sea might even be lapping at our cancerous feet. Climate change, what about that? Your house over there in England will be overcome by refugees. Your family will fall victim to mobs of howling mutants and, just to survive, your children will be forced into depravities beyond your wildest imagination.'

Her head was spinning. Was this the official Christian view?

'Unless?' said Bill, smiling warmly, letting the question hang.

'Unless what?'

'I told you, power of prayer, missy, power of prayer. If this is the end-time that the prophets foresaw, have no fear, 'cos the Lord will provide. For them and for us.'

Lights ahead, hurricane lamps hanging on the side of huts. They slowed down. Bill was leaning forward, squinting through the glass, trying to see the road, and neither of them saw the old man on the bicycle come wobbling out of an alley. The minibus hit the bike with its left front wing and there was a dull thump followed by some shouting.

'What was that?' said a voice in the back.

'I don' know.'

They pulled over on to the verge and Faith got out. Bill had a torch. The old man was lying on his front on the edge a deep drainage ditch, twenty yards back, screaming for all the world to hear. As she approached, Faith could see blood gushing from a wound behind his ear, a lot of it. They both stopped and stared for a moment and the old man fell silent, his eyes wide in panic. He was watching them watching him. Bill took a step closer and the man began to squeal again.

A couple of elderly ladies got out of the bus and stood watching from a distance.

'What shall we do?' said Faith.

Bill wasn't sure and bent down to look at the man, maybe to get him on his feet, when, without warning and silhouetted in the faint light from the distant village lamps, two men and a woman came running down the road, shouting and waving sticks.

Bill began to walk warily towards the approaching figures. They were yelling in a language Faith couldn't understand.

'Be careful,' said one of the old ladies, but, as Bill proffered his hand and before he could speak, one of the approaching villagers had smashed him across the head with what looked like an axe. Bill stumbled and fell, and as he went down, the man hit him again. And again. He seemed to be trying to get up but he couldn't.

Faith started to back away.

'Get in the vehicle,' she shouted at the ladies.

She wondered about getting in herself, maybe locking the doors, but she was hesitant, reluctant to run. She could see more villagers approaching, the ones already there kicking Bill and shouting. He was struggling, trying to protect himself. 'Please,' she heard him say, but the man brought the axe down on him once more, backwards, like a hammer. Then again. And more kicks. In less than a minute Bill had ceased to move.

The attackers stopped wailing and an eerie silence ensued. They began to walk towards her. Faith stood her ground, watching. No one spoke. The man with the axe was light skinned and appeared to be weeping, certainly Faith could hear strange, strangled whimpers. She took a step back and the crowd somehow took this as a signal. A woman from the front of the crowd suddenly ran at her, stopping a few yards off, screaming at the top of her voice.

Faith retreated another step. 'It was an accident,' she shouted. 'We didn't mean to hit him. He didn't have any lights, he didn't stop at the junction.'

She was breathing heavily. She looked towards Bill who was lying on his side, quite still now, the blood on his face oozing and glistening in the light of the torch.

More villagers arrived, mostly young men and women. They inspected the now silent old man, still lying on the edge of the drainage ditch. Faith understood she had to negotiate, had to buy time. The longer she could talk, the more chance there was of tempers cooling. Two youths approached, their faces expressionless.

'I can pay,' said Faith. 'How much is it worth?' She put a hand in her jacket, fumbling for her wallet.

One of the young men bent down and, almost in one motion, grabbed a stone from the road and hurled it at Faith. It missed. Faith reckoned it was wiser to keep still. 'It was an accident,' she said again. 'He should've been wearing brighter clothes. We could provide reflecting jackets. For the whole village maybe.'

The man snatched another stone. This time it hit her on the shoulder, but Faith felt nothing.

'It was an accident, for Christ's sake. *Please*, it wasn't our fault.'

The next one caught her heavily on the side of the mouth and she heard the crack of a tooth breaking. She was aware of more people arriving. Another stone and she felt herself wobble. She was aware she mustn't cry. That would not be helpful. She could taste blood in her mouth. She was suddenly angry. This was not fair. She was their friend. Several people were gathering stones now. Why were they doing this? This was an *accident,* a terrible mistake.

An image of her father came to her, a picture from long ago, a family camping holiday, the last one together, down on Milford Sound, South Island. It rained but they didn't care and she helped her father put up the tent. She remembered the way he smiled when the job was finished and some kind words and how they all huddled around the billy while he prepared tea.

She realised she'd fallen, that she was on the ground, that her clothes were ripped. She felt the crowd come closer. One man was struggling with a big boulder, having trouble carrying it. He stood over her and heaved it up, high above his head.

'Please,' she managed, and felt her mouth and nose fill with blood. 'I'm working with NADS. I'm only here to help.'

And then the rock hurled down on her with all the strength the man could muster. It tore her face and smashed her shoulder. She felt the crushing blow but somehow without much pain.

Then a voice. 'Call a doctor. We need a doctor.' Was it from the crowd? Was it inside her head?

Someone was holding her legs. More people coming forward with rocks, picking them up and smashing them down again. And again. And again. And again.

Part V

NINETEEN

November 2011

It was inevitable they'd come. He was expecting them. He'd always known he'd have to face them eventually.

He dismissed the doctor, hauled himself from the bed, adjusted his hospital gown, made sure he was decent.

'Yer lookin' good, Bent,' yelled the encephalic dwarf as he barrelled in, 'nice to see you to see you.'

Baxter felt a tremor, as if his confidence had already taken a fall. Maybe he should have put on some trousers.

'You remember Patience, Bent?'

How could he forget? His memory might be patchy here and there and he sometimes got his left and right mixed up now but there was no forgetting the face. In stylish tweed suit and Grace Jones hairdo, skin black and smooth like marble, she looked a million dollars. She wore the rig like she was born to it. Fantastic legs, terrific poise. From security guard to Adderbury's PA in a matter of months and no indication she'd ever been otherwise. No hint of the village, no soil under *her* manicured nails.

'We got her in on the MODE Young Professionals scheme,' said Adderbury. 'She took to it like a natural.'

Adderbury winked at Patience, 'Watch yourself, sweetheart,' he said, 'this is the guy who finally did for Dr Pugh. I don't know what ye said to him, Bent, but it fair did the trick.' The old man patrolled the room, checking the 1950s decor, the faded curtains, the Formica table, the portable TV currently showing children's cartoons. 'One disnae like to have to use force,' he continued, almost talking to himself, 'but he ran amok on the pitch and putt, digging up the greens, pissing in the flowerbeds, frightening the secretaries. I heard it took four good men to hold the bastard doon. Very sad, of course, another casualty of the War on Terror.' Age was catching Adderbury now, Baxter saw, marching across his face like those armies of the Khan he so esteemed.

Baxter made some Nescafe and they all perched together on the sofa by the window.

'We were so sorry about what happened,' added Patience, gesturing towards his bandaged hands.

Baxter realised it was the first time he'd heard her say a word. The last time he saw her was at the High Commission party where her fur coat had done all the talking.

'We heard you could have callers now,' said Adderbury, 'that you'd established a certain equilibrium.' Equilibrium was a term economists liked. Static equilibria, it defined their whole existence.

Baxter smiled, that was nice, but why hadn't they made contact before? The only communication he'd had with MODE HQ was a voice message on his bedside answering machine, a cheque, seventy per cent deducted from the original fee due to time penalty, it said, and an unsigned get well card stamped with the departmental logo.

'We heard,' Adderbury went on, 'that you were preparing to rejoin the world.'

'The doctors think I can,' said Baxter. He waited. He knew they hadn't come for the coffee. He was *much* better, that was true. There was still a scar on the side of his head where they had operated but his hair had grown in and covered it now.

'Will you be looking for work do you think?'

'Actually,' said Baxter, slowly and dreamily. 'I've got a change of plan.' He had intended to wait a while before dropping his bombshell but he hadn't been able to hold himself back. He'd blurted it out already. 'Yes, I thought I'd try to stop the clock for a bit, do a bit of writing. Maybe some new thinking.' He, of course, had written nothing so far, submitted nothing. How could he? On the day of the deadline, he was having frontal lobe surgery, his arms and legs all in plaster. But getting a platform for some writing had proved surprisingly easy. His dramatic medevac from Kampala had been shown live on CNN and an astute media agent had converted this into minor celebrity status. A gaggle of reporters had camped outside his house for a few days, he'd had an interview in the Daily Mail and a get-well email from the staff at COMPASSION. He'd become an expert on development more or less overnight and the Guardian was offering him silly money for a regular column starting with his views on the latest Nairobi bomb outrage and its impact on the tourism industry.

Adderbury didn't look convinced. 'What line will you take?'

He rubbed his eyes then stopped, self-conscious about his bandaged mitten hands. 'I thought I would try to move the development debate forward, maybe use the NADS story as an illustration. They want me to be provocative.'

'Really?'

'That's the role of the columnist.'

'Sure.'

'They said I should put my personality into it.'

'Absolutely.'

'In the first column I'm going for the jugular, starting off with a jolt. I'm taking a jokey tone but the idea is to develop an argument for a new level of discipline.'

Adderbury said nothing.

'It's half jokey...'

'Right...'

'It's also serious. It's a call to wind the tape back, bring in some rigour, wipe the slate clean, Calvinism with a bit of Pol Pot, you should know about that.'

Adderbury was impassive.

'Just take Uganda. I'm exposing those fat cats in their Benzes, the MPs, the Permanent Secretaries, the Commissioners .... the donor *kapos*. I'm suggesting there might be something to gain if someone was to smash their glasses and force march the bastards to Masindi. Through the swamp. A brisk ten-day hike, no water.'

Adderbury looked like he was considering this. 'Could be thought a bit belligerent, Bent?'

'And don't forget the new paradigm,' said Patience. 'I learned about it on a course.'

'This will be a *new*, new paradigm.'

'Oh,' said Patience.

'I'm calling it capital logic.'

'Expand,' said Adderbury.

'The idea is that people will be much better off if they understand where they are in the hierarchy of capital. Most of our stakeholders are at the bottom of the poverty pyramid.'

'The poverty pyramid? You mean Peter Piper's Poverty Pyramid?' said Adderbury, laughing. 'Blimey, I underestimated you, Bent. I didn't realise you were an intellectual.'

'It's not new,' he shrugged. 'I know that.'

Adderbury crossed his arms, hunkered down in his chair, seemed to be deliberating on the poverty pyramid, parsing the arguments deep down inside his vast intelligence.

Patience was fiddling with her handbag.

Through the window, Baxter watched some patients exercising outside on the lawn, pacing up and down, stretching their arms and legs, as if they were learning to walk again after a long period of incapacity.

'Maybe it's a side effect of your injuries?' said Adderbury.

'What?'

'All this belligerence. Probably it'll pass. The brain is a great healer.'

A wave of dizziness passed through Baxter. It seemed as if his chair had wobbled, as if he might be sliding on a bed of oil. 'I'm already on the mend,' he said, not altogether convincingly.

'The thing is Bent, what happens once you've written your articles, got the anger off your chest? You'll run out of things to say but by that time you'll have pissed off all your friends, run out of money…'

'How will you make a living *then*?' asked Patience.

'Then,' said Baxter, perhaps a little stiffly, not used to having to talk so much, 'I'll start a *new* journey. I've already taken the first steps. I'm going to seek transcendence. I'm working on it here. I am learning to tread the path alert to every possibility.'

'We did hear,' said Adderbury, talking softly, almost to himself, 'that you might have developed some, what should I say, *unorthodox* ideas.'

'I'm keeping my eye on the horizon,' Baxter continued. 'In time I shall make contact with the man within, the man I never knew was there.' This was the sort of thing the doctors had encouraged him to say but he hadn't expected to hear himself repeating it in this company.

'You're assuming, Ah suppose,' said Adderbury, 'that the transcendent man can subsist on spiritual essence alone?'

Pain behind his eyes but he knew he had to hold on.

'Look, Bent,' Adderbury went on. 'Let me be frank. Ah've been in this business nigh on forty years and I would say almost every development worker that's come through my department, every one, has at one time or another, sworn to me that they cannae stand it for one day longer. Some of them have broken doon. They've sat in my office and cried like wains.'

Adderbury seemed almost fatherly now. Perhaps the mask the old goat put on each morning had, in the fullness of his long years, gradually worn down until, finally, underneath, all that was left was the core, something inside that was softer at least than the once indissoluble shell.

'Aye, they bawled like wains. Oh, they want to be at home with their families, oh, they drink too much, oh, their wives have run off with a priapic gym teacher, oh, they'd like to spend time thinking, sitting on their yachts, writing their great novel. Oh, they'd like to run a boatyard in Jamaica, be a crofter in Ireland, a Jungian analyst, a motion-picture director. Even one or two fancying themselves as Florence Nightingale or Mahatma fucking Gandhi, writing a column in the fucking Guardian.'

He'd raised his voice there but he was kindly again now. 'But these are dreams, Bent. It's much too late. You're caught, we're all caught, trapped, addicted. Hotel breakfasts, free laundry, limousines, suntans in the winter.'

'I don't want to do it anymore,' he said, defensively, lugubriously. 'I don't believe it in anymore.'

Adderbury sighed.

Patience looked puzzled, confused, *hurt*. She hadn't come all the way from Africa, signed up to the MODE career structure, to hear this.

Adderbury stood up, began to pace around, one more tour of the facilities.

A long silence. It seemed they might be finally getting to the point.

'They told me about Faith,' said Baxter, jumping in. The name was spoken at last. It seemed to him as if they'd spent an hour manoeuvring around the only subject worth discussing.

Patience fumbled in her expensive handbag once more, as if looking for her car keys, as if she might be about to jump to her feet and rush off.

Adderbury shook his head. 'A dear girl,' he said.

Another silence.

'They did find some body parts,' said Patience, trying to be helpful.

'Her parents were on the box,' said Adderbury, 'her mother demanding compensation. It's so difficult, isn't it? People have no understanding. They think we do it for charity.'

Even Faith had never thought that.

'There was an article in the Daily Telegraph,' said Patience. 'With a picture, I think.'

Baxter took a deep breath.

'The Ugandans left no stone unturned,' added Adderbury. 'It's very, very unusual for a European to be...' he paused, 'and the government was mortified. The Minister told me personally. He *demanded* reprisals. The police raided a village, burned a few huts, shot a couple of people. It was an eye for an eye situation, he said. *Somebody* had to pay.' He finished the last of his coffee and let a new and more ominous silence fill the room.

'As for you, Bent,' he continued eventually, perhaps sensing he could lose the initiative, 'The President wanted to offer a special thank you. A holiday was suggested, a safari, a few nights in a swanky game lodge, something like that. It won't make up for it but it might be good for you, eh?'

'What about the rioting? What happened in the end? It seemed the country was going up in flames.'

'A storm in a teacup, Bent. You knew it yourself. The country offices always get it wrong. The trouble with experts these days is they never leave their armed compounds. It was just high spirits. Folk letting off steam.'

'And NADS?"

'You can give yourself a big hand for that, Bent. The donors are putting in another two hundred million. Everyone's delighted.'

'But it was falling apart, it was a slush fund for the President and his cronies, a bad project.' Why did he say that? He had almost closed them out and suddenly he was letting them back in, arguing points of detail.

'No, no, no, Bent, come on. Let's not exaggerate. And remember, you have to look at the big picture.'

'Which is?'

'There's no secret, Bent. There's nothing sinister about it.'

'Well?'

'Uganda is on our side, big man, join the fuckin' dots.'

'Crisp,' he said, after another pause, 'didn't think the project was even economic.'

'*Who*?'

'Charlie Crisp, the journalist. He said NADS had made no noticeable difference to production, even that yields might be *falling*. Soil erosion is at catastrophic levels, population is growing at one of the highest rates in the world. It's a disaster waiting to...'

'Give it time, Bent, you got to give it time.'

'But how long before the gravy train hits the wall? Crisp said eighty per cent of the budget was being spent on handouts.'

'Crisp! Come off it, Bent. What does he know? He's an amateur, a dilettante.'

'But even the experts say...'

'Experts for fuck's sake! What do *they* fucking know?' Adderbury was irritated now. 'Far too many experts in this game, Bent. If the people who built the terraces in Indonesia, or the great cathedrals of Europe, or the Pyramids, had asked the experts, had done yer cost-benefit analyses, where would we be today? I'll tell you. We'd still be sitting roond some vicious campfire, savage shitheads in the wilderness. Don't you know that?' He turned to the window where he could admire himself in reflection, the literate toad, his sheer brutishness made almost overpowering in the sideways angle of the light. Turning back, he closed his eyes and took a breath that seemed to last forever. 'Now, this business with the papers…'

Somewhere in his mind Baxter was not a little flattered that they were trying so hard to woo him but he knew he had to hold fast.

The silence stretched to minutes.

At one point Adderbury stroked his chin, rustled around in some papers he'd pulled from his jacket pocket. 'By the way, what happened to Godfrey Hilleard?' he suddenly asked. 'Any news?

Baxter had heard nothing.

'There wuz a rumour he might be somewhere oot in South America.'

How would Baxter know? He had had no contact with anyone for weeks.

'Of course, it wuz that Aral Sea Project that finished him, the legal bills, aw that unpleasantness. Those Kazakhs are terriers once they get on a case.'

Another moment of silent reflection. All Baxter knew was that HSC management had done a bunk one night and what was left of the old office had been simply asset stripped by the new owners, the Bosworth Bollinger group. They'd changed the name, brought in American money and merged with some accountants the group discovered it was already employing. They wanted to reposition themselves for the emerging climate change agenda. Another new, new paradigm. Perhaps the new, new, new paradigm.

'And MODE, us, we're building a new team,' said Patience, jumping in, trying to lighten the mood. 'I'm working with the recruitment committee.'

'It will be a new dawn for aid,' said Adderbury. 'We'll make poverty history, that'll be the slogan. It's the '68 generation, our time has come, everything is possible. It's so exciting!'

Baxter must have looked surprised.

'Aye, the age of empire has gone, Bent. There will be no more gunboats. No more bombing. Participation and empowerment that's the story.'

Baxter had never heard Adderbury talk like this.

'And, of course, we need a new strategy, Bent, a new approach, and we'll have to pull together.'

Baxter waited.

'Ye see, Bent, between you and me, we're worried about you, worried ye might get taken advantage of. These press people are hard as nails and you, how shall I put it, are a wee bit exposed right now, a wee bit shaky, a wee bit flaky. You give 'em an inch and they'll take the whole fucking Sudetenland, you know what Ah'm saying?'

The room went quiet. The old man seemed to be thinking.

'Let me be frank, Bent. We don't like this idea of you writing in the papers. Don't get me wrong, I love the Khmer Rouge idea but it'd be wasted on that lot. And, it could cause us a lot of difficulties. An old salt like you going soft on us, Bent. Those Bifferty articles were bad enough but a distinguished thinker like yourself, it would be much more damaging.'

Baxter smiled. That was nice.

'Don't take it the wrong way, Bent, but I thought we should offer you an alternative, if I can put it like that, an inducement...'

Baxter frowned. What was coming?

'Unfortunately we can't give you a real post, that's not possible anymore. You're much too old. Ask Patience. The recruitment people set the deal and they won't direct hire anyone over forty. They've had enough of folk saying they've seen this before, it didn't work then it won't work now, and all that kind of jive. They only want youngsters. They've changed oor logo: "we value enthusiasm over experience". They'd push me out too, Bent, if they could but, of course, I know *exactly* where the bodies are buried.' He let that hang in the air, perhaps for Patience's benefit as much as for Baxter's.

So what was it going to be then? Baxter could hear a clock ticking somewhere.

'There are, however,' said Adderbury, all tantalising smiles, 'still one or two vacancies for our few remaining transcendent souls'.

'People whose values we can trust,' added Patience.

'We thought,' said Adderbury, 'it should be something that gives you a regular income, a steady stream, and a pension. We hear your wife might appreciate that...'

'I'm not going to Afghanistan, if that's what you mean.'

Adderbury tried laughing but Baxter wasn't having it. 'We've been sending people there for a hundred and fifty years,' he shouted, 'and it only ever gets worse. If Pettigrew's team couldn't do anything for the place, how could I?'

'Fair enough, Bent, fair enough. What about Diego Garcia?'

'Diego Garcia?' Wasn't he a golfer? Were they joking? Were they trying to humiliate him? He looked to Patience who seemed curiously blank.

'It's not a well-known gig but it *is* under the Africa desk. Trouble is, Bent, it's got a problematic history and we need someone we know to… It's a bit delicate… the point is, it's in the rear, not in the front line, if you get ma gist. MODE intends to establish a marine park there. Cutting edge stuff. You would be the perfect candidate.'

Baxter closed his eyes. This was what he had prepared himself to resist. He turned his head away. He would *not* be bullied or cajoled.

Adderbury climbed out of his chair again. 'Look, Bent,' he said, pacing purposefully now. 'I didn't want to bring it up but… you see… the problem is… there's also these holdovers we need to clear up.'

'Holdovers?'

'This Kazakh business, you mentioned it yourself?'

Had he? His head was hurting now.

'You know we've been negotiating on your behalf, Bent, trying to help oot.'

Baxter tried to gather his wits, tried to find space to consider what was being said.

'You see, in the end, the EU found they hadn't the resources to collect the debt, thought MODE might be better placed, more contacts and all, more leverage, and as we're all in the same boat, we had to assist. And as ye know, debt relief is all the rage these days.' Adderbury was smiling, a half grimace that had Baxter believe, for a strange unsettling moment, that he could see through, even into, the eyes of a man from another world. 'Three hundred thousand smackers they reckoned, at the final count. I cannae think how you got through it all.'

Three hundred thousand now!

'Including interest and our respective commissions, o' course, but that's standard these days, you'd expect that in any debt purchase arrangement.' Adderbury smiled again, brooking no challenge. 'The thing is we need something back on this, Bent. The Treasury is insistent.' Adderbury's lower lip twitched, the perfect theatrical touch. It was a darker colour than the top one, with just a hint of green, like some mould on ancient wine. His eyes were hooded now, black and sunken. 'What other news have we got, Patience? Poor old Bent's been oot o' the loop for months.'

'Lord Pareto?' said the girl.

'Och aye, oor man from COMPASSION.'

Baxter had barely thought about Pareto since he'd seen him off at the airport in Entebbe.

'A malicious tip-off, I'm afraid. Who could it have been? We don't know. Apparently, on the way oot, Ugandan customs objected tae some pineapples he was carrying. It sounds absurd, Ah know, but perhaps they suspected that his, shall we say, mercantile calculations were a little adrift. Anyway, they detained the poor soul for a week. He claims he was beaten senseless and repeatedly sodomised by phytosanitary officials. Ah mean what *uz* it these days? Do people have no respect? Can ye not even trust the *old* values?'

Baxter recalled Adderbury, drunk, in the restaurant in Kampala. Hadn't he asked a similar question then? There was clearly something about this line of work that put the answer in doubt.

'And Macpherson's made a sworn deposition. I don't believe a word o' it of course but yer pals at the Guardian are lapping it up. The public care nothing about the new paradigm but *more* stuff about anal sex and the British Aid Programme, even if it *is* consensual on this occasion ... it'll never look good however we try tae spruce it up.'

Say hello to your old friend nausea, thought Baxter. It was down there, it had got in somehow. It was a dark toxic sludge, slopping around in the bilges, easing through the cracks in the rotten wooden planking that was his only support, seeping up the walls. As long as he kept still, he thought, tried not to get excited, he might be all right.

'Apparently,' Adderbury continued, 'it could go to the American courts and you know what *that* means. There might be a class action.'

'Class action?'

'Class action, aye. And the Kazakh lawyers might get tae look at the files.'

Baxter tried unsuccessfully to smile. Again. He seemed to be doing a lot of smiling.

'This position in Diego Garcia, Bent... Two years there, it'd be great... You'd have regular dosh comin' in, you could do some thinking...'

Was that his sentence? Two years in Diego Garcia?

'*And*, oor boys think that'd be long enough for the Kazakh scent to go cold.'

Baxter remembered that woman in the restaurant. Martha was it? In the Penal Colony. Kafka. This was it, they were beating at his door now. The only question was where they would put the tattoo.

'It's part o' oor wider Good Governance for the Poor Programme. What's the story again, Patience?'

'It's a marine park, supporting a rare kind of jelly fish,' said Patience, almost as if reading from a cue sheet. 'Under the Gender and Environment Unit. We've been asked to provide assistance to the local policewomen's union. Mostly baton training and the use of rubber bullets.'

'It's a sensitive one, as you can imagine, Bent, but the weather's grand and the girls delightful, last I heard at least.'

Baxter nodded, turned to gaze out the window.

'Business-class tickets of course, you won't have tae fly with the numpties. Ah know the benefit-cost ratio on that one, Bent. That's one bit o' economic theory Ah *do* fuckin' understand.'

Baxter was having trouble breathing. 'Good Governance for the Poor?' he managed eventually, almost as if thinking out loud. 'Environment, with a bit of a gender slant? You really think I'm the man for that?'

'No question, Bent. Abso-fuckin'-lutely.'

An autumn afternoon, wet and windy. Bare trees. Leaves blowing about the empty street like scattered scenes in other people's lives. A good day to hail a cab, or so it felt. Baxter walked out of his ward, past reception, easy enough, through the front door, no problem. No one stopped him, no one even noticed. And there it was, a big black taxi, coming his way.

He settled into the back seat and pressed his face to the glass, snoozing fitfully as the anonymous streets slipped by. They'd been driving an hour when he asked the driver to pull over, handed him a wad of notes. As he got out he saw he was on Rosebury Avenue, in sight of Sadler's Wells. He'd once had an office near here. He walked aimlessly, with no real idea of time or where he was trying to go.

Along the Aldwych there was a small electronics shop, two tramps huddled in the doorway wrapped in a filthy blanket. There was a television screen in the window and he stopped to watch the silent pictures flickering in the cold neon twilight. The tramps didn't stir. They could have been dead. On the TV, a talk show. Two talking heads, one of them a well-known pundit, the other a lean, handsome white man in an expensive suit, the latter faintly familiar. And suddenly everything fitted. Faith was dead, Hilleard was in hiding, and here was Charlie Crisp, on British TV, talking to the world. *He* had found a way through.

Baxter couldn't hear a word through the heavy glass window but he understood instinctively what he was seeing. A shot of black farmers in tatty trousers, some *kwashiorkor* kids, an elephant, an Ebola patient in an isolation ward. It must be Africa. Shots of the audience clapping. Crisp stood up, seemed to be conducting the applause. It went on and on. What had he done? The camera panned. Baxter squinted into the window. Another man, a third man, coming on now. A shot of the host, smiling. The new entrant, a man in battle fatigues with long black hair and pissy eyes, silly pink sunglasses. More shots of the audience clapping. Then Baxter realised. It was his old chum from the Munyonyo party.

All three men embraced as if they had found their long lost brothers, the audience still clapping. After a moment, they all sat down and started talking again. A close-up of Crisp looking happy. He was laughing. What was the joke?

Baxter pushed his only coin into the freezing hand of one of the sleeping tramps and turned once more into the cold evening wind. Past the Waldorf and the old RSC theatre, across the road and on to Waterloo Bridge. Commuters were rushing in all directions, no one stopping to look. He scanned the faces, all intent and busy and full of purpose. He walked to the middle of the bridge where a man in a tracksuit was leaning across the balustrade, staring intently at the water below. Baxter wondered for a moment whether the fellow might be preparing to jump.

As he watched, the man turned and saw him. 'What you staring at?' he shouted, mad-eyed, pushing his little dog-face forward.

Baxter shook his head, embarrassed. 'Sorry, nothing, I didn't...'

But the man wasn't dissuaded. 'What you looking at? What's so interesting? Are you a fucking sociologist or something?' But before Baxter could reply the man was legging it away, scuttling along the bridge, disappearing into the crowd.

The light was fading now and as Baxter looked west along the river, it was as if a scarlet flame was stretched across the sky, some vast fire burning far away. As he watched, he thought for a moment of the dead girl's parents. What would they be doing? An aeroplane was flying low into the red evening light. Where was it going? Where was anyone going? Suddenly, it all became quite still, there among the crazy bustle of the oncoming night. Something had come and gone and he felt a breath, just a whisper, of understanding. For a moment, he experienced a kind of balance, as if, for a second, he had been granted a fleeting illumination. And then the moment was gone.

PRESS RELEASE

HILLEARD CONSULTANCY SERVICES ANNOUNCES A NEW INITIATIVE

January 17th 2012

Hilleard Consultancy Services (HCS) is proud to announce its rebirth as a first rank British company specialising in the provision of technical expertise and management services for poverty alleviation worldwide. Arising from the ashes of the former Hilleard, Semple and Crooks Ltd (HSC) and backed by the funds and expertise of Bosworth Bollinger Inc. of Minnesota, HCS intends to bring the hard reality of economic rigour to the soft needs of poverty planning and to be 'simply the best'.

Since acquisition the company and the team have undergone fundamental change. Most fundamentally the skills of the former HSC have been merged with the considerable but sometimes overlapping track records of other Bosworth Bollinger subsidiaries, notably Consultancy Alternatives (CA), Economic Realities Inc. (ERI) of the USA, Real Consultancy Ltd (RCL), and Alternative Realities of Stroud to provide a unique synergy sufficient to catapult the new HCS to the very forefront of poverty best practice.

Staff of HCS have unparalleled expertise. Individuals have participated in some one thousand economic development projects and studies, from Africa to Asia, Central and South America, the Caribbean, East, Central and Western Europe. Their reach extends to every geography and demographic and their experience covers the full range of technical assistance needs, from advice in research, to planning and project design, from programme implementation to the management of small, medium and large projects. In addition contract staff are employed and a comprehensive register of freelance consultants is maintained on a computer database. HCS's clients are governments, multilateral and bilateral development agencies, private companies, other consulting firms, indeed anyone with a problem. As with the old firm, MODE is expected to be a favoured customer.

Bosworth Bollinger Inc. has been established for over 125 years and buys, sells, processes, manufacturers, stores and transports almost everything.

SHORT CVS OF HCS STAFF AND ASSOCIATES

HCS's in-house staff, and the associate experts that the company can call on, represent a pool of expertise in the development field that is unrivalled outside these islands. HCS is proud to present its core personnel as follows:

Dr GODFREY HILLEARD: Formerly Managing Director of Hilleard, Semple and Crooks, Godfrey Hilleard has been lured back from retirement to preside over the birth of the new company. He is the Director of HCS and oversees all the work of the business. He is an economist of unparalleled experience who has been involved in poverty work since the 1960s. Recent assignments in which he has been the Team Leader include the Great Man-Made River project in Libya, the Ethiopian Airlines Buyout and the ongoing Halliburton stabilisation programme in Iraq. He has worked for MODE, UNDP, EU, and the World Bank.

Dr WILLIAM CROOKS: An enviable reputation as a mover and shaker precedes Billy Crooks wherever he goes. He has spent over five years in long-term residence and has undertaken numerous poverty assignments, many as Team Leader, for both private and public sector clients (incl. MODE, the World Bank, EU, UNAP, UNIP, UNEP, DAC, and UNICEF). From 1999 to 2007 he was business manager with HSC, presiding over a period of great change for the company. Since the acquisition, Dr Crooks has continued to work hard for HCS, developing the vibrant Iraq and Afghanistan portfolios.

Dr WILFRED WRENCH: One of the sharpest analytical minds in his field, Wilf is a historian and Associate Professor at the College of Further Education, Aylesbury, where he teaches poverty economics. He heads up the new NGO Department at HSC, with change management responsibilities with CARE, CONCERN, CONSIDERATION, COMPASSION and COMPLIANT. He has had an advisory role in the establishment of the new NGO DISQUIET. He is working on alternative crops for the opium producers of Afghanistan, taking a very long-term view.

Dr JAMES PETTIGREW: James 'Jimmy' Pettigrew is a human geographer with many years' experience of poverty development and community based planning. For ten years, he was resident in Thailand where he undertook feasibility studies and project preparation (using LFA, RRA, PRA and PPA) and where he was also responsible for evaluating ongoing projects (using the ZFA and LOOTOL methodologies). Mr Pettigrew has worked extensively all over South East Asia, keeps a house in Bangkok and lives there sometimes with his friends. He oversees the MODE projects in the Pakistani North West Frontier and expects to be doing more assignments in Yemen and Libya.

Dr ANGUS MACPHERSON: Professor Macpherson is a lecturer in the Poverty of Development and the Development of Poverty at the University of Kiev with 25 years' experience as a teacher, trainer, scientist and analyst. He has undertaken consultancies in some 30 countries (although, these days he limits his travel to a few carefully selected destinations). He keeps ahead of the game with testing assignments on a range of subjects, from evaluations and programme reviews to institutional reviews, poverty alleviation missions, and public sector reform programmes. In addition to USAID, he has recently been heavily involved with the ILO, WHO, DIF, DAGS and DIDGE.

Dr BENT Q. BAXTER: After a short time out for learning and reflection, Dr Baxter has returned to the poverty alleviation world. He has forty years' experience of poverty issues and has worked in over 80 countries. His recent assignments have included spells in Uganda and Kazakhstan, the purposes of which have been wide-ranging: from project analysis in Uganda to transport policy for the newly engendered city in Kazakhstan. He is currently halfway through a very long assignment in Diego Garcia where he is on a MODE contract to teach vocational training to prison guards and police officers. He has worked for all the usual agencies: the World Bank, DIDGE, DODGE etc.

SIR MORGAN ADDERBURY: Previously Professor of Economics at the University of Aberdeen and Permanent Secretary at MODE, Professor Sir 'Zoo' Adderbury is now on retainer with HCS. Recently knighted for services to the poor, he is Director for Poverty on the Board of Bosworth Bollinger PLC and Principal UN Adviser to the Three Gorges Dam Project in China. He has published very widely and has established a worldwide reputation as a thinker on the economics of poverty, sustainable poverty and global poverty worldwide. Professor Adderbury has worked in a consulting or advisory capacity for the World Bank, the EU, UNEP, UNCTAD, DIF, DAG, and DIDGE, as well as a plethora of private sector interests. In 1994 he was elected to the United Nations Global 500 Roll of Honour for services to poverty.

Printed in Great Britain
by Amazon

13783842R00139